Ganny

W9-BCO-416

Divorcing
Your
Grandmother

Divorcing Your Grandmother

· A NOVEL ·

by
Jean
Gould

WILLIAM MORROW AND COMPANY, INC.
NEW YORK

FOR MY MOTHER

Copyright © 1985 by Jean Gould

"We're Off to See the Wizard," Words by E. Y. Harburg, Music by
Harold Arlen, copyright 1939, renewed © 1967 by Leo Feist, Inc.
Rights assigned to CBS Catalogue Partnership
All rights controlled and administered by CBS Feist Catalog Inc.
All rights reserved. International copyright secured. Used by permission.

All rights reserved. No part of this book may be reproduced or utilized in any
form or by any means, electronic or mechanical, including photocopying, re-
cording or by any information storage and retrieval system, without permission in writing from the Publisher. Inquiries should be addressed to
Permissions Department, William Morrow and Company, Inc., 105 Madison
Ave., New York, N.Y. 10016.

Library of Congress Cataloging in Publication Data

Gould, Jean, 1939-
Divorcing your grandmother.

.I. Title.
PS3557.O863D5   1985   813'.54   85-347
ISBN 0-688-04970-2

Printed in the United States of America

First Edition

1 2 3 4 5 6 7 8 9 10

BOOK DESIGN BY JAYE ZIMET

· NEWS ITEMS ·

By mid-July, *The Globe* reported it was one of the hottest summers on record in Boston, with no letup in sight. Water was rationed, and lawns turned brown.

The Red Sox were temporarily in first place. No one could believe it. Red Auerbach announced that Larry Bird would be a Celtic forever.

According to the results of a survey on love conducted by *Psychology Today*, fifty percent of married men and women reported they had had at least one extramarital affair by the age of forty. Ellen Goodman wrote a column about lack of commitment. Everyone talked about narcissism.

An old woman in Melrose was eaten by her thirty-five cats. When you're a woman alone anything can happen, people said.

Five young men, charged and convicted for raping an aging beauty queen, were acquitted in a second trial. It was reported that the jurors said the rosary while they deliberated.

7

· JEAN GOULD ·

• • •

The Cambridge Center for Adult Education began its summer courses, which were oversubscribed the first day of registration. New sections of the following were opened: The Single Life, Life Begins at Thirty, Life Begins at Forty, Life with Children, Life Without Children, Is There Life After Fifty? And so on.

CHAPTER

· ONE ·

Saint Margaret's Church in the Back Bay was anonymous enough, Kate decided. But the confessional smelled musty. Like an old bureau drawer at the rural college where she had just attended a summer workshop: New Techniques in the Dissection of Small Mammals. There had been a dead mouse in the drawer.

"Confession is good for the soul," her mother always said. "And it's cheaper than psychoanalysis," she had come to add in recent years. Well, sitting here was punishment enough, Kate thought. Like being put in the closet when she was small and had misbehaved. Even Rose Kennedy put her children in the closet when they didn't mind her.

It had been thirty years. As a child, she had loved closed-in places when it was her own choice. She played "tent" under tables with a blanket and was sad when she grew too big to hide in the kitchen cupboard under the sink.

Her father joked that the confessional was a coffin on its end. But he forced himself into it once a year just before Easter. Kate wondered what sins he would confess, what penance he would say with his large paws folded in atonement. She knew, of course, that her mother never sinned

9

and imagined that she and the priest talked about the altar flowers or the next novena.

She heard the muffled voices now of the priest and the sinner on the other side of the box. You could faint in here. Or kill yourself, like the little mouse in the bureau. An odd taste pushed itself up from her stomach. She found a Life Saver in her purse and popped it into her mouth. It was peppermint. There was a sigh. And the wooden partition slid open.

"Bless me, Father, for I have sinned," she began. At least she still remembered how to cross herself. Sister Perpetua had been good for something; they'd spent most of first grade crossing themselves and learning to genuflect.

"Go on," the priest said. His breath came through the screen like a heavy cloud. Garlic.

"What?" Kate said.

"Continue," he said.

There was something about garlic that was supposed to open your pores. "I don't think I can do this," she said. In the shadows she saw the white hair and profile of her confessor. His ear was pressed to the screen.

"Yes, you can," he said.

"I always wanted to be an altar boy," Kate thought to herself but said out loud. She swallowed the Life Saver whole. It caught in her throat.

"Dominus tecum," the priest said.

Kate put her fingers to the screen. It was like a jail screen. "Bless me, Father, for I have sinned," she used to say. "I told three lies," she would lie. She had to say something, after all. And what else could she think of at seven? One boy in her class claimed to have peed in the confessional. Michael Dolan. He had become a high-school principal. Kate had secretly worn a rosary around her neck then. She had taken Magdalene as her confirmation name and made everyone call her Maggie for a whole year.

"I'm hedging my bets," she said now.

"Yes, my child," the priest said.

Kate had wanted to be an altar boy more than anything. She had wanted to ring the bell that made the Faithful stand, kneel, and sit. She'd longed to look inside the tabernacle. And if she'd been able to serve mass, she'd have known once and for all whether or not Father Moynihan had scotch or wine in his chalice.

"Yes, my child?" the priest repeated. It was a question this time.

They always said "my child," Kate remembered. Probably no matter how old you were, they would say "my child."

"They're going to kill me," she said. "Tomorrow they will cut me open. And I'll be dead."

"Surgery?" said the priest.

"Yes," she whispered.

"And how long is it since your last confession?" The voice was steady now, like a march.

"Twenty years," she lied. Thirty years was just too long. How could she admit to thirty years?

"Now," the priest said, "I'll hear your confession."

Kate took out her list. She was good at making lists: for groceries, for students, for errands, what to take to the hospital. She would finally read *Ulysses* in the hospital, she decided. She even had a list of chores for George while she was away, as if her husband would forget to feed the dog or change his clothes. But now it was too dark to see. Should she go and get a votive candle? She dropped her sins on the floor.

She closed her eyes. Did she have to tell why she'd left the Church as a teenager? Did she even know? She shoved three Chiclets in her mouth and blinked her eyes open. What would her mother say if she could see her now? "If

11

you would just find a nice priest, Kate," she had been saying all these years. "A nice, old priest. Not one of those young ones." Her mother had been instrumental in retaining Latin at Saint Luke's.

The nice, old priest was winding his watch. It was probably quitting time.

"Abortions," Kate said.

"How many?"

"Several." Why were numbers so important?

"Several?" he said.

"And infidelities."

"What?"

"Adultery. Thou shalt not commit adultery. Remember?" Kate said. She cracked her gum. What was she doing here?

"How many times?"

Quantity again. He is feeding the sins into a computer, she thought. At the end of the day, he'll get a printout. At the end of the year, the Church can issue a statement like the FBI does. "Envy is big this year. Up by fifty-three percent."

"I gave all my students A's last semester," she said. Was that a sin? Was it a sin that she had been too tired to look at their work? to check their cut-up cats? their drawings of the fetal pig? It was getting hard to breathe.

The priest was scratching his listening ear with his index finger.

She must tell. That's why she was here, wasn't it? She must say that she'd just come from an afternoon of margaritas, fresh pâté, and lust.

"I don't believe in sin," was what she said. She stuck her gum on the wall.

"Yes," the priest said. "Now say the Act of Contrition, my dear."

"No," said Kate. "I won't." She found the door handle.

She fled down the aisle. She was hot and thirsty. Was she hyperventilating? She sat in a pew in the rear of the church to calm herself. There was a dime on the bench beside her. She put her head between her knees and tried to remember the Act of Contrition.

Too many margaritas. That's what it was. Charlie had outdone himself this afternoon. He had rented the best suite at the Hyatt Regency. He had the luncheon catered by Maître Jacques. Fresh pomegranates and avocados. A creamy Brie. Sole meunière. White wine. A Riesling. Flowers of all colors in their bed.

They had popped grapes on each other's cheeks and rolled on the thick blue carpet. They had eaten the crème caramel with their fingers. It was disgusting and delicious. She was a little crazy from so much excess, she told herself. Why else would she have come to a church?

She sat up cautiously. She was very thirsty, and the sweat was dripping off her nose. She touched it with her tongue. It was salty. Like a margarita. Like all those wonderful margaritas.

At the door, her eyes were drawn to the holy-water font. Well, why not? She dipped a Kleenex in the water and wiped her face. She looked around, and cupping her hands, she scooped the sacred liquid into her mouth. It tasted like perfume. She couldn't swallow it. She imagined the headline: WOMAN DIES AT SAINT MARGARET'S. POISONED BY HOLY WATER. She held it in her mouth and went out into the early evening. There were too many people on the street. She eased the water down her throat.

When she was halfway to her car, she realized she'd left her sandals in the confessional.

CHAPTER
· TWO ·

"This is the worst part," the young resident grimaced to Kate, as he pulled what seemed to be an Ace bandage out of her vagina. A rabbit from a hat, she thought.

She always smiled when she was annoyed. Be a good girl, she reminded herself. She didn't want to offend the resident, after all. He'd already said this was the worst part.

"Almost finished," he sighed, careful not to meet her eyes. He had pimples on his chin. He had her chart. I could be his mother, she mused. His glasses slid halfway down his nose.

It was the first day after the surgery. There were balloon bouquets dancing on the ceiling. Blue and green. Was there a special color for hysterectomy?

She reached for the telephone and dialed long distance. "They're trying to kill me," she whispered to an old lover in San Francisco.

"Who is this?" he grumbled. It was four in the morning on the coast.

"Never mind," Kate said. "It must be the morphine." She hung up and rang for the nurse, who appeared instantly, like a genie or a fairy godmother.

15

"Yes, Mrs. Cummings, what can I do for you?" Her voice was warm. Her brown eyes were clear and direct. I could be her mother, Kate thought.

"Yes?" said Brown Eyes, still patient.

"About Dr. Pimple," Kate began. Was she slurring her words? "I mean Dr. Whipple. The resident. You know?"

"Yes, I know him," the nurse said.

"Does he have acne, or what?" Kate said. It had seemed the most vital thing in the world a moment ago. But as she heard herself now, the words seemed not to belong to her, although she recognized the voice. "Will you hold my hand?" She reached out. The nurse's nails were perfect. "I'm malignant, you know."

Later, George came with some flowers and a hot-fudge sundae from Bailey's. Her husband had always been partial to red carnations. Like blood. Lots of blood. "What was it like when they slit me open?" she'd asked the resident.

"Oh, it wasn't bad," he'd said. "They drape a sheet over you, so it's all very private." She wondered if he bit his nails.

"But was there much blood?" She had to know. When her students did dissections, there was never any blood. She often reminded herself how glad she was she didn't have that job: draining the blood out of laboratory animals. In fact, she made mental lists of jobs she didn't want: blood drainer, turnpike toll collector, dentist, or entrepreneur. From time to time, she thought she'd like to be a waitress. The notion of matching face with food appealed to her.

"Dr. Parks is a fine surgeon," the resident was saying. "The best. A real clean job."

"And what did they do with my insides, once they were outside?" It was only half a joke.

"Pathology," he said. If she were him, she'd squeeze those

16

pimples until they popped. His color wasn't good, she noticed, as he changed her dressing.

George put the hot-fudge sundae on the tray in front of her. It had nuts and no cherry, just the way she liked it. But the ice cream was melting.

"Oh dear," she said, as she watched him lick his lips. "I don't think I can eat anything yet. You have it."

The woman in the next bed groaned. They had amputated her leg below the knee that morning. Kate wondered when her next shot of morphine would be. Perhaps she should have taken a private room.

But she hated being alone when she was sick. She'd been quarantined with scarlet fever when she was ten; it was awful. This time, she arranged her friends' visiting schedules beforehand and decided to have a roommate. Unfortunately, she knew that neither George nor Charlie would agree to a schedule, and the prospect of their meeting in the hospital seemed almost more dire than her surgery.

George slurped the last of the ice cream. "I wanted to bring you something you'd like," he said.

"You. I like you." She grinned. "Come and lie down with me." She reached out her arm with its plastic tube.

"I gave the dog a hamburger for breakfast," George was saying. "She misses you."

"Let's not talk," Kate said. Words were harsh now and chipped at her like jackhammers. She put her head back and closed her eyes. Maybe she would sleep. She felt herself rocking.

"Remember the swing contest?" she said half aloud. Was it third grade? They had dared each other to go higher, higher on adjacent schoolyard swings, until Sister Marcella had come roaring out of the school to make them stop. Neither of them had been afraid of anything then, not even the Sisters of Mercy. "Oh, how I like to go up in a swing,"

she remembered Stevenson's poem. "Up in the air so blue."
Was she reciting it out loud?

The phone rang and roused her. She had drooled on the
pillow. George had gone, and there were more flowers. Red
roses. More blood. And yellow mums. Two quarts of pus,
she had heard them say. The balloons continued their own
vigil above.

"Yes," she hissed. The phone had no eyes. She had never
liked it. She licked the holes in the receiver; it was an old
habit.

"It's Charlie." The voice was very far away.

"I think I was just dreaming about you," Kate said. I
could be a drug addict, she told herself. "When can you
come?" If she weren't so tired she would cross her fingers.
What time was it anyway?

He had phoned from the lobby. He had wanted to be
sure the coast was clear. "I love you truly," he crooned
as he came through the door to her room. The furniture
grew smaller in his presence.

"Here's your get-well gift," he said, as he put a striped
paper bag on the tray in front of her, where there were
still a few drips of vanilla ice cream.

It was a water pistol. Kate pointed it at him and pulled
the trigger, firing over his head.

"Not at me," he said. "For your enemies. It's for all those
nasty people in white hanging around here."

"Don't make me laugh." Kate held her stomach with
the folded blanket on it. She was surprised to find moisture
on her cheeks. Had the water pistol backfired? "Oh, Charlie," she said. "It's over. And I'm still here."

"What else?" he said. "And two days ago you made me
stage the last supper."

She remembered the thick blue carpet and licked her lips.
She needed to brush her teeth.

* * *

She badgered them until they put down the sides on her bed and she was allowed to get up and walk around on the IV leash. She could almost smell the ocean as if she were on a liner. The ground was not quite steady beneath her feet, and it was a relief to get back into the hospital bed. She wanted to weigh herself, but had forgotten.

"I picked Charlie up in a drugstore," she told a freckled nurse. "He's married, too, of course," she added. "I was refilling a pain prescription. He was getting antidepressants for his wife." Oh dear, was she turning into one of those poor souls who spill their guts to anyone who will listen?

The nurse had a heart-shaped diamond on her left hand. Kate had not wanted an engagement ring, but George had insisted and they had compromised on a sapphire. She agreed to the wedding in her parents' church, although she refused to allow her father to give her away, claiming she had never belonged to anyone in the first place. And so she had walked down the aisle by herself. Her father had forgiven her; her mother had not.

She dared to look at her belly now for the first time, as the nurse changed the dressing. "My god, staples!" she said. "Desk staples!"

"It leaves a better scar, Mrs. C.," the nurse said in a monotone.

Kate looked away. "When I found out I had to have this surgery," she said, "I knew I had only one last chance. Do all your patients tell you that?" She wished Brown Eyes were here. This nurse was probably thinking about her china pattern and place cards at the wedding. Kate went on anyway. "I had to have him. Charlie. You only live once, you know," she said, annoyed as she heard the cliché. "And sometimes not even then," she added.

"Would you like to try a little Jell-O, Mrs. C.?" the nurse asked. "It's red today."

Why am I explaining Charlie to her? Kate wondered. "Listen," she said. "About the staples. I mean, there must be twenty-five metal staples holding me together." No one had told her there would be staples. She thought about the story of the wolf who fell asleep with the lamb inside him, only to wake up with rocks in his belly. "How do they take them out?" She began to feel faint. "Never mind. Bring the Jell-O."

In the bathroom, later, she looked down at her stomach again. She would get used to it, she supposed. But her belly was flabby now. It would be a long scar. And she had liked making love with the lights on.

Charlie brought a plastic duck that boogied across Kate's tray table. It was the funniest thing in the world to watch it stumble across the surface and fall over the edge.

"We'll go to Vermont for a weekend," Charlie was saying. He was lying next to her on the bed. It hurt to be jostled.

"The thing is, Charlie," she said, "I hadn't planned on this. I'm malignant, you know."

"Let's play strip poker." Hadn't he heard her? He dealt out the cards. The woman with no leg peeked through the curtain around her.

They'd had a long wait that evening they'd met at the drugstore in Newton Highlands. Both were impatient. Kate was in pain and angry she'd let her prescription run out. Charlie sat next to her on the bench, tapping his foot.

"Do you have to do that?" she accused.

"Maybe I do. And maybe I don't," he said.

"I suppose next you'll have to get in line to die," Kate said.

Charlie picked up a pack of cards from a bin with dessicated-liver tablets and athletic supporters. "Let's play," he said.

Kate raised her eyebrows and looked down her long nose at him. He twinkled all over, as if he were filled with punch lines. His lightweight sweater had mangled lift tickets hanging from its edge. She liked him.

"Why not?" she said.

"At your service," he said, standing up and making a little bow. Like a plant in a time-lapse photograph, he grew before her into a giant of a man. He must even have to stoop going through doors. "And I'm still a growing boy," he said. Indeed, Kate was sure he was much younger than she. He was probably thirty or thirty-five.

"Now for serious business," he said, folding himself up like a yardstick. He shuffled the slippery cards and removed the jokers. "Gin rummy or crazy eights?"

"My deal," she said. They laughed, cheated, dropped the cards on the floor, and bought a pad and pen to keep score. Kate forgot the awful teeth gnawing at her gut. She and Charlie went into a restaurant next door to the pharmacy to finish their game. She took her codeine with a Lite beer.

"I'm tired of gin rummy," she remembered saying. "You cheat." She was light-headed. "Let's play war."

The game had been ferocious. She knew the other patrons had noticed them in their booth slapping their cards down, screaming over their triumphs, bemoaning their losses. Kate had even seen one of her neighbors come in to pick up a pizza. She didn't care.

A week later, she sent Charlie a nine of diamonds in the mail. And their affair began.

Now, in the hospital, watching the crinkles around his eyes, she said, "I don't know anything about you, you ~~ .~~" In those weeks before her surgery, they had played ~~ ~~ made love. She had taken her pills with Jack ~~ ~~ had become the double-solitaire champion

"OK," he said, "we won't play strip poker. How about fish? Give me all your threes," he began.

Kate knew it was just luck that George hadn't come in while Charlie was there. She should never have told Charlie it was all right to visit. She vaguely wondered now what she'd say and felt her left eye begin to twitch. For a moment, it was as if she had seashells pressed to her ears. They would not meet, these two. She would not hear them speak to one another. Perhaps she would die after all.

It didn't happen. George visited twice each day, but never when Charlie was there. Somehow, he'd found buttercups and put them in a small glass by her bed. Had he actually picked them himself?

"How're things going?" It had been his opening line for a long time. He kissed her on the forehead.

"Have you ever played canasta?" she said. They'd stopped playing bridge years ago when they agreed to disagree about games.

"Tell me"—he held her hand, twisting the gold band on her finger—"have you moved your bowels yet? They told me you can come home after you move your bowels."

Some balloons were drooping a bit now. Like tired breasts, Kate thought. "Be sure you bring some chocolates for the nurses before I leave," she said.

"And shall I bring you some prunes?" George enjoyed bathroom jokes. He liked to have things in order. The pennies in his loafers were shining. She always knew what to expect from him, and it was a comfort to have him so predictable.

Once, at a party, they were asked to describe their favorite animals. It was a psychological test, someone said. Actually it was supposed to be a description of your mate remembered she'd chosen a dog and said it was a warm, and constant. Well, that was George

22

an eagle, saying it was free, powerful, and unpredictable.

"Ellen called today," Kate said. What would her daughter say if she knew her mother had a lover? "She'll be home by Labor Day weekend."

"Of all the places to go for the summer, she had to pick the Maine wilderness," George said. He didn't like it when his daughter was too far from home. "And was does 'disadvantaged' mean, anyway? Is she safe with fifteen teenagers? How on earth did she find a telephone?"

Kate remembered Ellen's special sweet fragrance as a baby, her breath, her skin. She was a singing lily of the valley. "Let's not talk," she said to George. She wanted to hum a lullaby, but was suddenly embarrassed by the rush of feeling for her child. She wanted Ellen here.

Brown Eyes came in to take temperatures and blood pressures. "Prime rib tonight?" she joked. "Or would madam prefer the roast duckling?"

George went home. He looked tired. Had she thanked him for coming? Thanked him for the buttercups? Had he brought them today? Or yesterday? She would call him later.

She ate the Jell-O on the tray and lowered the head of her bed. Where was her uterus now? What did it look like? Pear-shaped, like all the books said? She had never seen a human uterus. At nine, she had wanted to take her tonsils home in a jar. They had called her morbid; she had looked it up in the dictionary. Morbid. She still kept the small cardboard box filled with all her baby teeth and molars.

"Which one is your husband?" Kate's roommate came to life. "Buttercup? Or the card shark?"

Kate was grateful for the interruption of her reverie. "Are you talking to me?" She peered across at the bold face with the tiny features; it was like small print on a large menu. It had the highest forehead Kate had ever seen. The woman's teeth were too small for her mouth, but her smile was friendly. Kate sat up and pulled back the drape. They introduced themselves.

"Mine left me after I lost my first breast," Rhoda said. Kate pictured a breast rolling down a sidewalk, like an errant softball. When she first started teaching, lab animals were usually male. The distributors claimed there were too many complications with females: enlarged mammaries, ovaries with too many eggs all over the place. Now each batch had equal numbers of males and females, and usually one pregnant specimen was included.

"Your husband left you?" Kate said.

"Yup," Rhoda said in a firm, alto tone. "Packed his stuff and the cat. That was it."

"You don't sound sorry."

"He smashed my violin before he left," Rhoda whispered.

Kate wondered if she had missed something. She was having a hard time concentrating. At this rate, she would never get to *Ulysses.*

"A three-thousand-dollar, two-hundred-year-old violin," said her roommate. "Splinters and broken strings. The bastard." Rhoda, it turned out, was a violinist and teacher at the Boston Conservatory.

"But I thought it was your leg," Kate said.

"Oh, sure." Rhoda seemed to take it all in stride. "The leg this time. But first one breast. Then the other."

Before she could stop herself, Kate's eyes went to Rhoda's chest. "But," she said, "you look so"—she paused—"normal." She knew it was not the right word.

"Plastic inserts," Rhoda said. "I'm more plastic than a Barbie doll. They put in the plastic and then pump you up like a football." She giggled. "Or a basketball." Her dark hair framed her face in parentheses. "Wait until you see my new leg," she said. Kate wondered what had become of the old leg. It would be too grisly to ask.

"So, he left you? He really walked out because of your mastectomies?" Kate went back to a safer topic.

Rhoda explained their rivalry as fellow musicians, their various arguments. She cooked baked potatoes too long, he'd said. Paid more attention to her instrument than to him. Her voice softened when she spoke about her music.

Kate had never considered leaving her marriage. Had George? It wasn't that she didn't believe in divorce. But she and George had been as good as family before they married; they had known each other their whole lives. It would be like divorcing your grandmother. It would be impossible. People just didn't divorce their grandmothers.

It was very late, past visiting hours, when Charlie came in with his green visor and several decks of cards. He wore khaki shorts with his ostrich legs.

"Pick a card. Any card," he said.

"Don't make me laugh," Kate said. "I'll pop my staples."

"I'll pick a card," Rhoda said. Her teeth had grown larger. She drew a card from the middle of Charlie's arrangement.

Charlie shuffled the remaining cards with great fanfare. He put them next to his forehead. He raised the deck toward the ceiling. He did a polka step to the left, a waltz motion to the right. At last he announced, "I have it! The six of clubs!"

"Wrong!" yelled Rhoda. "The ten of diamonds."

"Oh, no." He put his head in his hands. "It must be a bad deck." He threw his cards into the wastebasket, reached into his pocket, pulled out another deck, and gave it to Rhoda. "Your deal," he said. "Name your game and your price: blood, money, or love." He drew out the last word, so it had two syllables: lo-ove.

"Did you have to say 'blood'?" Kate said.

"Did you have to say 'love'?" said Rhoda.

"Time's a-wasting," Charlie said. "What'll it be?"

"Hearts," Rhoda said. "What else?"

Kate drew a chair up by Rhoda's bed. It still hurt to sit up straight. But as she imagined losing a leg, her pain subsided. She must remember to congratulate her mother on the wisdom of encouraging her to be a hospital volunteer when she was a teenager. Of course, seeing people in real agony was one of the things that had made her lose her religious faith. But her respect for the body's determination to survive had endured.

Rhoda shot the moon on the first hand. "I've decided to play for money," she said.

They played all night. Just before midnight, Charlie sneaked down to the residents' cafeteria and brought back peanut-butter sandwiches and root beer.

When the nurse came in to check on them, Charlie hid in the bathroom. Rhoda and Kate told the nurse they were fine. They were just fine. It was the first time Kate had had an appetite since the surgery.

· THREE ·

George was glad he had his office at home. On a quiet side street, the house was made of rugged fieldstone and was full of the permanence he liked. He and Kate had bought it after the last year of his training, with help from their parents. The former owner was a retired psychiatrist who'd hanged himself from an old beam in the garage. The beam cracked, the ceiling fell in on him, and he had survived. They'd got the house for a good price. And while they had planned to live closer to the city, Newton was, at most, twenty minutes from downtown Boston. Besides, it was home. Was there anything wrong with living in one place all your life?

As he sat in his chair looking at Ethel Simpson, George felt his eyebrows knit together. How could he concentrate? He was trying to listen, but he could only watch her lips moving. It was like a TV with no sound.

Mrs. Simpson was a woman about his own wife's age. She was slightly overweight, slightly short, slightly dumpy, in fact. He liked her. He liked all his patients. "I'm feeling mar-vel-ous," she said. The sound did not match the mouth movements. Delayed reaction, George told himself.

He had seen her through her husband's heart attacks and death and her own grief. It had been a long siege, and she still was not happy with widowhood. She'd adjusted to it, she said. But she would never like it. George knew he would feel the same way if he were widowed.

"Doctor," Mrs. Simpson was saying, "I'm so grateful . . ." He didn't catch it all.

Why had he become a psychiatrist? There was already enough pain in the world, wasn't there? He had to look for more? Well, he hadn't wanted to touch anyone who was sick. That was one reason. And it was true: There was some triumph in the process of emotional healing that made him feel good. The ability of the human spirit to restore itself never ceased to fascinate him.

Ethel Simpson was "terminating" today. She spoke rapidly, eager to get on with it. Her eyelashes flicked back and forth; she had taken to wearing eye makeup in recent months. Kate never wore eye makeup. George kept seeing her lying in the hospital bed, hearing her ask how much blood there was, watching her face close off against him. She didn't want to talk, she said. She couldn't.

He couldn't remember her ever being sick in bed. She was even the first to get up in the morning. Usually he woke to find his coffee steaming on the night table and Kate standing on her head by the closet door. It was good for her brain, she said. She didn't want her brain to get varicose like her legs. He loved her legs, he told her.

How much longer could he go on avoiding this Murdoch guy? If only Kate would get over him on her own without a confrontation, just as she'd gotten over that Paul Applegate in high school. Applegate: the all-American boy, superjock. George had vomited his lunch every day for the two months of that romance.

"But we've always loved each other," he finally blurted out to her one day after school, feeling he had swallowed the jar of paramecia from biology class. He wished their parents hadn't let them transfer to Newton High, although he and Kate had begged to go to public school.

"Oh, George," she said, her dark hair shimmering. "We'll talk about it sometime." She'd worn a tartan skirt with pleats. Her green eyes were fringed with black lashes that were too long. Everyone said she looked like Audrey Hepburn, but he couldn't see it. He had known her too long for such comparisons. Her nose was too long, she said. Her legs were too short. She was average, she claimed. He thought she was perfect.

"I see you've got on your bagpipe skirt," he said. He had teased her about it before. His mouth felt as if he'd been licking envelopes for a long time.

She drifted away. "I'm late," she called out to the crisp October air. Probably she was going to watch Applegate at football practice. "Bye," she said, as if she'd just remembered he was there.

Kicking dead leaves, he told himself he would find someone else. There were lots of girls around. Nice girls. Why should he wait for Kate? He spent a few days looking at the shiny lips and pointed breasts of other girls. He decided to wait. After two months, she came back to him. And where was Paul Applegate today? George had a sudden urge to know.

"Razzle-dazzle. That's what it was," Kate explained. Her lips formed a small heart.

"I guess I'm not very exciting," he said, hoping she'd contradict him. "Maybe," he continued with a grin, "I could be one or the other."

She looked puzzled.

"Razzle or dazzle," he said.

"I learned all the new dances," she said. "His parents took us to the country club."

George had taken Kate to the movies every Saturday night since the eighth grade. Once they'd gone bowling. He had never been to the country club. Probably he'd trip at the door or use the wrong fork. Probably he'd burp after dinner or blow his nose in his napkin.

"How about going to the movies on Saturday?" he said. He needed to be more spontaneous. That was it. But he liked holding hands in the movies, the popcorn between them.

She had come back. He guessed now that she had always been elusive. Once she told him she had married him because he let her breathe. Loving was easy, she said. It was breathing that was hard.

". . . and, Doctor, I've taken a house at the beach for the rest of the summer . . ." Mrs. Simpson went on in the background. The lines on her face curved up instead of down now. He wondered if he'd had anything to do with it. He wished he were pottering about in the heavy moisture of his greenhouse, where he could really relax. The progress of his plants was more easily measured than the progress of his patients.

Had Kate thought of leaving him? He glared at the pattern of the Oriental rug that covered his office floor. They had furnished this house together, saving some of the best and some of the worst things for George's office. This carpet had been in the house when they had moved here; it was threadbare and full of character, they agreed. They had both liked it. He was drawn now into the whirling of its faded colors. Had it moved? Had it turned to a heavy scarlet syrup? No. No. He jerked his head up and caught Mrs. Simpson full in the face. Kate would never leave him.

He glanced at his watch. His jaws ached from suppressed yawns. He never slept well when he slept alone. This was his last appointment of the day. It was warm. When could he get out of this suit? Only fifteen minutes had passed. What was Kate doing now? Was that jerk with her? Perhaps George would wait outside the hospital and follow him. He could push him in front of a car. He could even hire somebody to do it. God! He felt like eating licorice, black shoestring licorice. His mother had said it wasn't good for him, but he used to sneak it when he was a boy. She would always find out when he came home with blackened teeth.

"Do you like licorice?" he interrupted Mrs. Simpson's monologue. He would even settle for Smith Brothers cough drops.

"Pardon me?" She crossed her legs. "Well," she took a deep breath. "I am trying to lose weight. Last night, for example, I ate only half portions." She continued, outlining her menu for the rest of the week.

George thought of his ten o'clock patient, a woman who weighed three hundred pounds. They had wired her jaw shut and fed her liquids through a straw, but she'd lost only one pound in a month. Now she was contemplating having part of her stomach removed. Or was it her intestine? George had hated his surgical rotation. The operating room had no color: silver and white glare. Even the blood seemed gray, the dialogue stilted, like a bizarre meal where no one eats but everyone carves the roast.

They claimed Kate's malignancy was arrested; they had gotten it all. Did he want to watch? they asked him. As a physician, he could watch. Surely he would want to watch. He looked at the clock across the room. Twenty minutes to go.

It was different when Ellen was born. They'd had fun. They were young and had not been so scared. They did not plan for problems, and none had occurred. They'd read Dylan Thomas aloud, done the breathing together, and delivered a normal, healthy baby girl. Sure, there was blood. It was an operating room. And Kate had bellowed with pain. But they knew no one would die.

He did not watch them cut Kate open. He saw his early patients, as usual, and jogged around the track at the Y, as usual. He was there when she awakened. "It's going to be all right," he told her. She groaned. She had not opened her eyes. Yesterday he had spent an hour picking buttercups for her. He'd had a cancellation. Yellow was her color. She even liked dandelions. They were livelier than roses, she said. Often, at the end of summer, she filled his office with sunflowers. She seemed to know what he wanted even before he did. Small things like sunflowers. Or more important things like knowing when the house needed a new roof or arranging his mother's funeral. Sometimes at night in bed, when he drew into himself, she would curl up against him, her head nestled between his shoulder blades. She would try to bite his spine or print messages on his back.

Mrs. Simpson was getting up. She was holding out her hand. George's leg was asleep. If he got up, he might fall. "And so, Doctor," she was smiling, her lips twitching just a bit, "perhaps we'll meet again."

He had failed her. This had been her day, her time. He had let her down, and she hadn't seemed to notice. He got to his feet, his leg cramping. He would offer her another session with no fee. Closure was crucial. He watched a spider crawling up the wall. Years ago, that would have embarrassed him. "Mrs. Simpson," he began. But she was already barreling toward the door.

She turned. She was sniffling. "Thank you for everything." She smiled.

Why did they always say that? He should hug her. They should cry together and applaud their good work. But she crossed the threshold, clicked the door shut behind

32

her, and was gone. George was relieved.

He tore through the house looking for licorice, the way he and Kate had ransacked pockets for change when he was in medical school. Why had they decided to give up sugar? It was a half-hearted attempt. Anyway, they both kept their stashes. He searched all the usual places: the bread box, the bookcases, the medicine chest. But he came up empty.

He phoned Kate at the hospital. "Did I wake you?" She sounded groggy, distant.

"Who is this?" Yes, she was definitely groggy.

"I'm dying for licorice," he said. "Do we have any in the house?"

"There's some in your old backyard on Thompson Street." She was awake now. "We buried it with the chameleon when he died. Don't you remember? We mummified the chameleon and buried him with treasure, just like the pharaohs. Fifth grade? Or sixth?"

"What's the penalty for grave robbing?" It felt normal to banter with her.

"What time are you coming tonight?" she asked. "I'm awfully tired."

Oh, no, he thought. She'd rather be with someone else. Somehow, it seemed less real if he didn't call Charlie by name. "I'll come right now. Is there anything you want? Ice cream? Prunes? Prune ice cream?" He suddenly felt fine, just fine. He was almost high.

"Nope," she said. "See you soon." She hung up.

George found himself driving across town to his parents' Thompson Street house. He had changed his clothes and was more comfortable, but it was still warm. He refused to have air conditioning in his car. As he stepped on the brake at a light, he realized he had not changed his socks.

Kate wouldn't like it: Bermuda shorts and black socks. Well, at least he was cooler than he'd been all day. " 'I like to catch brass rings on the merry-go-round,' " he sang, " 'the merry-go-round, that's me.' " It was a reflex, as he drove into the old neighborhood. It had been his mother's favorite tune. What was he doing here? The folks were dead now; he hadn't been here since he'd sold their house. He felt a bead of sweat roll down his side, playing his ribs like a xylophone. Had he really come here to dig up the dead chameleon and forty-year-old licorice? He slowed the car down. There were children playing stickball in the street.

And then he saw his house. They had painted his house green. Not forest green. Or mint green. It was the color of lima beans. The house looked puffy and tired. Once he had left lima beans on his plate and found them on top of his cereal the next morning. His house had always been white. Who would ever paint a three-story frame house green, anyway?

He drove to the end of the street and turned around. Kids were roller-skating on the sidewalks. He smiled at them. None smiled back. He passed his house. "Damn," he said aloud. "Goddamn."

Two blocks away, he thought, Kate's parents were watching the evening news or finishing their dinner. Their house was white with blue trim, as it had always been. He could go by and say hello. They wouldn't mind his black socks. They would offer him an iced tea. They would ask about his tennis game, although he had given it up two years ago. Isn't Kate making fine progress, they would say. And he would say, oh, yes, she certainly is. He decided not to stop.

He turned on the radio for the eight o'clock news. It was still ninety degrees. The National Centers for Disease Control had announced that herpes was now a nationwide epidemic. The daredevil Evel Knievel had broken his fiftieth bone earlier in the day trying to leap over twenty-three cars on a motorcycle. George turned the radio off. He was late. Would Kate even notice? The clock regulated his life; he was never late. What if he just didn't show up at all? He could go to a movie or walk the dog or just drive around singing old songs.

The cold air shimmied its way into his veins as he passed through the hospital lobby. He didn't even look around for Charlie. If he was here, too bad. That's all. It would just be too bad.

Kate's cheeks were sunken as if a small animal had nested on either side of her face. Her hair hung limply across her shoulders. He remembered that she had chewed on the ends of her braids when she was in kindergarten. Now she looked either much younger or much older than she was. He couldn't decide.

It was OK that he was late, she said. There had been other visitors. The balloons drooped like old condoms, George thought. She was kissing his hand; she was chewing on his fingers. She hated sleeping without him, she said. Her feet were always cold.

"Here," he said. He took off his black socks and gave them to her, glad to be rid of them.

"I can't reach my toes yet," she said. "Even when I was pregnant I could still reach my toes."

He put his socks on her. For a medium-sized person, her feet were big; his socks were just the right size. His own bare feet felt strange in his loafers. He never wore shoes without socks.

"Rhoda has plastic breasts," Kate said, as she and George took their hike down the hall. "And she's getting a plastic leg," she added. "Her husband left her."

35

"How was your afternoon?" George was suspicious of plastic parts. His father had had a Teflon aorta and had died anyway. "You can't expect too much from a Cracker Jack prize," he had warned the family.

"Rhoda's a violinist," Kate said. She was leaning against his shoulder. Her grip on his arm tightened with each step. He hadn't known her hands could be so strong.

George's neck was already starting to stiffen from the air conditioning. His stomach growled. "They painted the house green," he said. "The house on Thompson Street."

"Don't you think I'm walking better now?" Kate said, making an effort to stand tall.

"It's a lima-bean color," George went on. "And the front yard is full of weeds."

CHAPTER
· FOUR ·

Charlie looked at himself in the plate-glass window as he entered the bank on State Street to make a withdrawal. He was always surprised to see how long he was. His father had called him "beanpole" when he passed six feet in the seventh grade. Charlie had never seen a beanpole. He supposed it was something like a peashooter, only longer. He brushed back the lock of auburn hair on his forehead and went inside the bank. The air was clear and cool. Three days of consecutive ninety-degree heat, much less a whole month, was unusual for Boston. But it was July. What could you expect? And once the ski season was over, it might as well be summer anyway.

He stood in the roped-off line tapping his foot. Why couldn't people make their own queues as they always had? Each teller had a small light and a bell to tell you when to move ahead. Whoever sold those contraptions was making a bundle. Charlie looked around. The man behind him wore a bulky raincoat, which was odd for such a hot day. He could have a weapon underneath. Charlie shuffled a few inches forward. He was anxious to get his money and leave. There was a tomblike quality about banks he didn't like. The shoulders of the woman in front of him were red. Maybe she had eaten lunch outside. She might even have had a salami on rye with half-sour pickles. Charlie was hungry.

What could he buy Kate? He had already sent a large bouquet of gladiolus. "It looks like a funeral arrangement," one of the nurses had said. She was right. The bell rang, and the light went on.

"Go ahead." The man in the raincoat nudged him in the shoulder.

"Sorry," Charlie said, as he jumped toward the teller. She wore a light-blue suit and glasses with her initials on one lens. He and his brother had often been "bankers" when they were children. They had never let their sister play. "Girls aren't bankers," they told her. One stood behind a spoked dining-room chair and arranged the Monopoly money in neat rows. The other was the customer. Sometimes it took them all day to set it up. How could it have taken so long? And why, he wondered, looking again at the man in the raincoat, hadn't one of them been a robber? They hadn't even thought of it. It might have been fun to be a robber.

The teller gave Charlie his money, and he loped out into the crowded street. He had left the office for the day. The market had been going crazy for months. Business was good, but crazy nonetheless. No one could predict what would happen from one day to the next. Luckily for him, his clients were speculators who were after big bucks. But then, commodities traders never had to deal with the nickel and dime stuff. So at two in the afternoon he was free. Most of his clients were on the golf course by now anyway. He should play more golf. It was good for business. If only it moved a little faster. He loosened his tie as he headed for his car. He should call his sister. He should have let her play "bank."

He had double-parked a few steps from the bank's entrance. A cop was just starting to write up the ticket.

"It was an emergency, Officer." Charlie ran up to him. "My wife's in the hospital. I needed the cash." He had forgotten how hot it was. Sweat dripped from his forehead.

The policeman stared at Charlie, unconvinced. He stood with one hip thrust out, his arms folded across his chest.

Charlie made his eyes wide as a boy's. "She's had a cancer operation. I had to buy her flowers," he stammered. The sweat stung his eyes.

"I've already started to write the ticket, mister," the cop said. He was old enough to be Charlie's father. If *he* were a cop, Charlie thought, he would want to be a mounted policeman on one of those huge Morgan horses that Sears dame had donated to the city.

"Please"—he made one last attempt—"I'm in a hurry. She's liable to come out of the anesthetic any minute. I want to be there."

The policeman's eyes narrowed. "What hospital?" he said. He had a slight lisp.

"Mass General." Charlie whimpered on purpose, knowing he'd won.

"OK, mister," the cop said. "Move along. But don't do it again. Boston streets weren't meant for the automobile, you know."

"Yeah," said Charlie. "They shouldn't allow cars within city limits." Cops liked that idea.

The cop smiled on one side of his mouth. "Good luck to you," he waved as Charlie got into his car. "And to your wife."

Charlie sighed with satisfaction as he started the engine. He had waited his whole life—thirty-two years—for this Mercedes. And even now, after two years, he still did the tune-ups himself. He turned on the air conditioner. He was

39

soaked, and his pants stuck to the leather seat.

Where should he go now? If he went to the hospital, one of Kate's friends was sure to be there. Had she told any of them about him? He could go and pretend to be visiting Rhoda. Now there was a gal for you. Half plastic, but all woman. No. He wouldn't go. He would have to wait until after ten tonight.

"Get on top of me," Kate had said the last time he was there. "Come on."

"Later." He was too long for the bed, anyway, he said. He was afraid of hurting her. Besides, what would he do if her husband came? Whip out his cards and do a trick? He thought he had seen George Cummings once in the lobby, but he wasn't sure. They had gotten on the same elevator together, and this George, or whoever he was, had gotten off at Kate's floor. Charlie had kept going and had ended up in geriatrics.

He had been a patient in a hospital only once. He had broken both legs in a skiing accident. At least they didn't hang over the end, since both were in traction. They had told him he was too big to be a skier, and that was all the challenge he needed. He had tackled the advanced trails within a few weeks, skiing bareheaded, barehanded, even in the coldest weather. His father had called him "bare-brained." But he was eighteen then. He had had a lot to prove. "Basketball," his father insisted. "Six feet six and he doesn't want to play basketball." His father had been a star at Boston College, but didn't have the height to turn pro. He had settled for a job as athletic director at Winchester High.

The car was cool now. Charlie drove along the Charles River. Nearly naked summer-school students lay on the banks. He wished Kate were his wife, as he had told the cop. At least then he could see her during normal visiting hours, instead of sleazing around.

He parked illegally again along the river. But it wouldn't be the same cop, he thought. He left his jacket in the car and walked down to the water. A soft breeze took the edge off the oppressive heat. Some kids were trying to fly a kite, but there wasn't enough wind to get it up. They ran along, the bat-shaped mass behind them in the air. When they stopped, the kite took a nose dive. They laughed anyway; they were having a fine time.

He and Janet had had one of their first dates right here on the Esplanade. It had been a Fourth of July concert. Arthur Fiedler had been magnificent, and "The Stars and Stripes Forever" became their song. But the past few years his wife hadn't wanted to come here anymore. She was too tired. Or it was too hot. Or the kids would get too restless.

"Fiedler's dead, so what does it matter, anyway?" she said.

"Postpartum depression," the doctor told him on the phone.

"But it's more than a year since the baby was born," Charlie said. "She never wants to do anything." Was he whining? "Some days she never even gets dressed. She wasn't this way with the other two." He remembered the phone call. He had just come back from a weekend of skiing at Stowe. He shouldn't have gone. But what was he supposed to do? Sit home all the time? And the powder had been packed and perfect.

"I'll prescribe some antidepressants." Charlie could imagine Dr. Deardorff's jagged face as he wrote on his prescription pad. You could never tell what he was thinking.

Janet hadn't wanted another baby. The others were in school now, and she wanted to go back to work. She wanted to get away from the house. Maybe she even wanted to get away from him. They had discussed abortion. Mostly, she had discussed it, he remembered. She was always big on discussions. Round-table discussions, she called them, although their kitchen table was rectangular, Charlie would point out. He could never seem to say what she wanted, as if there were some magic words she expected that he didn't know. Still, he liked the angle of her dark eyebrows when she was serious.

"If you want an abortion, it's OK with me," he'd said. "Or if you want the baby, that's fine, too." Maybe he should have taken a firmer stand. But it was her body.

She couldn't make up her mind. They went over the pros and cons again and again. He lost patience with the discussions. Finally, he said, "Look, you either do it or you don't." He had just bought the Mercedes. They were eating spaghetti at a local restaurant. Janet was twirling her pasta on her fork and had stopped after he'd spoken. She stared at him for a long time. He could still feel the power of the perfect engine of his new car; he loved its rich maroon shine. Then she threw the fork at him. He had laughed; he had always loved her spirit. A strand of spaghetti hung over his eye, another on his shoulder. His face and shirt were spattered with sauce. As he dipped his napkin in the water glass so he could wipe off his face, he saw that she was crying.

"You think it's so easy," she said. "You think everything is so easy. Do it or don't do it." He thought she might spit at him. "Do it or don't do it," she repeated in a singsong tone. She shoved the plate of food away from her.

"I always say the wrong thing," he said, following her outside. He noticed some dirt on the rear fender of his car.

So she had had the baby, a girl this time. They had both wanted a girl.

Janet had been taking the antidepressants for several

months now. Charlie had taken them himself at first, when she refused.

"I'll take one if you take one," he said.

"This is silly," she said. But it had worked. And after a few weeks she claimed she was feeling better. At least she got dressed every morning now. All the drugs had done for Charlie was to make his mouth dry.

He was thirsty now. Why didn't somebody start a beer concession along the river?

The kids would be home from day camp by this time, and the baby would be having her nap. He could play ball with the boys. He had bought Jimmy a new baseball glove last week and showed him how to condition it with linseed oil.

A jogger panted by, followed by two golden retrievers. Some people never used their arms when they ran, looking like wooden soldiers. The last time he had gone home early in the afternoon, he had found Janet sitting by a window in the living room. It was winter, and the shadows had already gathered.

"Shall I turn a light on?" he asked.

"Go away," she said. "Leave me alone."

He had not known what to say, so he had said nothing.

He would not go home this afternoon. The river lapped gently at its bank. Someone was feeding the squawking gulls. In his father's day, you could swim in the river; no one would take that chance today. He would take Kate sailing here when she got out of the hospital. She would love it.

He got to his feet. There were grass stains on his pants. He would buy Kate a present, a terrific present. It would make her laugh. He saw that his car had no ticket. What luck. He believed in luck. You had to, to be a broker, he smirked.

He found solid gold earrings at Churchill's on Newbury

43

Street. They were handmade. Kate would love them. They
cost eight hundred dollars. They were golden kites with
their corners askew. He got two boxes—one for each ear-
ring—and put one in each pants pocket.

He was home in the Oak Hill section of Newton by five-
thirty. Did Janet actually smile as he came in the door?
"I'll get you a drink," she said. "Shall I get the boys? They're
swimming next door."

"I'll mow the lawn before dinner," he said. Was she wearing a new dress? "I'll change my clothes."

It was hot. It was crazy to mow the grass, which hadn't
grown in two weeks because of the heat. But he had to
do something. The yard was a good size, and he was soaked
before he even started up the engine. But he liked the noise
of it, the power of it. You couldn't hear anything else. He
liked jobs like this one. Up and down. Back and forth.
You could see your progress; the job had a beginning, middle, and end, like courting a new client.

Afterward, he felt light-headed and thirsty. He gulped
a cold beer right from the bottle. Janet hated that. All
women hated that.

He took the bottle upstairs and finished it in the shower.
The smell of cut grass hung in his nostrils.

"I knew it," Kate had said when they first showered together.

"Knew what?"

"You're the kind of man who doesn't dry his back," she
said.

"What does that mean?" he said.

But she hadn't told him. She had put her arms around
him and laughed. She'd found soapsuds on his collarbone.

"I can't stay for dinner," he told Janet when he came downstairs to the kitchen. She was holding little Janie on her

hip. She was still smiling. Maybe Deardorff had changed her prescription again.

"I've got a late meeting," he said, throwing the empty beer bottle across the room into the wastebasket. If his father were here, he'd have reminded Charlie he could have been a Boston Celtic; they might even have retired his jersey by now. Not long ago, Janet would have said, "Larry Bird for two!" The boys would still say it. He'd gotten season tickets last year and taken Jimmy and Mike to nearly every home game.

"I've made gazpacho for you," Janet said. She'd gone to one basketball game at the Garden last winter. But she insisted they leave before the first quarter was over. It was too hot and too smoky, she said, and it smelled like beer. The Celtics had been playing Philadelphia.

She looked at his bare legs now. Gazpacho was his favorite. What kind of meeting could he go to with bare legs? her eyes said. She knew how carefully he dressed for business. Nevertheless, he often had meetings with clients at odd hours. She was used to it. He felt the two small packages in his pockets.

"I was thinking," she said, putting the child down on the shiny, speckled linoleum.

Oh no, he thought. He had gotten used to her silences.

"I was thinking of planting vegetables. Do you think it's too late? Cabbage and corn. Peas and tomatoes. Beans and cauliflower." She went on and on. They had played Categories late at night when she was pregnant and couldn't sleep. Avocado. Kale. Alfalfa sprouts.

Little Janie had overturned the wastebasket. The beer bottle rolled across the floor. Charlie scooped up the baby, while Janet picked up the bottle and some Popsicle wrappers.

"I know it's July already," she went on, her voice sound-

45

ing like soft wind chimes. "But I'd like to try."

Charlie shifted from one foot to the other. He guessed he could stay for dinner, he said. His feet were wet inside his moccasins. He should have put powder in them. The baby squirmed in his arms. She had prickly heat on her neck.

"I could turn over the garden tomorrow," Janet said. It was a question. All her words were questions.

CHAPTER

· FIVE ·

George was saying good-night when Kate saw Charlie at the doorway, a small package in each hand. There was only one light on in the room.

"Darling," Charlie said, sweeping his arms behind his back. "Pick a hand, any hand." He strode to the side of her bed.

"Do you think you have the wrong room?" Kate managed to say. She had to say something.

There was a long silence. George stood up from his chair. He was so much smaller than Charlie he looked shrunken; she'd forgotten he was also ten years older. She'd never noticed George's receding hairline before. Now she saw that Charlie had twice the amount of hair that George had. George's mouth was slightly agape, as if he might drool a bit, as he did when he slept heavily, or when he had first learned to kiss.

They were in the backseat of someone's car after a prom. She was crushed in net and full skirts. Her shoes were pinching her feet. It was a big deal—this soul kissing. Afterward, George said he had been too nervous to swallow. That's why all the saliva had dripped down onto his jacket and onto Kate's corsage. She looked at her hands, clenched into fists now. What was the matter with her? How could she think about kissing at a time like this? She should have told Charlie to stay away. And now it was too late.

Rhoda flipped on the TV. It was a rerun of *Hill Street Blues*. "I like the guy who plays the dog," she said. "He reminds me of my ex-husband. Just watch him when he bares his teeth."

"I'm sorry," Charlie said. "I guess I do have the wrong room." He started to back out, like someone being presented to the queen.

"Don't be silly, Charlie," Kate said. What was the use? "Come and sit down." They could all be civilized, couldn't they? There would be no homicides here. Could she ever make them understand that one of them had nothing to do with the other? "Charlie, this is George. George, this is Charlie."

There was a commercial for a douche called Summer's Eve on Rhoda's TV.

"Well, how do you do," said Charlie, sticking his hand out to shake George's. He still had the package in it. But it was a small package with a small pink ribbon. Who could even tie a ribbon so small? George offered his hand. Kate could see the box between them as they made the gesture. She felt the veins on her own hands growing larger.

"Oops, sorry," said Charlie, putting the package in his pocket. "I've heard a lot about you," he said to George. "You're a shrink, right?"

"Yes," said George. He would be polite, Kate knew. Of course, he would be polite. What other choices were there? Her incision throbbed. Maybe she would never heal. Maybe the staples were rusting. Maybe they had left an instrument inside her. A scissors.

"I always thought Furillo's nose was too big for a leading

48

character," Rhoda said, as her program continued.

"I'm a broker, you know," said Charlie. He was on familiar ground now. He sat down on a chair on the other side of Kate's bed from George. "A commodities broker." He slipped off his moccasins and wiggled his bare feet along the antiseptic floor.

"Yes, I know you're a broker," George said. Kate turned to look at him. She could not see both men at the same time. How did George know? How did George know anything about Charlie?

The TV program was in its last few minutes. There was a shootout: the bad guys, the good guys, the yelling. "The thing about this program," Rhoda said, "is that justice isn't always served. Ho hum." She sighed.

Kate knew she should say something, do something. On the other hand, she thought, this is nothing. A few days ago, she was nearly dead. "I think I'll go to the bathroom now," she said. No one could get angry with her for going to the bathroom. I'm a coward, she told herself. But how could they get mad at her? She could be dead. And then where would they be?

Both men jumped to their feet to help her out of bed. "I can do it myself," she said. "Just get my legs over the side." The floor was cold on her feet, like the metal instruments in the operating room. Had they been cold? Or did they actually heat the utensils the way she heated plates for dinner?

She moved slowly between Charlie and George, between Rhoda and the TV. With one hand she moved the IV unit; with the other she held the back of the hospital gown. "Don't look," she said. Maybe they would both leave before she came out. Whenever she and her mother had argued, she had always run to the bathroom to hide, locking the door behind her. Her mother told her she had never grown up. Was she right? They had no locks on bathrooms here. A patient might need help or even die; the nurses had to get in.

She looked at herself in the mirror expecting to see a pale skeleton and was surprised at her tan, at the brightness of her eyes. She felt as if she'd been reading Poe for a long time. " 'Once upon a midnight dreary,' " she said aloud. There had been other relationships. Other men. But if George had known, he had never said anything. Now that he and Charlie were out there breathing the same air, she would have to explain herself. And what could she say? That she was sorry? She looked for some remorse in her eyes and felt a surge of energy. She couldn't help herself: The situation was exhilarating. Had she become one of those risk-taking junkies who can only be happy living on the edges of disaster? Had she become so self-involved that she didn't care about anyone else?

The vitality faded as quickly as it had come. She didn't want to face anyone. She couldn't. Maybe she could signal Rhoda to call for a bedpan. Then they'd leave. She would write Rhoda a note and pass it to her as she went to bed. Where was a pencil? This is dumb, she reprimanded herself. "I'm very tired," she practiced to the mirror. "Would you both please go home?" And then she would ring for a morphine shot. That's why she'd been thinking of Poe. He'd been addicted to morphine, hadn't he? Well, they had already started cutting back on her pain-killers. Tonight she would insist. But if both George and Charlie left at once, what would happen? What did she want to happen? She had never considered it. Since she had known she would die, she had lived only in the present. Well, she hadn't died. It was getting to be a problem.

As she maneuvered her way back to bed, she heard the eleven o'clock news. The Red Sox had won in twelve innings. Big deal. The heat wave would continue. A beer commercial. Rhoda winked at her. George and Charlie were still there. Had they been talking to each other? Three marine recruits had been killed in war games in California. There was a shot of President Reagan on his horse at the ranch. Kate got herself up on the step stool and into the bed. She lay back with a groan.

"Everything all right?" asked George. Was he going to say something about her bowels?

"Still here?" she said.

"George is treating Janet," Charlie said. His eyes looked cornered in his face.

"Janet?" Kate said.

"My wife," Charlie said.

"Your wife?" She could only repeat what had been said. It would be safe. There was a glass of ginger ale on the tray still blowing its bubbles.

"Dr. Deardorff referred her to George," Charlie said.

"Dr. Deardorff?" Kate would have to stop this.

"Oh, boy," she thought she heard Rhoda say as the news ended.

"Her obstetrician," Charlie continued.

"Well," Kate said. "There's no need to get excited." Where was her morphine? Where was the nurse? "Why didn't you tell me?" She turned to George.

George looked at his loafers. He looked at Charlie. "I didn't make the connection until tonight," he said. "They have different last names, you know." He scratched his knees. "I think I'll be going now. This air conditioning is killing my neck." He rubbed it. "Or maybe it's the tension." Why did he always talk about tension in that velvety voice? Why was he always so reasonable? He stood up. "I don't know how you girls can stand this cold air," he said.

"Women. Women," Kate corrected him.

"Yes, women," he said. "Good night." He kissed her forehead, waved to Rhoda, and nodded to Charlie.

"George," Kate called to him as he moved to the doorway.

He turned around. One shoulder was higher than the other. "Yes?" he said.

"I'm sorry about your house, George," she said.

"Good night," he said.

"It's *The Tonight Show* with Johnny Carson," the TV blared. Rhoda turned it off. "Oh, boy," she said.

"Maybe I should go, too," said Charlie.

"Oh, no," said Kate quickly, reaching out her hand to him. "Don't go." She thought of a dream she often had of sitting down to a meal where there was no food on the plate. She was a guest and had to pretend the meal was delicious as she clattered her knife and fork against the empty white china. She would wake up, her jaws tired from smiling and from chewing the air.

"I can't believe he knows Janet," Charlie said, drinking the ginger ale. "And that Dr. Deardorff sent her there just this week."

So Charlie's wife had kept her maiden name. "I don't want to talk about Janet," said Kate. By now, George would be pulling out of the parking lot.

"I don't blame you," said Rhoda.

"No wonder she seemed so cheerful," Charlie continued anyway. "She finally decided to go to a shrink after all this time."

"Truth is stranger than fiction," Rhoda said.

"Give me all your aces," said Kate. George had known about Charlie all along. She knew it now.

Charlie stood up and reached into his pockets. "I nearly forgot," he said. "I have a present for you." He gave her both boxes at once.

Her fingers were tired. They seemed to be made only

52

of bone. She could hardly open the tiny boxes. "They're lovely," she said, reaching for an enthusiasm she knew was beyond her.

"Kites," Charlie said.

"Yes," she said.

"Put them on," he said.

"But I don't have pierced ears." She and George and Ellen had often made kites at the beach. "Go fly a kite," they had shouted to each other.

"My mother made me promise never to pierce my ears," Kate told Rhoda after Charlie had left and she'd had her sweet shot of morphine.

"How come?" said Rhoda. She had refused her injection, claiming that feeling something was better than feeling nothing.

"Only certain kinds of girls have pierced ears, you know," Kate mimicked her mother. "I think she was afraid I'd turn into a gypsy."

"There are some marvelous gypsy violinists," Rhoda said. "Are you sure that shot is what you wanted?" It was dim in the room now. There were shadows tapping at the walls.

Kate didn't want to think about George or Charlie. She didn't want to think about Rhoda or the hospital. "If only I could dissect a nice fetal pig now," she said.

"What?" Rhoda said.

"That's what I do for a living."

"What?" Rhoda repeated.

"Dissect fetal pigs. Well, not only pigs," she said. "Cats are good, too. But they're harder to get. They like to give us rats." The morphine was making her tongue thick. "I teach anatomy and physiology, you know. To nursing students. That's why we only get pigs. Medical students get the real cadavers."

"And all this time I thought you were a lady of leisure,"

Rhoda said. "Sneaking off to hotels in the middle of the day. That aristocratic nose fooled me."

"It's the circulatory system I like best," Kate said. She had trouble saying circulatory. "Each vein, each artery has its own function. Like a motor. Did you ever take a motor apart?"

"You should have been a surgeon," Rhoda said. "You could have done my leg."

"Clocks," said Kate. "I love clocks."

"Those earrings are gorgeous," Rhoda said. "I got my wedding ring at that shop. When we split, I took it back. They gave me more money than we'd paid for it. The price of gold's gone nuts. Will you have your ears pierced now? We could do it right here. I'll bet Blue Cross would even pay for it."

"I wonder if I gave them each a clock to dissect the first day in anatomy . . ." Kate thought aloud. It was a splendid idea. "They're so squeamish about the crayfish." She pushed the button to lower her head. It was the wrong button. Her feet went up. She was nearly at a right angle before she realized it.

CHAPTER

· SIX ·

The next day, George decided he was going to stop pretending. He had spent a sleepless night obsessing about his wife and her lover. Why had he left them together in the hospital? Wasn't he man enought to fight for her? And what kind of dumb question was that? Man enough.

Well, he was a creature of habit. It was true; it was a comfort. He saw his early morning patients and went jogging. He liked running in the heat. He was up to twenty miles a week now, and his gait was easy.

He'd spent a long time just sitting in his greenhouse after coming home last night. The dog had crawled underneath one of the low tables where it was cool. She wasn't allowed in the greenhouse, but George could never get her to behave when Kate wasn't around. His feet made a crunching sound on the moist pebbles. The dog was panting. George sat on a stool in the middle of the enclosure. There was no question about it: His thumb was green. Nothing would die under his care. Of course, many of his plants were outdoors now for the summer. But he kept his pets inside. Succulents he had grown from seed. A new variety of staghorn fern. Donkey's tails.

People always expected that he raised orchids since he had a greenhouse. But he liked more ordinary plants. Oh, he had tried orchids and other exotic things. But somehow they seemed too fragile; they needed special treatment, special diets, like Olympic athletes or operatic sopranos. Imported soil and light at odd times.

Janet Jerome had wept the full fifty minutes of their first appointment. She sat on her hands. And the tears fell silently down her cheeks. She was small and dark with almond eyes. Like a miniature Joan Baez. It was the day before Kate's surgery; she'd gone off for the afternoon claiming she needed to be alone. He knew she was with Charlie. But he had not connected Charlie with Janet until he and Charlie had talked in the hospital.

"I wish my wife would see a psychiatrist," Charlie had said. "She's been out of it for more than a year now." And he had told George the story. People always seemed to think George was dying to hear their dismal tales. Didn't he hear enough problems as it was? But he supposed Charlie got his share of requests for free tips about the market and investments. Kate was lucky that way. Who would ask her about cutting up small animals? Except at Thanksgiving. There was always a great to-do about sharpening knives at Thanksgiving.

Well, it had finally happened: He'd caught Kate and Charlie together. And the two men had chatted about Charlie's wife as if they were nothing more than strangers on an airplane, while Kate hid in the bathroom. Charlie went on about the baby, the depression, how his wife wouldn't go anywhere, do anything.

George felt a hot circle on the back of his neck. "Your wife's name isn't Janet, is it?" he asked after a time, certain that it wasn't. He shouldn't have mentioned her name. But Charlie's voice was beginning to bother him; it was a hail-fellow voice full of sharp edges. At the same time, George sensed that silence in the room would precipitate disaster.

This Charlie seemed like a nice enough fellow, he kept telling himself. He was young though, awfully young. The detective George had hired hadn't said anything about how young he was. George would never tell anyone about the detective; he was ashamed of himself. But he'd had to know. He'd got Marabel Greenleaf from the Yellow Pages: the Star Detective Agency. Imagine it: a woman detective. Well, what else could he do? Ask a friend? Do the snooping himself? Do nothing? He was spying. He knew he was spying. Kate might even have had other relationships, but he had never considered spying.

The Greenleaf woman had made him feel worse instead of better, as if he himself were a criminal. He was doing it out of concern, he'd told her, and out of love. She looked at him as if he'd brought an odd odor into her office. She'd worked for Kevin White in three mayoralty races; that's how she got interested in the detective business, she said, as if that explained everything.

For several months now, he had stopped by her office each week for her reports. It had become a humiliating addiction. Two hundred and fifty a week he paid her for the predictable information.

"You're a real Samantha Spade," he tried to kid her the first time they met. But he was never very good at kidding.

"When do you think you'll go to court?" she asked. She would get photographs, she said. And he shouldn't worry about alimony, she told him. The courts were different today. And did he want to have dinner at her house?

She looked more like a Girl Scout leader than a private eye, he thought. She wore sensible oxfords and no-frill clothing on her ample frame. She was divorced, she told him. Four teenaged kids, she said, and an alcoholic ex-husband.

They did not go to dinner. He had never been interested

in other women. Most men, it seemed, could never get enough. Or at least they felt they should say so. But Kate—and Ellen—were his life.

Mrs. Greenleaf had not taken long to get the preliminary information: Charles Milton Murdoch, stockbroker, married, three children, University of Massachusetts, Harvard Business School. A good credit risk. Marathon runner. Of course, he would have to be a marathon runner. He probably made it in under three hours, too. No. George would not tell anyone about the Star Detective Agency.

He saw Charlie half rise from the hospital chair, as if he'd been goosed. "Do you know Janet?" he said.

Of course, if George had been paying attention, he'd have put Janet and Charlie together before this. He'd met other relatives of his patients. Boston was not that big a town. And George kept his mouth shut, never talking about his patients to anyone but Kate. And then only occasionally.

Before he could correct his blunder, Charlie said, "Janet Jerome. My wife. You do know her. I can tell. You do know her."

George looked hopefully toward the lavatory door. There was no way out of this. "She was referred to me by Herb Deardorff," he said. Well, it was out now. Let the bastard stew a bit.

"As a patient? A patient?" said Charlie, sitting up in his chair again. "Did she tell you about me? What did she tell you about me? So that's how you know I'm a broker. What else did she say? What did she say about me?"

Me me me. He was beginning to see at least one dimension of Janet Jerome's problem.

"I have dreams of murdering my husband," she'd said between tears. "He never stands still."

Indeed, Charlie had jiggled his legs the entire time George sat with him in Kate's hospital room. There was no denying

58

it: He had a certain electricity about him. No wonder Kate liked him. He was that Applegate kid reincarnated.

"I see him lying in a pool of blood," Ms. Jerome had said, "on the kitchen floor." She paused a long time, and then she said, "and I'm glad he's dead. But I'm sad," she sniffed. "I'm sad because the blood is sticky and won't come off the linoleum." She laughed a very small laugh. "Lady Macbeth Syndrome?"

Well, he would have to decide what to do about Janet Jerome. He could hardly treat her now. However, he could hardly tell her, "I can't see you because your husband is sleeping with my wife." He would have to think of something. Maybe he could refer her to a group. Or, he thought, smiling to himself, maybe he could persuade her to kill Charlie after all. "Yes," he would say afterward, "I was treating her. She was psychopathic; we just couldn't keep it under control. Yes," he would testify, "I spoke to Mr. Murdoch on many occasions about hospitalizing his wife. But he wouldn't hear of it. Yes," he would say, "it's terribly difficult for families to accept mental illness in those closest to them." And Charlie would say nothing. Charlie would be dead.

He sprayed the new roses he was growing from cuttings. They had thorns even in their infancy. There was nothing much wrong with Janet Jerome, he decided. She was depressed and angry, to be sure. But she'd begun to take charge of her life again. She would be OK. A high-powered husband and three small children weren't easy for anyone to manage. Did Charlie know she had already made plans to leave him?

When George stopped by the hospital that afternoon, some of Kate's friends were there. They always kissed him, her friends. And after dinner her mother was visiting. He was sure Kate had asked her mother to come; she usually didn't go out at night. He was relieved they didn't have to talk about Charlie.

"Did you know they painted George's old house green, Mother?" Kate was saying. She was eating an enormous peach from a basket of fruit someone had sent. A dark eyelash lay on her cheekbone.

"I guess I overreacted," said George. But his stomach sank as he thought of the color. Bile, he thought. It's like bile.

"After all these years, Kate," Mrs. Logan said. "After all these years, I just can't imagine why you would do it." She wore a print sundress; her shoulders were freckled; small wads of flesh hung from her upper arms. She uncrossed her legs and then crossed them again. George could hear the rustle of her stockings. Even in summer, she wore stockings.

Does she know? George wondered. Does she know about Kate and Charlie?

"And does George know what you've done?" she clucked. She does know, he realized.

"It's really not worth talking about, Mother," said Kate. "Who's living on Thompson Street now, George? Must be new people."

"But you promised you'd never pierce your ears, Kate. You did promise. You know the sort of girls who pierce their ears. I've even heard that some men do it now." She frowned. She looked at George. "Don't tell me, George," she began. "You haven't mutilated yourself, have you?"

"Don't worry, Mrs. Logan," George said. He had never gotten used to calling her anything else. "Don't worry. I'm still in one piece." So that's what it was about: ears. And not about Charlie. George glanced toward Rhoda's bed. The curtain was drawn around it.

60

"She's had a bad day," Kate said. "They've doped her up."

"What's this about pierced ears?" George said. He wondered if Rhoda would die. She could be dying behind that curtain right now.

"Show him. Show him," said his mother-in-law.

"Oh, Mother," Kate said. "I have students with pierced noses. Dr. Whipple did my ears for me last night. It seemed a good time to do it as long as I was here."

"I suppose you'll do your nose tonight." Mrs. Logan wouldn't quit.

George noticed the balloons were gone from the room. Expired, he guessed. "I'll water the flowers," he said. As he got up, he saw the glimmer of gold in Kate's ears. So that's what Charlie had given her in that small box: pierced earrings.

He left Kate and her mother to battle out the ear problem. He wouldn't worry about it. Kate had never liked jewelry anyway. Maybe he would just not say anything about Charlie. He would wait for her to raise the issue. And would she? He didn't know.

On the way home, he stopped at the Longwood Cricket Club. The U.S. Pro Tennis Tournament was in its third day. George had been a better than average tennis player until he'd hurt his shoulder and had to give it up. He found a parking space right on Hammond Street. He was glad he had the smallest car Toyota made; it was easy to squeeze in. The gates were open and the ticket takers had gone. It was a little after nine.

It pleased George to get in for free. When he was a kid, he and his friends would buy one ticket to the movies, and one boy would let the others in through an emergency exit. They'd never been caught. It had seemed very daring. When you're a kid, you can do anything; you're not supposed to be rational. Oh, adults would always tell you that you should know better, but it was clear from their manner that they didn't expect you to know anything.

The stands were half full. People still wore hats and sunshades as if it were daylight. He bought two hot dogs and a diet soda and walked up toward the top of the bleachers where he could get better back support. As he climbed up the center stairway, he spotted a man with small pheasants on his trousers. "Tennis is sure a preppy sport," Ellen had once said. He missed her. Even though she had her own apartment now, they saw each other often. She was an only child by their choice, but he had often wondered how one person could handle so much love. He had wanted brothers and sisters when he was growing up, and so had Kate. But in the end, they opted for the familiar. And Ellen was the only child they wanted.

The evening was pleasantly cool, although he could see, even from this distance, that the young men on the lighted court were soaked with perspiration. Usually Kate came with him to the matches, often inviting friends and making a party of it. They had not even talked about it this year. They had spent the past month talking about her surgery. If she died, he should certainly remarry, she told him. She would want him to find someone else.

"Hey, George," someone called at the same time that he felt a hand on his shoulder. It was Abe, his old tennis partner. "Where's Kate?" he said.

"At the Mass General," George said. "A little surgery. She's OK." He didn't want to talk about her. "Good matches?" The hot dog tasted good. He was glad he'd bought two.

"Sylvia went home," said Abe. "Said she'd had enough. She'd been here all day. Can you give me a ride?"

"Sure," George said. He hadn't seen Abe in a long time, probably since he'd hurt his shoulder and stopped playing tennis. He looked old and tired. They were the same age. Perhaps he just hadn't noticed before. He licked the mustard from his fingers. If the hot-dog stand weren't so far he'd get another one—or maybe two. Kate always brought something for them to eat; he'd never sampled the hot dogs before this. One of the players was questioning a line call. George had a few old tennis friends who used to call lines but had recently quit because of the abuse by the players.

"Can you believe what they get away with?" Abe said. "It's murder. Absolute murder."

The player, a tall blond from Czechosolvakia, threw his racket at the umpire's chair.

"He'll get a fine for that," Abe said.

The match proceeded. It must be great to be so good at something that people pay to watch you, George thought. He often had medical students observe him as he conducted case conferences, but it was not the same.

"How's business?" he asked.

"Not bad," Abe said. He owned several car dealerships. George couldn't remember how many. "But not good either. I guess I'm about even, which means we're doing fifty percent of what we did last year. Now, if we can ever get rid of what's-his-name in the White House, there might be some hope." He shifted on the bench and lit a cigarette. "God, my ass is sore," he said. He raised his husky frame and stretched.

"And how're the kids?" George said. There was something merciful about small talk. He was glad he and Abe had run into each other.

"Fine. Fine," Abe said, sitting down again. "Hey, you'll never believe what happened tonight. Listen to this. When I lit a cigarette," he paused and took a long drag, "the guy behind us asked me to put it out. Bothered his eyes, he said. What do you think of that?"

George had never smoked. He didn't like the taste it left

63

on his teeth. The Czech who'd had the tantrum was losing in the third set. George was wishing that just once *he* had thrown his racket.

"How's your tennis?" he asked Abe, but really didn't want to know. He missed playing.

"I haven't played in a year or more," Abe said. He blew the smoke away from George, but there was a slight breeze that made it sweep back across his face. "Knees. They finally gave out. I even had some braces custom made. I still had to ice my legs after I played. Too much pain. Not even fifty and I'm a has-been."

"I'm sorry," said George. But he was not sorry. While not exactly pleased, he was somehow relieved. It put them on more of an equal footing. He wondered if Charlie played tennis. Kate could have been a good player, but she was never much interested in athletic competition. She preferred walking or standing on her head. She'd been standing on her head since they were children.

"Of course, they wanted me to have surgery," Abe was saying. "Name me an orthopedic man who's not ready with the knife. Repair my knees, they said. Told me they have plastic kneecaps now."

The doubles match was starting. The play was quick and sharp compared with the singles game where both men had seemed content to slug it out from the base line. Spectators left the stands in small groups, their sweaters wrapped around them.

"What a shot!" Abe said. "Did you see that? If only once in my life I could make that shot . . ."

George took a deep breath. The worst that could happen would be that Abe would tell him it was none of his business. "Abe," he said. "Have you ever cheated on Sylvia?" He was startled by his own question. It was the wrong question. It wasn't what he wanted to ask at all. The sound of the ball hitting the players' rackets was magnified: bounce-hit-bounce-hit.

Abe lit another cigarette. "I know car salesmen are supposed to be shifty," he said. "Sort of like Nixon," he went on. "Beady eyes. Pin-striped suits. Sweaty upper lip. You know what I mean."

"I'd never compare you to Nixon," George said. Abe had a thing about Nixon. Well, for that matter, who didn't? George noticed a dark spot on the court. They were supposed to have bought new lights this year. He looked up and saw through clouds of bugs that one light was out. More than likely, some player would file a protest about it.

"He'll probably run again." Abe was still talking about Nixon. "He'll probably get elected. He'll sign an exclusive contract with the Japanese and put me out of business." They both laughed.

Abe appeared to have forgotten about George's question. Just as well, George decided. It was the wrong question.

And then Abe said an emphatic "Nope." He dropped his cigarette butt under the bleachers. "Life's crazy enough. I don't have to tell you that," he said. "Five kids. A hectic business. A wife I like most of the time."

"So you've been faithful," George said. The word sounded ancient. It echoed. He was embarrassed.

It was nearly eleven. There would be another doubles match after this one. The players were newcomers to the men's pro circuit. No wonder they were given the late starting time. They were warming up in the dark behind the stands.

"Once she got so mad at me she threw out all my power tools," Abe said.

The stands were nearly empty now. There couldn't have been more than a few hundred people left.

"Once I got so mad at her I took off for three days," Abe continued.

George remembered the best talks he had had with Ellen as she was growing up had been in the car when they were headed somewhere, when they were captives, when there was no TV, no phone, when there was no eye contact, when they were side by side. Still, he couldn't frame the question he wanted to ask Abe, although this talking was easy. Maybe he ought to have gone into analysis years ago, as his supervisor had suggested. But George and Abe were here to watch, not to talk. It was as if this were a casual conversation that really didn't matter. That's right. It really didn't matter, George convinced himself.

"I could go for some coffee," Abe said, shivering. "Did you really think I'd step out on Sylvia?"

"What about her?" George said. "Has she been as true to you as you've been to her?" Finally, he'd said it. But again, the word *true* seemed antiquated. What did it mean, anyway?

"Jesus, George," said Abe, still watching the tennis. "What's this all about? Sylvia? My Sylvia? Come on. Sylvia writes greeting cards for Hallmark. Sylvia believes in true love, for Chrissakes."

CHAPTER
· SEVEN ·

Dear Ellen Sweetheart, wrote Kate. *And how is the forest primeval?*
The sun was filtering through the sunroom windows.
George was seeing his patients. Her mother was in the
kitchen. Charlie had already called twice that day from
his office.

I wish you were here. It was true: She longed for that rush
of feeling she experienced just from looking at her daughter.
Some people loved babies for that very reason. But Kate
had never gotten over the miracle of Ellen's very existence.
Sure, there'd been the usual problems, but both Kate and
George delighted in Ellen's zest for her own life. They had
learned from it. *I miss you,* Kate wrote. Sometimes she wondered if they'd put too much focus on Ellen's ability to
charm them. Kate had been trained to be wary of such
passion.

You'll be pleased to know I've been reading Ulysses, she wrote.
For two weeks. I'm on page 8. Ellen had majored in English
literature in college. You couldn't be a real, live person
without reading Joyce, she'd told her parents. When and
if she had a child, she would name it Joyce, or James if it
was a boy.

Won't you be glad to sleep in a real bed with sheets and everything?
Kate continued writing. She had tried all summer to imagine
in what ways her daughter would enjoy being in the Maine
wilderness with fifteen teenagers. *And eat regular food? Something besides nuts and berries?* Ellen had been a vegetarian since
junior high. Kate knew that part of the Outward Bound
"experience" was determining what part of nature was
edible. *If you're eating mushrooms and tree bark, don't tell me.
Are you?*

The phone beside Kate was ringing. It was Charlie again.
"I've got to see you," he said. She imagined what would
happen if Charlie and Ellen met. They wouldn't like each
other, even if Ellen never suspected Charlie were her mother's lover. Charlie the capitalist and Ellen the naturalist.
El in her Goodwill clothes and Charlie in his Mercedes. It
would never work.

"I'll climb the vines to your window," Charlie was saying.
"Listen. What are you doing for excitement?"

That was the thing about Charlie: He always made you
laugh. Kate heard her mother rattling dishes in the kitchen.
A photograph on the wall was askew. It would take Kate
ten minutes to get up, cross the room, straighten the picture,
and get back to her chair. "I have to go, Charlie," she said.

Charlie wanted to come over. He wanted Kate to sneak
out. What would he do if he had to go another day without
seeing her? He made smooching noises. She laughed. They
hung up.

The photograph was of Kate and George on a trip to
the Grand Canyon. Ellen had taken the picture. She had
hoped for more than scenery and had even left food out
for bears, which never came. Kate got up and straightened
the picture. She was surprised her mother hadn't noticed
that its frame was dusty.

They had made up a whole series of stories about bears

in the Grand Canyon after that trip. "Once upon a time," Kate would begin. And Ellen would continue, "there was a bear who lived in the state forest." One bear had eaten all the witches in the world and had burped up Milky Ways. Another had turned snakes into stars. One had decided to join the convent. Ellen loved stories about nuns. The convent bear had taken the name Sister Mary Franceline. She had eaten her rosary beads.

If you were here, Kate continued her letter, *maybe we could spend the day telling stories. Once there was a little bear named Molly Bloom who went off to the woods to seek her fortune. . . .* What was her own story? Of course, she could never tell Ellen the real one: Once a middle-aged woman met a younger man and the chemistry overpowered them. It was not a children's story, was it? Besides, it was not the whole story. She began again: Once there was a little bear who took Magdalene as her confirmation name. She giggled. It was too silly.

Your father's been playing tennis again, she wrote, *with more vigor than I thought possible. He claims the inspiration of the Longwood matches cured his shoulder.*

The dog padded into the room and put her muzzle against Kate's leg. "Good girl," Kate said, running her fingers over Clancy's teeth. *Once there was a dog who liked to have her teeth tickled. Clancy misses you, too.*

I want you to know that every day Daddy asks if you ever get a chance for a hot bath. Please tell us. We are holding our breath. There was no point in writing that George was overdoing the tennis, that she knew he was too upset about Charlie even to talk it out.

The garden is gorgeous. Gram brings in fresh tiger lilies every day. Of course, she wears gloves so the orange dye won't ruin her hands. Ellen teased her grandmother about her rubber gloves.

I'm trying to think about my courses for the fall semester. That was a lie. She couldn't really concentrate on anything. *The new edition of my book should be here any day.* Ellen had been in seventh grade when the first edition had been published. Her first book was going to be about people, she'd said, not animals. And for sure, it would not be about taking animals apart.

Mostly, I do crossword puzzles and hold your father's hand, and think about you. It was true: She and George had resumed sleeping with their fingers entwined, as they had when they'd first married. "Maybe I should sleep in another bed," he'd said the first night she was home. "I might bother you if I move around." "Oh no," she'd said, easing her body next to his.

Someone from the Women's School called about your fall survival course. I gave your Maine address and said you'd be home in a few weeks. Tell me I got it wrong. You're not really going to climb Mount Washington in December, are you?

Kate poured herself a glass of iced tea from the pitcher her mother had left by her chair. It was half lemonade, just the way she liked it. She lowered her glass to give Clancy a drink. An ice cube rolled to the floor and melted.

I turned the TV on once or twice, Kate wrote. *But all the shows were about hospitals. Even on PBS someone was performing brain surgery.* Could they have televised her hysterectomy? They had a closed circuit at the hospital. *And on the evening news, they show new surgical techniques in living color.* She had not watched much TV before this. *Do you suppose people actually eat dinner while looking at heart transplants?*

We're looking forward to Nantucket. It'll be good to get away from this heat. In truth, she and George had hardly talked about their vacation. She wasn't even sure if she'd made the reservation for the car on the ferry. And she hadn't mentioned to Charlie that she'd be away for a whole month. *I wish you were going with us.*

70

· Divorcing Your Grandmother ·

I'm so glad you decided to stay in Boston after you finished school. I know that children (pardon the expression) need to spread their wings. But you were born with spread wings, weren't you? When Ellen moved her things to her own apartment a year ago, Kate and George had drunk two bottles of wine and cried in each other's arms. Ellen had lived in a dorm at school and had really left home then. But she had come back for vacations. And somehow the shift had occurred without their awareness or preparation. Clearly now, they needed her more than she needed them.

I had my ears pierced in the hospital, she remembered to write. *What do you think of that?*

I wish I could give you a big hug right this minute. Kate tried to imagine how Ellen would feel in her embrace, but couldn't do it. She could, however, remember the feel of Ellen's small hand in hers as they crossed streets together long ago.

Kate wrote her *xx*'s and put the letter in an envelope. If she reread it, she might not send it.

CHAPTER
· EIGHT ·

Charlie had to see Kate. But it wasn't going to be easy, now that she was out of the hospital. He couldn't visit her at home, and she wasn't well enough to go out.

They spoke on the phone. He said he would climb the vines to her window. There were no vines, she said. He said he would come by and pick her up. She was too tired, she said. Yes, she missed him. But her stomach jiggled when she moved, she told him.

He couldn't stand it. He was beginning to forget what she looked like. He drove by her house. He had never been curious about it before, but now he thought he might go up and look in the windows. He had always thought it strange when Janet told him she liked driving by people's houses in the early evening before they drew their curtains. Now he understood.

Janet had more of her old pep, although the two of them continued their pattern of mutual avoidance. Lately, when he pulled into the driveway, he would find her playing ball or Frisbee with the boys. She seemed always to be wearing something striped and cool-looking. He used to kid her when she said stripes made her taller. Nothing would make her taller; she was as small as he was big. But there had been no kidding for a long while, and when she saw him, she would stop the game and head for the house, gathering Janie in her arms. She would say something about starting dinner. And Charlie would take off his jacket and tie and continue the game.

He guessed that George was probably a good shrink— or even a better-than-good shrink. But Janet hadn't told him she was in therapy, and Charlie didn't mention it. He was savvy enough to know you didn't bring it up until the patient was ready. One thing he knew for sure: He didn't want to get involved with it. Joe Drake, at the office, got roped into something called "couples therapy." It was the pits, he said. One night a week, six couples got together with a shrink and talked about their problems. Joe said they asked you how often you screwed and what you thought about when you were alone.

This George Cummings didn't seem like that kind of guy, if that night they met in the hospital was any indication. It was those people who had to say everything that got Charlie. The ones who acted more like shrinks than the shrinks did. They were always asking how did you feel about this, or how did you feel about that, when, in fact, you had no feeling about it one way or the other.

Well, he didn't mind if George knew that he and Janet hadn't slept together for more than a year. He didn't even mind if Janet told George about him—whatever there was to tell. What would she say about him anyway? He'd like to know. But he sure as hell wasn't going to any shrink himself. If she'd just get a little exercise and work up a good sweat now and then, maybe she'd forget all this gloom and doom stuff. She hadn't even come to watch him run the marathon this year.

They never argued; they were even friendly to one an-

74

other. But at night, in bed, he was careful to sleep at the edge of his side. Like California, he thought. It wasn't easy, since it was only a double bed. They'd bought it when they were full of passion for each other. And now neither of them had been able to say a larger bed would make more sense.

"You move even when you sleep," she said. "Can't you just lie still?"

But when he was just falling into a dream, he would jerk his leg or his arm, shaking the whole bed. And they would have to start all over.

Kate had been home exactly two weeks when Charlie went to her house with the balloons. He knew George would have patients all afternoon, and that her mother was there taking care of things. He parked the car on a side street. George would surely know what kind of car Charlie had, wouldn't he? At least, he could be that cautious; he didn't want to run into him again. There had been no fireworks that night at the hospital, and nothing had come of their meeting, according to Kate. But just the same, it had been uncomfortable. While he had not felt any real guilt, the encounter had rubbed his nose in the truth. And he had not liked it.

Kate's house was old and made of fieldstone. Who would want such an old house? The ceilings were probably high, and it must cost a fortune to heat.

The door had one of those bells you turn; he could hear it ringing inside. When the door opened, Charlie announced he had a delivery for Kate Cummings. Peeking through his balloons, he saw a lady with blue hair suck in her lips.

"I'll take them," she said.

"Are you the lady in question?" he said in a falsetto voice. "I have to make the delivery in person. I have a singing message."

"I don't know," she hesitated. He could see her ankles were swollen in her white pumps. "I'm Mrs. Cummings's mother."

Charlie walked by her into a large hall. Never hesitate with a salesman, he thought. He looked around. He had been right: twelve-foot ceilings.

"Which way, Mother?" he said to the bustling woman.

A small smile spread slowly across her face. She looked up at him. There were curtained French doors to his right. George's office must be beyond them. So this was where Janet came. How often? Probably Kate's mother had even answered the door for her. He noticed a young woman, the next patient, on the other side of the hall sitting on a bench. She stared at the floor, looking as if she hoped to be invisible. It could have been Janet. What if it had been Janet?

The balloons rustled. The girl at the balloonery told him that sometimes when they were too tightly filled with helium they would pop, that helium expanded within the first hour after filling. He imagined George charging out of his office. He would think someone had been shot. The next patient was already so frightened she would probably slide right off the bench and disappear into the thin carpeting.

"Well, I suppose it's all right," Kate's mother was saying. What was her name? Had he ever asked Kate her maiden name? He followed to the back of the hall, where it narrowed to a corridor. The balloons brushed the walls as he passed. One string caught on a blue abstract painting. Did Kate paint? Or George? Or the daughter? What was the daughter's name?

The passageway ended, opening into a glassed-in room, a porch made into a sunroom. Nice, he thought, estimating how much it must have cost. He wondered if it was insulated, as he saw the baseboard heating. There was one gigantic plant in the room. It was almost a tree. What was the point of that? Somebody could sit in that space.

Kate was on a summer lounge chair with her feet up. She had polish on her toenails. She had once tried to paint his toenails. They'd been at the Copley Plaza. She'd brought Magic Markers, nail polish, and poster paint. She said white bodies were as boring as earthworms in the lab, he remembered. She'd drawn maps on his body: Yugoslavia. She was crazy about Yugoslavia, she said.

"This is Mrs. Cummings," the mother said. Kate was reading. She wore glasses. He had never seen them before. The ends of her dark hair curled up.

"Yes?" She looked up without recognition. What was her best feature? Her huge green eyes and those amazing lashes? Or her fragile cheekbones? How could he ever forget how she looked?

" 'You are my sunshine,' " he started to sing. The balloons were yellow. " 'My only sunshine,' " he continued.

The mother laughed aloud. Kate looked beyond his shoulders. He began to feel silly. What was he doing here anyway? A grown man holding a bunch of balloons singing about the sun? A gigantic white dog sauntered up to him sniffing his crotch. It would probably get hair all over his seventy-dollar trousers.

" 'Please don't take my sunshine away,' " he concluded the first verse. "Do you want the second verse, ma'am?" he said.

"Yes, please," Kate said. She was wiping her eyes. She was crying. What in hell was she crying about? My God, the damn dog wouldn't let him alone. He finished the song and made a little bow.

"I've never known George to do anything so frivolous," the mother said. She was still attractive for her age. He tried, but couldn't find Kate in her face. "Is there a card?" she asked. "Read the card."

He saw what looked like annoyance creep across Kate's brow. He wished they had talked more about important things. He wished he knew more about her mother. Did they get along? How could you not get along with your own mother?

"It's a private message, ma'am," he said. "For her ears only." He let go of the balloons, which moved together like magnets to the ceiling. He bent down toward Kate.

"Be my valentine," he whispered and kissed her on the cheek. She was too pale for the bright room. Was she really all right? Of course. She would have to be all right.

"Thank you very much," she said. Her hand touched his calf. She was pulling his trousers behind his knee.

"My pleasure," he said, standing up straight now, backing away.

In the car, on the way home, he knew something had changed. He wished he were heading to the Copley Plaza to meet her. The hotel had billed him on his American Express card for the sheets. And he had worried that day that Janet would notice the paint on his clothes and in his hair; it had not all come off in the shower. He had cleaned out the garage when he got home, he remembered, and taken the kids to McDonald's. Janet had said nothing.

Some dog hair floated up in his face now as he closed the windows and turned on the air conditioning. He was glad Janet had never wanted animals in the house. Now he would have to clean the interior of the car. He could already see the short white hair on the brown leather of the other seat. He didn't mind if the garage and his office were messy. They were supposed to be messy; it meant you were busy. But his car and his clothes had to be perfect.

Janet said it was his "Mercedes mentality," whatever that meant.

He saw a place where he could vacuum the car and stopped. It cost fifty cents for five minutes.

"Not a bad business," he said to the guy next to him with a rusting fifty-six Chevy. "Your car's a classic," Charlie told him. The guy was about Charlie's own age. He had long greasy hair combed back in a fifties style.

"Yeah," he said. "A classic." There was a barefoot boy about Jimmy's age standing next to him.

"Your car's a classic, too, mister," the boy said, rubbing his hand over the fender, as if it were a strange animal he thought might bite him. He left finger marks.

"The car's full of dog hair," said Charlie. "It's a mess." He saw that the Chevy's upholstery was ripped. His first car had been an old Dodge Dart with plastic seats. It had cost two hundred bucks, and he drove it only a week before it died. He spent a whole summer and all his money fixing it up, buying new parts. He took the engine apart daily. His mother yelled that he was always filthy, that he'd never get his fingernails clean again. His father told him he should be out practicing his hook shot. "Bill Russell," he said. "You could be the next Bill Russell."

"Can I look in your car, mister?" the barefoot kid was saying. He had mosquito bites on his arms, which he had scratched into scabs.

Oh, well, what did it matter? He would give the car a really good cleaning at home. "Sure," he said. "Go ahead. Sit behind the wheel, if you want."

The boy sat tall, fingering all the buttons on the dashboard, reaching his legs to the pedals. He moved the steering wheel to the left, to the right. He was dreaming, Charlie thought, about his own car, his own steering wheel and dashboard.

"Thanks," the boy said and got out.

"Thanks," the father said, hanging up the vacuum hose on the machine.

Charlie's time had run out, and he hadn't even started yet. He put in more money. He heard the kid say something about the car to his father, as they drove away. Charlie watched the dog hair vanish into the long hose. How could Kate stand having a dog like that?

When he finished with the car, the machine was still going. He turned it on his trousers, but even from the distance of a few inches, the material puckered. He pulled the nozzle away, but not before a grease smudge made its mark on the gray fabric. Seventy bucks. Oh well, he could afford it.

On the way home, a light rain began to fall. Nearly every day this summer there was some precipitation, when the heat became liquid. Everyone said there had never been a summer like this one. He put the car on cruise control and reminded himself how much he liked zigging along the side streets. Janet had made him promise never to do it when the children were with him.

He admired his modern split-level, mostly glass house, as he drove by it into the driveway. He liked square corners and angles. He and Janet had designed the house; mostly, he had designed it. If only he'd had the chance to experiment with it, as he had the old Dodge, he'd have known more about what he wanted. But they had lived in the duplex next to his parents in Winchester until they'd bought this house. He'd change a few things, if he could: more closets, fewer windows, a bigger family room. Still, he was satisfied. He'd learned about solar heating and was pleased with his ingenuity. He'd insisted on all the modern gadgets possible, although Janet had, from time to time, said the whole enterprise was entirely too capitalistic for her, he recalled, as he pulled up next to her old VW bug. He had wanted her to get a little sports car, an MG, even a Corvette, but she said the VW was a fine car. "It suits my character," she said, whenever he brought it up. But it was that dull red color that happens with time and not enough waxings; he had always thought the engine was a toy. No wonder the poor girl was depressed.

He was surprised that no one was in the kitchen. It was raining steadily now. He would wait until tomorrow to clean the car. As he started up the stairs, Janet came out of the lavatory.

"Oh, good," she said. "You're home I've been waiting for you." She wore a raspberry-colored dress; her hair was tied back with a ribbon.

He could hear the water flushing and refilling the tank in the bathroom as he followed her to the kitchen. "Where is everybody?" he said.

"Sit down, Charlie," she said. She rarely called him by name. It sounded strange. "Want a drink? Coffee?" She spoke crisply, as if he were a guest in her house.

"Is this going to be a round-table discussion?" He smiled, outlining the edges of the angular table with his long fingers. He sat down and leaned back in the chair on two legs. "Oh, sorry," he said, when he saw her look. She said it was a bad example for the children, that they'd break their necks trying to be like him.

She brought him a beer and a tall glass and sat down across the table. "I've been thinking about this for a long time," she said.

"Well, I don't think you can plant a garden now," he said. "At least not vegetables." He poured his beer down the side of his glass. He never thought it really made much difference how you poured it; the taste was the same. And he always burped after the first swallow anyway.

Her eyes were brighter than he'd seen them in a long time. Did she even have makeup on? She looked small and delicate in the chair. There was more than a foot's difference in their heights.

"I hope we'll always be able to communicate," she was saying. "And I hope you can understand why I am doing this."

"Where's the baby?" he said. "Where are Mike and Jimmy?" The house was too quiet. Usually on a rainy day, the TV was on.

"They're all at your parents' house for the night," she said. "I wanted to talk without interruption. I wanted to try to have a discussion."

She was finally coming out of it, he thought. That George Cummings was really something, a regular miracle worker. In only a few weeks, she was back to her normal self. Janet was going to tell him about it. She was going to present some plan for their future together. She would say she was sorry for the past. He would tell her it was all right. He would promise her they'd have no more babies. He would even get a vasectomy. There was still time left in the summer for them to take a vacation together. They could take the kids camping in Maine. They would go to Bar Harbor, go hiking. They would all love it. He would charter a boat, and they would sail off the coast.

"I'm leaving you," she said.

"I think the toilet's still running," he said, going to the hallway to check.

"Did you hear me?" she said.

He came back and sat down next to her. She moved to the other side of the table, where he had been sitting. He wondered if she felt the seat still warm from his body.

She told him she had planned to leave before she was pregnant with Janie. She told him they had nothing in com-

82

mon. He had once fallen asleep in the middle of their lovemaking. She hated their life-style, she said. It was killing her.

How could he have been stupid enough to think George had helped her? "Are you having a breakdown?" he said, forgetting to swallow his beer, which dribbled down his chin onto his blue shirt, the stain spreading.

She explained that she was "in therapy with a wonderful man," that she should have talked with him sooner, that she thought she had known herself, but was now uncovering new layers. She told him this was the most exciting time of her life. She had found an apartment in Cambridge. She would move in at the end of the month. She was beaming. She had found a job as a social worker, using some of her old contacts. She would be able to support herself without any help from him.

Charlie saw the ends of his legs under the table but felt unconnected to them. "What the hell kind of discussion is this?" he said. "This is a decree. You've got the whole thing done, finished, ended. Is that it?" His voice sounded too loud, even to him.

"There are beginnings, middles, and endings to things, Charlie," she said. "You often say so yourself."

"Don't call me Charlie," he said. "Besides, cutting the grass is a little different from what we're talking about here." If he pounded his fist on the table, would she understand it better?

"We're at the end," she said. "We want different things."

Charlie had not given much thought to what he wanted, with the exception of the Mercedes. He supposed he wanted what everyone else wanted. He got another beer from the refrigerator and took a gulp from the bottle.

"Excuse me," he said, as he burped. Nobody in his family had ever divorced. Did she mean to divorce him? Or was she just going off for a while to find herself?

"It'll be all right, Charlie," she said. "You'll see. Are you hungry? Let's go have some dinner." She seemed to have it all worked out.

They went to the same Italian restaurant where they'd argued about whether or not she should have an abortion. Had it really been two years ago? It was the first time they'd been out together in a very long while. They ordered a bottle of Chianti; it was almost a celebration. Charlie spilled spaghetti sauce on himself. He was a mess. That's what he was, he thought, a goddamn mess: full of grease, beer, and spaghetti.

She would not take the children with her, she said. She had thought it all out. It would be good for them to spend more time with him. He was a wonderful father, she said. And besides, she had to get her career back in swing. Wasn't the veal Parmesan delicious, she wanted to know.

He ordered another bottle of wine. He looked at the tiny legs of the young waitress. Maybe this wouldn't be so bad. It would all work out. Things always worked out.

They were still talking as the spumoni melted in its dishes in front of them. "I thought we had nothing to talk about," Charlie said, as they walked arm in arm to the car, both laughing.

"Let me drive," she said.

She had never wanted to drive his car before. She had called it an obscenity. She had talked about how many people it could feed. She screeched out of the parking space, just grazing a tree. The shattering of glass was a delayed noise as the jolt spread through his body.

"Jesus Christ," he said, leaping out the door.

"It's nothing," she said. "It's only a tail light."

She was right. It was only a tail light. He stooped to pick up the pieces of the red glass, stuffing them into his pockets.

"You'll cut yourself," she said. But he had already cut himself, right through his pants pockets. There was blood running down his leg.

"I'm sorry," Janet was saying. "I'm really sorry. I know you think I did it on purpose, but I didn't. I really didn't."

Charlie wasn't thinking about Janet. He was thinking that he hated these goddamn pants. He was thinking that he would never wear them again. "Let's go," he said. "I'll drive this time."

It was only a mile home. The house was dark. It was odd not to have to take the baby-sitter home.

"It's funny not to have the sitter here," Janet said.

"We have a lot in common," he said.

In bed, they touched in what almost seemed like the first time.

"I love you," he said.

"Yes," she said, stroking his back.

The next day, she packed her clothes, a few books, and left. She didn't want to wait until the end of the month, she said. She would be back if she needed anything. She had gotten some furniture and dishes from the Salvation Army store, she told him.

He wondered if she was seeing another man.

CHAPTER

· NINE ·

When Kate was pregnant with Ellen, they told her she was built for having babies, and she had believed them. They had not told her about the episiotomy until after the delivery. She was a science person, she was smart. How could she have been so stupid? How did she know they would cut the opening to her vagina to make it wider? How did she know they would sew it up again? And that it would hurt so much?

It was one of those times she wished for sisters. None of her friends had had babies yet. And while her mother considered herself modern, to hear her talk, you'd think Kate had been born by magic. Why, they didn't even have maternity clothes when her mother was pregnant.

The incision from the episiotomy had healed slowly. Kate took warm baths in baking soda. Between Ellen's feedings she gave herself treatments with a sixty-watt bulb. Someone had told her light promoted healing. She smiled as she thought of it now. Had George actually held the lamp while she lay there, vulnerable? She would have to ask him; she couldn't remember.

Why was she thinking now about pregnancy and childbirth? She didn't believe in those "loss of womb" reactions she'd read about. She was thinking about the healing. The long vertical incision on her abdomen ought to heal more quickly than the episiotomy, she thought. Of course, there were things inside that also had to heal. The doctor had said those stitches would dissolve, but she couldn't picture it.

It was three weeks now since the hysterectomy. She expected to be fine. Instead, she felt tired and sore. She was used to moving quickly, and now she had to calculate each step in advance. She rested. She thought about her fall classes. She stepped on the scale: one hundred and fifteen, exactly the same as before the surgery. Apparently her uterus had weighed nothing. She looked in the mirror. She tried to imagine if there were any poisonous cells dancing under her skin, the way she scrutinized empty dogwood branches for buds before spring. She measured her scar. She would have to stop thinking about herself. She would pull up her socks. She would march on. She asked her mother to play a tape of the Mormon Tabernacle choir.

She supposed the encounter between George and Charlie in the hospital could have been worse. She and Rhoda and the nurses had actually laughed about some of the possibilities, which didn't seem so funny now.

She had tried several times to bring up the matter with George. "There's something I want to talk about," she said. Or, "You know how much I care for you." There was no easy way to begin. But each time the light would go out of his eyes, or he would look away. And Kate changed the subject.

"I wonder why they haven't suggested radiation," she said once. "Perhaps I'm too far gone." She had to stop feeling sorry for herself. But it would have been easier for her to talk about Charlie.

George's body relaxed with gratitude. He was an expert on everyone's feelings but his own. She knew he loved her for accepting that irony about him. She knew her death was less painful for him to discuss than her betrayal.

"They haven't suggested radiation because you're cured," he said. "They got it all." It was becoming a refrain. She remembered their first apartment. The exterminators had promised that they had got all the roaches, and Kate had believed them. But the apartment was in the Back Bay, where there were always roaches. They had all learned to live together despite their reservations and the exterminator's promises. She and her body would learn some kind of peaceful coexistence.

At night, Kate and George still held hands as they went to sleep. Clancy lay on the floor next to Kate's side of the bed. She snored. Their last dog had also snored. They talked about their month on Nantucket, where they went every year. It was familiar conversation. Each July, George examined his temptation to let some of his patients come see him while he was on vacation. It was such a small thing, he said. It would only be an hour or two of his time and would make such a difference to them. Kate presented her case: that all this business about separation was designed to make the therapists feel less guilty; that a commitment to someone was a commitment. If his patients wanted to see him, why not? But George always ended by following the rules. These vacations were supposed to help his patients deal with other separations in their lives, he said, reciting it like a catechism. Separation didn't make their wounds deeper; it helped heal them.

Charlie called on the phone every day. If her mother was suspicious, she never said anything. Kate wore his earrings, reminding her mother she would do as she pleased. How old was she? Forty-five? And was she still rebelling against her mother? She decided to take the earrings off.

She didn't know what she was going to do about Charlie; she was too tired to think about it. When he called, he seemed very far away, like a pleasant dream whose details she couldn't recall.

When he arrived that day with the balloons, she felt as if she were watching herself watch him. She had just persuaded her mother to let her use the crushed tiger lilies to dye her toenails. The bending to do her toes had worn her out. But she loved the splendor of the orange; the effort had been worth it. When Charlie came in singing to her, she felt almost aphasic. She couldn't think of the right thing to say or do. She wanted to show him her toenails, but it would have opened the door to something memorable; she could neither remember nor forget it, whatever it was. So, instead, she had grabbed his pants leg, as if she were a prisoner of some kind, giving a secret signal. And with a rush, her connection to him was restored. How could she say no to such vigor?

She remembered now, without any difficulty, why she liked Charlie so much: He was an energy transfusion, a pain-killer. She thought about the afternoon they'd played Chinese checkers and tossed marbles at each other. Was it at the Marriott? They put marbles in their mouths; they had a contest to see who could fit in the most marbles; they spit them at each other. Of course, George would have to have known. All those afternoons were unaccounted for. What had she told him? And what would she do now? Had anything changed? Calculations and analyses took away from pleasure. She did not want to add up the pros and cons of her choices. But she hadn't counted on George's finding out. That changed everything.

She had to see Charlie again. She called his office. He was gone for the day. Was there a message? "Yes," Kate said. "There's a message. Tell him Mrs. Marble called. He has my number."

"Who was that?" her mother said, as she came into the room with a pitcher full of something cold. She couldn't help herself: She still wanted to monitor Kate's life. She looked up at the balloons and smiled. "If only your father would think of something like this," she said, pointing to them.

Kate understood. Her father tended his rose garden and listened to opera records, when he wasn't at his insurance office. He was a methodical man, not given to fancy. And he was a gentle man. He had played center on his high-school football team and was uneasy at being so big. When Kate watched him in his garden, she couldn't imagine that he could ever knock anyone down. He touched each plant as if it were fine glass. She often thought he was born into the wrong body. Looking at her mother now, she understood that probably her father was not very romantic, that he lacked imagination. And for the first time she considered how like George he was. Had she really followed the usual pattern, in spite of herself, and married a man like her father? She did not like to think of herself as ordinary.

She closed her eyes. She heard her mother tiptoe from the room. Her mother had a stage tiptoe. You always knew of her comings and goings.

Kate dozed. She hated to waste time sleeping. Yet each afternoon her body folded into itself and napped. Her thoughts wandered. Maybe she and George would remodel the house. It would be interesting to knock down a wall or put in a skylight. Sledgehammers weighed sixteen pounds, someone had once told her. Could she lift one and eliminate a wall? Would she want to? She had heard there were places you could go and take your turn at destroying a car with a sledgehammer. It was a little like those rock musicians who destroyed their instruments after they'd finished playing. Was she that angry?

Every afternoon, she had the same dream: She was building something. Was it a house or a person? She could never make it out. She had long strips of wood, which she fastened together to make a freestanding structure. She attached pieces of metal and glass to the wood. How did she do it? A staple gun? She smiled to herself, even in her dream. This staple business just wouldn't let her alone. She'd never get over the fact that her belly had been held together with staples. The metal parts of her project glistened in the sun. She was outdoors in a place that was always spring and lush. She floated on the air as she worked on the apex of her creation, as if the rest of it were underwater. "Look, look," she was saying to someone and pointing to her work. She was lying on the grass now; it was tickling her legs. And then she woke up, her mouth still moving, her hands still gesturing. She never knew quite where she was or what she'd see when she opened her eyes. Her first thought was a fear that she had called George by the wrong name.

She liked dreaming, but never attached any significance to her dreams and usually didn't remember them. She forgot both the good ones and the bad ones as soon as she entered the real world. Duty and responsibility forced her to plan ahead. She knew she was compulsive about making lists. But her greatest pleasures came from giving herself to the present moment.

"Are you sure you should be playing so much tennis?" she asked George one night as she rubbed Ben-Gay on his neck and upper back. It surprised her that she had stopped calling him by name.

"I'm in great shape," said George. "Just feel those mus-

92

cles." He was lying across their king-size bed in his tennis shorts.

Kate put a dab of the cream behind George's knees. It was cold. He jumped. She thought of Charlie. It disturbed her. She had always been able to compartmentalize her life, her relationships. Charlie had no place here, now, in her bedroom with George. The doctor had said to wait at least a month before making love. There was little more than a week to go. Of course she wanted George. What was the matter with her, anyway?

He was telling her about his muscle tone. It was great to be back at the tennis club with his old friends, he said. He hadn't realized how much he missed them. Running was OK, but it was too solitary for him. Tennis was more his style. It was a bit like psychotherapy, he was saying. The parallel eluded her. It was unlike him to be so effusive.

Kate was thinking about Charlie in spite of herself. "I'm going to remodel the house," she announced. "What do you think?" She got off the bed, went to the small desk across the room, and drew a diagram. The Ben-Gay was slippery on the shaft of the Paper-Mate pen.

George was talking about his drop shot. He was still lying on his stomach. "I love the smell of this stuff," he said out of the side of his mouth. "It makes me feel like a real athlete, instead of such an egghead."

"I thought I'd knock down the wall between the two back bedrooms," she said, "and have the entire wall glassed in. What do you think?" she asked again. "And I'd like to add a skylight."

George was getting up. It was not a new idea, her notion to redo the house. "I'll take a shower now," he said. "You know I like skylights," he added.

"There's nothing wrong with being an egghead," she said. "Should I rub a little Ben-Gay on your head?" She grabbed

93

him around the waist. "Ellen calls those people airheads. Is that what you want to be? An airhead?" She felt his twelve-hour beard on her cheek and remembered he sometimes shaved before they went to bed.

"Airheads have their moments," George said.

Kate was puttering around in the garage the next day, not sure what she was looking for, when a short worried-looking man approached her. As he came closer, she saw that he was young, probably just out of college. And why do I assume everyone is interested in going to college, she corrected herself.

"I'm sorry to bother you," he said politely. Perhaps he was one of those religious kids, a Mormon doing his year of missionary work. But those young people traveled in pairs, she remembered. "Dr. Cummings doesn't answer the door," he said. He was a patient. The procedure was for the patients to ring the bell, walk into the hall, sit down, and wait their turn. "The front door is locked," said the young man. "It's my regular appointment hour." His eyebrows wandered over his forehead.

Kate clapped her hands together like two blackboard erasers. She was dusty. She'd been looking through the twenty-year rubble in the garage all morning, taking a sort of inventory. Dr. Hirschhorn had left an entire workbench behind. There was no sledgehammer. Kate was sitting on the floor looking at the rafters when the displaced patient entered. The day was cool, in the low eighties, the first one in weeks. There were yellow jackets buzzing on the roses that climbed on the garage walls.

The patient shuffled his feet on the cement floor. "What shall I do?" he said.

"Oh, yes," Kate said. She and George had collected bees in old Miracle Whip mayonnaise jars. They had put holes in the lids so the bees could breathe, and honeysuckle inside so they could eat. She got up off the hard floor. The zipper of her jeans tugged at her scar. "I'm Mrs. Cummings." She brushed the dirt from the seat of her pants and walked toward him, extending her dirty hand.

The patient walked too fast for her, as they went to the front of the house. Would she ever be mobile again? Everything reminded her of her infirmity. The front door was locked. They went to the back. He followed her through the house, the dog sniffing him up and down. George's door to the office was ajar; he was gone.

"You must be Mr. Anthony," she said, looking at George's appointment book. Was it really two o'clock? What had she been doing in the garage all this time? She looked again at George's schedule. He had a full afternoon of patients.

"Yes, I'm Anthony," the young man said, reminding her that he was still there.

Was there something special about Mr. Anthony? Had George told her about him? Was he dangerous? Clancy was licking his hand, but that was no indication. Clancy liked everybody. It was already two-thirty.

"He must have had an emergency," she said. "But it isn't like him not to leave a note. Perhaps you'd better go along. I'm terribly sorry. I'll have George call you when he gets home. Does he have your number?" She knew George had all his patients' numbers. She wondered what this mild little man would talk about for fifty minutes with her husband. He'd probably waited all day for his time. She felt sorry for him. "Perhaps you'd like some iced tea," she said.

"Sure," he said, the disappointment in his eyes fading slightly as he followed her to the kitchen.

Mr. Anthony, it turned out, was an unemployed actor. "And I'm only a person when I'm on stage," he told Kate.

She wondered how he was paying for his appointments with George. He lived with his mother on Beacon Hill, he said. He had had the lead in *Fiddler on the Roof* in college. He knew he could be a star if he just made the right connections. Her husband was super, Mr. Anthony told her. He thought it must be swell to be married to a psychiatrist.

Just before three, the front bell rang. It was the next patient, Miss Flaherty. George had still not called. Kate asked the young woman to come in. She couldn't have been much older than Ellen. Her face grew grim as Kate explained that George had been called away on an emergency.

Yes, Miss Flaherty would have some iced tea. "You must call me Betty," she said. Mr. Anthony made no move to leave. The dog settled herself under the table. Miss Flaherty—Betty—was a graduate student in English at Harvard. Kate saw that she had eczema on her arms.

"My problem," she began, "is that I can't relate to men." She glanced sideways at Mr. Anthony. She seemed determined to have her therapeutic hour with or without George.

"You must call me Tony," Mr. Anthony said. Apparently Anthony was his first name. Or, Kate thought, it could be his last name. Would his parents have named him Anthony Anthony? No wonder he had problems.

The two young people chattered on, comparing notes about their therapy, the way students often do about their teachers or their parents.

"I find him tremendously responsive to my needs," Betty said. She was chewing on an ice cube.

"Don't do that," Tony said. "Please. It makes my teeth hurt."

Kate decided to phone the hospital to see how long George would be gone. He hadn't been there, they told her. She called her mother. Perhaps he had gone there while

96

she was buried in the garage. Had she told him she was going to the garage? He probably thought she was resting upstairs. No, her mother hadn't seen him. She was just about to do the grocery shopping and come by to fix dinner for them. Was everything all right? she wanted to know. Yes, yes, Kate said, things were just fine.

When she went back to the kitchen, the two patients were having a fine time. They were laughing about their first appointments with George.

"I was so scared I couldn't say one word," said Tony.

"And I was so scared I couldn't stop talking," said Betty.

"Imagine being afraid of Dr. Cummings," they both said at once and laughed harder.

Tony held his sides. "I tripped over my foot," he snorted. "Size seven feet and I trip."

"I dropped my purse and everything fell out," Betty said. "I had five lipsticks, and they all rolled in different directions. Now I don't even wear lipstick." Tears were rolling down her serious cheeks as she laughed a laugh that made no noise. "You must think we're crazy," she said. And they all three laughed together.

The four-o'clock patient was a Mrs. Becker who scurried away before Kate could ask her to come in. She was a woman of about fifty with rings on every finger and a straw hat with a wide brim. As soon as she heard George was not in his office, she turned on her spike-heeled sandals and clicked away down the cement path to the sidewalk.

Kate had just set out some crackers and cheese for Betty and Tony when Mr. Brader rang the bell. He was the five-o'clock patient. Kate knew George had been seeing him for years. It was a familiar name: Martin Brader. The bell rang again. Mr. Brader was impatient.

"Why don't I get the door and say that I'm the shrink of the day?" Betty said. She had been telling them about her thesis on Jane Austen with such enthusiasm that Kate made a resolution to read *Pride and Prejudice*. She had used the Cliff's Notes for it in high school.

Mr. Brader stamped his foot like a small child when Kate told him George was away on an emergency. He was bald, which made his head look too big for his body. He did not want to leave. Clancy sniffed his feet suspiciously.

"I have nothing else to do now, so I'll just wait for him," he said and walked past her into the hall. He thumped himself down on the old wooden pew she and George had bought at auction years ago for two dollars. It amused them to have a pew in their house. Kate decided not to ask Mr. Brader into the kitchen.

When she went back there, she saw that her mother had joined the two young people at the table. She had a tumbler of pale fluid that Kate knew was J & B scotch with water. Her father was a teetotaler, and they never had liquor in their house.

"Isn't it nice of Ellen's friends to come over to see you while she's away?" her mother said. Would she ever take the time to get things straight? Would she ever learn to listen? Kate's father called her Bubbles.

Betty and Tony looked at Kate. She knew her mother hadn't given them a chance to identify themselves. Betty was scratching her arms. Kate went over and put her arm around her and raised her eyebrows at Tony in what she hoped was a reassuring gesture. Her mother continued talking and making her assumptions. Of course, they had all been at school together. Of course, they had all grown up in Newton. And wasn't it odd she hadn't met them before? She knew all of Ellen's friends, of course.

"Do you think we ought to be going now?" Betty said to Tony. Kate wondered if they were going to be a couple.

They got up and went to the door. "Thanks for every-

98

thing," Tony said, as if he'd been a weekend guest.

Kate found a tear blocking her vision in one eye. She put her arms around Tony first and then Betty. "You'll come by again soon, won't you?" she said.

They opened their mouths in surprise.

"I really mean it," she said. She missed Ellen, she knew. But as the screen door banged behind them, she knew she also missed the give-and-take she had with her own students. She loved their openness. She often thought she learned more from them than they did from her. When she told them so, they usually looked at the floor or changed the subject. They were unused to that kind of praise from adults. It embarrassed them, so she had become more subtle in her admiration.

She was feeding the dog when George arrived at about seven in his tennis clothes. Her mother had finished her drink, put a casserole in the oven, and left for home. A determined Mr. Brader sat in the hall.

"Hi!" George said.

"Where have you been?" she asked. It was obvious where he'd been.

"You should see my backhand volley," he said.

"Mr. Brader's in the pew," Kate said. The dog was gulping her food. George's sneakers and socks were red from the clay at the tennis club. Had he been there all afternoon?

"I've got to ice my elbow," he said. "I forgot about my patients," he smiled as he stood before the freezer putting ice in a plastic bag. "Isn't that something?"

He'd actually forgotten about his patients? She didn't know what to say. What could you say to a psychiatrist who forgot his appointments? Even if he was your husband? Well, maybe even psychiatrists were entitled to one mental-health day. "I forgot about Mother's dinner," Kate said, as she lifted the casserole out of the oven. The smell made her mouth water. She thought of all the kindness and good food her mother had lavished on her these past weeks. Theirs was a love that permitted impatience with one another. She wished they were more openly affectionate. Being the center of her mother's life had been a privilege and a burden for both of them.

Kate hadn't eaten all day. The one-dish meal was made of brown rice, crabmeat, and cheese. George was starving, too, he said. He would have to go on a special diet now that he was exercising for so many hours every day. He was thinking of becoming a vegetarian.

They forgot about Mr. Brader and were startled to find him still waiting in the pew in the hall when they turned on the light. It was after eight-thirty.

"Don't worry about being late," Mr. Brader said as he took George by the arm and led him into the office.

CHAPTER
· TEN ·

What was such a big deal about driving the car, Kate wanted to know, as she backed out of the driveway for the first time in four weeks. The big deal was that she was free. She smoothed her sundress over her lap and blew Clancy a kiss. The dog was playing with an old tennis ball on the front lawn.

This was going to be a perfect day. She was going to the college to order her lab supplies for the fall semester. She was going to meet Charlie for lunch. And after that, she was going to visit Rhoda. Yes, it would be perfect.

Of course, she didn't really have to go to the college to order her supplies; she could phone in the order. But she knew that just being in the lab and in her office would help erase the last month of helplessness. The smells of the lab would blot out the hospital odors. She looked down at her still-round stomach as she went over the bump at the end of the driveway. It still hurt to be jostled. But she knew her muscle control would come back. It was just that when you're older . . . She decided not to complete the thought.

George had come to bed and gone right to sleep after

seeing Mr. Brader that evening he'd forgotten his patients. While he slept, he mumbled something about attacking the ball. Had she been so self-involved these past months that she hadn't noticed him? Since that night, every morning when she woke, he was gone. Well, soon they'd have their month together at Nantucket.

Today was going to be hot again. She ought to have turned on the lawn sprinklers. But probably Clancy would dig holes and play in the puddles. What did you do with a dog who refused to grow up?

An ice-cream truck rang its bell and children appeared from nowhere. Kate was hungry. She hadn't eaten breakfast. Should she stop and eat a Popsicle or a Dixie Cup? She could almost taste the orange ice on her tongue. No. She could wait. After all, she was meeting Charlie for lunch in a little while. She could wait. She had waited all this time to be alone with him. She should surely have a good appetite. The car stopped at a red light. The children were lined up at the window of the ice-cream truck, holding their thin arms up for their treats. She could still park the car and get in line. Why had she skipped breakfast? Eating now seemed like a betrayal of Charlie, of his lunch, of his affection. Well, he wouldn't have to know. The car behind her was honking. The light had changed. She pulled over and parked and ran across the street. Her incision again reminded her that she was not like everyone else.

"Are you Judy's mother?" a small boy asked her. He had ice cream on a maroon shirt that said PROPERTY OF MIT ATHLETIC DEPT.

"No," she said. "I'm Ellen's mother." She was next in line.

"Judy went to the bathroom outside," the boy said.

Tattletale, Kate thought. "One orange Creamsicle," she

said to the ice-cream man. His mouth had the same sallow
look as Martin Brader's.

The college was nearly deserted in the summer. Although
it was in the city, the campus now was quiet in comparison
with the regular academic year. The skeleton staff asked
Kate how she was. Hadn't she lost weight? And wouldn't
it be wonderful, they said, if there were such a thing as a
school without students. It was so peaceful during the summer, they told her. There were no problems.

Kate sat in her second-floor office and opened her desk
drawers looking for order forms. She had been writing these
orders for fifteen years, and every time the bookstore
changed management there was a new form. Her desk was
full of junk: old test papers in an orange file she'd marked
"Graveyard," pencil stubs, rusty scalpels, telephone messages, a jar of peanut butter and a package of crackers in
the bottom drawer. She could still taste the orange Popsicle.
Probably her tongue was orange. She went to the mirror
in the bathroom to look. It was. Well, a little peanut butter
wouldn't hurt, wouldn't spoil her appetite for lunch. Her
good appetite had always been one of the things Charlie
liked about her, he said. Janet was a picky eater. He hated
picky eaters. Where was the knife she kept to spread the
peanut butter? She could use a scalpel. No. Probably she'd
get rust poisoning. She did not plan to die of rust poisoning.
She dug her finger into the sticky, chunky stuff and spread
it on a cracker, which broke in her hand. A glob of peanut
butter landed on her skirt. She scraped it off with the rusty
implement. The dress was patterned; no one would notice.
She licked her fingers, washed her hands, and wrote out
her orders on one of the old forms.

In the lab she saw Howard Hansell, the chief custodial
worker, scrubbing out one of the deep sinks. "Hi, Howard,"

she said, poking her head in the doorway. He had been at the college longer than anyone could remember. In the early days, it was rumored, he gave out the paychecks.

"Oh, Mrs. Cummings," he said. "Come on in." Howard was proprietary about the campus. His face was lined. He must be nearly seventy. She saw he was washing the glassware, not scrubbing the sink as she had thought.

"It gets the dirt off my hands," he said, as if he'd read her mind.

"I appreciate your doing it," she said.

"What's the matter with you?" he said. Howard was never one to waste words. "You look awful. You sick?" He was drying his big hands. Even at seventy, or more, his presence radiated power. What was it about him? His growly voice commanded her to come into the lab again. Even though he called her Mrs. Cummings and she called him Howard, it was clear to both of them who had the higher status.

"I have cancer," she surprised herself by saying. And before she knew it, she'd told Howard the whole story: about George and Charlie. She told him that the malignancy was supposed to have been removed. She was crying. She was telling him about Rhoda. She did not want to be plastic like Rhoda. Howard had drawn two high lab stools together, and he sat listening and patting her hand.

What was she doing? She and Howard had never exchanged more than a few words. And now she had simply let loose. She who had prided herself on her control. She who made lists and foolproof course syllabi to show how organized she was. What was the matter with her? She touched the peanut-butter spot on her skirt.

"There's nothing wrong with you," Howard was saying. "You've had a bad time is all."

"But you told me I look awful." She couldn't help it now. She felt sorry for herself. She hated herself. She hated her body. She wanted to go on as if nothing had happened.

"You look tired is what I meant," Howard said. Was he whispering? "And you're not as tanned as you usually are. But you're not dying. I'd know it if you were dying."

Kate remembered that Howard's wife had died after a long illness. Was it cancer? She was afraid to ask. She squeezed his hand.

He got off the stool and was rummaging in his toolbox. "I always keep a bottle on hand for times like this," he said. Kate wiped her nose on her bare arm. She hadn't cried like this since she was a child.

Howard handed her a bottle. She expected it to be brandy. If this were a movie, it would certainly be brandy. She felt as if she were, in fact, watching herself, as if it were a movie, as if this couldn't possibly be her, sitting in an empty lab with an old janitor, sniveling like a baby, about to drink brandy from a bottle.

"Shall I pour it into one of these?" Howard held up a beaker and then a test tube.

"No. This is fine," she said. But it was not brandy, as she had expected, or even cheap whiskey. Her throat had been ready for the assault of straight alcohol. Instead, she saw from the label, it was a bottle of Moxie.

"That'll put hair on your chest," Howard said. It was just what her father used to say when she was small. She supposed it was a sexist remark. But the affection on Howard's face was undeniable.

She took a swig of the dark liquid. It touched each cell of her mouth, her throat, her esophagus. She imagined it flowing down to her toes. "Wow," she said. They both grinned.

She was late getting to the Union Oyster House. As she looked for a parking place in the busy downtown section of Boston, she realized she had overscheduled herself. She had made it into a test of some sort, like walking across a log over a stream when she was a kid. If she could do it without getting her feet wet, she could count on good luck. But she knew that was silly. Wet feet had nothing to do with luck. And surviving this first day out was a test of foolishness, not of good sense.

She double-parked her car in front of the restaurant, wrote "handicapped" on a piece of paper and stuck it on the windshield. Howard had told her to follow her instincts. They had finished the whole quart of Moxie and had gotten as high on their new friendship as if the stuff had been two hundred proof.

"You can't park there, lady." Where had that policeman come from all of a sudden?

"Oh, yes, I can," she said. "I'm handicapped." She limped into the restaurant. She would take a taxi home if they towed the car.

Charlie had been waiting forty-five minutes, he said. He was getting worried. Where had she been? She looked wonderful, he said. He was so glad she was wearing his earrings. Did she still like them? And how was school? Where had she parked?

"You look marvelous," she told him. In truth, he looked gaunt and tired as day-old celery. Still, she was pleased to see him and fought the urge to sit on his side of the booth.

The lunch crowd was thinning out. She liked this place. It was full of men in brown suits and furrowed brows on expense accounts. She and Charlie had met here once before in the middle of the afternoon and dipped their oysters in beer. They had played tic-tac-toe on their napkins.

But George was right: She ought to have waited another week before going out. She was tired. Oh, God. She hoped he hadn't forgotten his patients again today. She hoped he wasn't out on that damn tennis court trying to prove something to himself. Maybe she should call home.

"I've missed you," Charlie was saying, as he put his hand on her knee under the table. She was glad his suit was blue. She was glad to be here with him. The beer in the frosted mugs was cold; she hadn't realized how thirsty she was. Business was picking up, Charlie said, although it looked like the farmers would take a big loss with their crops this fall. And weren't these oysters sensational?

Yes, the oysters were better than she'd remembered. She was beginning to revive. George would be all right. Howard had told her everything would be all right. She could still feel the weight of his large hand on hers.

"Have I ever told you about Howard Hansell?" she said. "He's the head custodian at the college." She tried to describe Howard—his gruffness, the Moxie, his insistence on having his fingernails clean. "He saved my life today," she was saying.

"Janet's left me," Charlie interrupted.

An oyster slid halfway down Kate's throat and stopped. She hadn't meant for this to happen. "I don't know what to say," she said. Was she going to start crying again? Where had Janet gone? And what about the children? And would Charlie expect Kate to leave George now? The oyster made its way up her throat, and she spit it into her napkin.

A jovial red-faced man came to the table and patted Charlie on the back. "So this is the little woman," he said, grinning at Kate. Did people still talk like that? "The little woman?" He was shaking Kate's hand. Charlie was introducing them. Had he told the man her real name? The noise from adjacent tables seemed to block it out.

It was all for the best, Charlie said, when the man went away. Janet had explained that she needed to have her own life. He supposed she was right. Maybe it had even been his fault. The only thing was, he said, that she'd left the kids with him. And what was he supposed to do with three kids under seven?

Kate was making a pattern on the sweat on the side of her beer mug. Where had Janet gone? Where did a woman go when she left a husband and three children?

"She's got an apartment in Cambridge," Charlie said. "A studio. She didn't take anything from the house. She got her furniture from a thrift shop. Between you and me," he said, his face darkening, "I think your husband's made her crazier than she ever was."

Kate wondered if they'd towed her car yet. She'd forgotten that Janet was a patient of George's. In fact, she didn't like to think of Janet at all. "She'll be back, Charlie. I'm sure she'll be back."

The children were staying with his mother, he told her. But how long could that go on? And what was he going to do with that big house all by himself? What was the matter with Janet anyway that she had to go off and become a goddamn social worker? What was her family supposed to think while she was out saving the world? He ran his fingers through his thick hair. Kate thought she saw the shine of tears in his eyes, but he turned his head to look for the waiter.

She wanted to comfort him, to give him the gift Howard Hansell had given her in the lab. But she said nothing. Theirs had not been a relationship of articulated feelings or shared histories. She suddenly felt intrusive.

"I've got to get back to the office," Charlie was saying as he fished in his pocket for his credit card.

"Things have changed, haven't they?" Kate said. What a dumb thing to say. It was obvious that things had changed.

He took a last swig of his beer and again looked around

for the waiter. Kate got up and sat next to Charlie in his booth. She put her arm around him and nestled his head on her narrow shoulder. She loved his smell, a sort of blue-oxford-cloth-button-down-collared-shirt smell.

He sighed. "You smell delicious," he said.

"Will there be anything else?" the waiter said, as he collected the credit card.

At the door, the light was so bright they both squinted. "When can I see you again?" Charlie asked.

Kate saw her car was still there with its "handicapped" sign. She was leaving in a few days for Nantucket, she told Charlie. She would be away until Labor Day. She always went to Nantucket in August, she said.

Oh, he said. He had never been to Nantucket. Did she like it? He didn't know if he would take a vacation this year.

As she got into her car, they made plans to be in touch by phone. Maybe they could even find time to see one another before she left. It was all a question of finding the time, they said.

"And Kate," he said, as she put the car in first gear. "Kate, have you ever gone to a shrink?"

"No," she said, surprised at the question.

"What really happens there, anyway?" he said, almost to himself, walking away before Kate could answer.

George had often commented on how his patients would say the most important things in the last minutes of a session. "Oh, Charlie," she said aloud as she headed into the afternoon traffic. She remembered the bag of marbles in her purse. She had thought it would be great fun to play marbles on the table at the Oyster House. But the moment hadn't presented itself. In the rearview mirror the sun caught the surface of the gold in her ears.

On her way to Rhoda's apartment, Kate startled herself

by thinking about Janet. She wondered again what kind of person would leave small children. Perhaps she was desperate. Kate had never before thought of Janet as an actual person, but as some sort of cardboard fixture in Charlie's life. Had she found out about Kate and Charlie? No. Charlie would have told her that. And George had said nothing about his relationship with Janet as a patient. Nor would he. Kate had assumed Janet's problems were minor. After all, Charlie wouldn't have chosen a really crazy wife, would he?

Rhoda's apartment was a brownstone on Beacon Street. The two women had talked on the phone nearly every day since Kate had left the hospital. Rhoda had gone on to a rehabilitation center and had only been home a few days. She was waiting for Kate at the door. Her dark hair seemed to have grown longer and her brown eyes larger in the month since they'd seen each other.

"Come in, come in." Rhoda was half a head taller than Kate. It was the first time they'd stood up together. And Rhoda was younger—maybe ten years younger. Kate saw that she had a cane, but as they entered the apartment, Kate had a hard time remembering which leg had been amputated.

"You're walking so well. You're amazing," she said. "I'm so glad to see you."

A huge orange cat pounced on the floor beside Rhoda. "Hermione, meet Auntie Kate," Rhoda said. "She's become a watchcat in my absence. I guess she missed me."

The apartment had high ceilings and long windows with old uneven glass. The woodwork was brown and warm. A grand piano took up most of the front room, where there were also a few pieces of overstuffed furniture.

"The furniture came with this apartment," Rhoda said.

110

"But the piano's mine. My ex came back and took everything one night while I was giving a concert. Fortunately, I was able to dig up a bill of sale on this baby," she said, patting the piano lovingly. She was smiling. Kate remembered how easily she smiled, how dazzling her teeth were.

"You're terrific," Kate said.

"Do you want the grand tour?" Rhoda was already moving to another room, with Hermione on her heels. "I couldn't stay in the apartment where Russell and I lived. I was lucky to get this place." The flat had five sunny rooms, two with fireplaces. Orange and yellow dominated, as if she'd decorated the apartment to go with the cat. There was no doubt about it: Rhoda exuded cheer. They carried a plate of freshly baked macaroons and a bowl of grapes into the living room from the kitchen. The old horsehair furniture was comfortable, and the light streaming through the bay window played on the surface of the hardwood floor, catching particles of dust in its wake.

"I'm afraid I have to leave for rehearsal in an hour," Rhoda said, chomping on a cookie.

"Rehearsal?" Kate was incredulous. "But I thought you were still recovering. How can you do it? How will you get there? Aren't you still in pain?"

"It was only my leg I had taken off, not my arms. Thank God." Kate noticed she did not use the word *amputate*. "Of course, my running days are over," she went on. "Actually, they were over long before this." How could she laugh so easily? so genuinely? "I've got hand controls on my car now," she said. "And in another week or two I'll be rid of this thing." She rattled the cane next to her on the floor. Hermione jumped.

"But you aren't recovered yet," Kate persisted.

"By the time I'm"—she paused—"recovered"—her lips drew together—"they'll be after the other leg."

"Oh, I'm sorry. I'm such a dope," Kate said. She certainly was a dope. What did she want Rhoda to do? Cry in her cookie batter? "It's just that I can't figure out where you get all that pep." She sighed.

Rhoda took a deep breath. "Somewhere along the way . . . Was it at Juilliard? or later?"—she looked at the ceiling—"I learned that success as an artist is only partially related to talent." She popped a grape into her mouth—"I always swallow the seeds," she said—"After all, there are loads of talented people out there. Success also depends on confidence, arrogance, and perseverance. Those who lose heart because of a poor audition or review and can't recover, give up. That's the real reason Russell left me. He felt I minimized the obstacles to his success. He was angry that I was so undaunted while he was always questioning his talent."

"Are you still in touch with him?" Kate asked.

"Oh, no," Rhoda said. "The last I heard he'd joined an orchestra somewhere in the Midwest. Oh, no. I understand him. But I could never forgive the despicable things he did to me." Her features pinched together as she spoke of her former husband.

"True love," said Kate. "Wonderful stuff, eh?" She detested Russell. How could love end in stolen furniture and silence?

"Ah, well," Rhoda said, changing her expression. "What's the news with old Charlie? How was your lunch?" The cat had settled itself on Rhoda's lap and was purring as she stroked it.

"His wife's left him," Kate said.

"Oh, boy," Rhoda said. "Does she know about you and Charlie?"

"I don't know," said Kate, eating the last cookie.

They exchanged recipes, talked about their prize students,

112

and laughed about their hospital ordeals. They talked about their plans for the fall, about Charlie, George, and Russell. Rhoda said she hoped to remarry. Kate said she wondered what it would be like not to be married. She gave her bag of marbles to the cat who alternately pounced on and guarded them. The best pain-killer was a good laugh, they agreed. Rhoda suggested they play a duet on the piano. They were good at "Chopsticks"; they were very good at "Heart and Soul." They sang "There's a Long Long Trail" together with Rhoda's accompaniment. They could do anything.

Afterward, Kate watched Rhoda hobble into her green sports car and head for Symphony Hall. The cat was sitting in the window licking its paws. Kate had been worried the cat would swallow the marbles, but Rhoda said Hermione was smart enough to know the difference between toys and food.

CHAPTER

· ELEVEN ·

George's first patient of the day, Henry Matthews, didn't seem to object when he saw George wearing tennis shorts. "You guys have it made," he said, straightening his tie. "Can you imagine what Leora would say if I left the house like that?" Mr. Matthews was the first battered husband George had ever treated. Leora, Mrs. Matthews, attacked her spouse with some regularity, actually with increasing regularity, according to him. She kept a jackknife under her pillow.

George felt sorry for Matthews. He was a self-made man; he owned a chain of hardware stores worth a fortune. But in his personal life, he could be intimidated by a piece of lint. He had scars on his arms and face from his wife's assaults. He loved her, he claimed. It was his fault, he said. He would have to try harder to make her happy.

George remembered that time after Ellen was born when Kate broke a whole set of dishes. Maybe she'd wanted to throw them at him, but she hadn't. She'd thrown them at the bright yellow walls in the kitchen, at the sink, at the stove. She'd cut her hands trying to pick up the pieces. She was so tired, she said. The baby hadn't slept. Her breasts hurt. When George had found her sitting on the floor in the broken mess, he'd sat beside her and licked the blood from her hands. He had rocked her in his arms. He had not known what to say. He was too frightened to say anything.

Matthews was getting up. He had a way of talking into the collar of his shirt that made it difficult to pay attention. It must be awful to sleep next to someone who had a weapon under her pillow. Matthews had finally talked her into seeing George, he was saying. Leora would take his next appointment. Would that be OK? He still had one more appointment scheduled before George went away, he said.

"Oh, yes, fine," said George. It would be interesting to see Leora the Terrible, as he had come to call her in his own mind. It would be nice if this couple could come to terms with each other, he thought. Matthews was a pleasant enough fellow, even though he was a little rough around the edges, as his wife had complained. People just expected too much from one another, didn't they?

George's plan this morning had been to see Matthews for just a few minutes and explain that he had an urgent appointment at the tennis club. But when he and his patient were face to face, he saw the folly of his fantasy. He had to give Matthews the full fifty minutes. You just couldn't say no to such desperation, although he was able to end the session a few minutes early.

While he was phoning the tennis club, Miss MacIntyre appeared in the doorway. He signaled her to come in.

"Emergency," he mouthed to her.

She sat in her usual chair, as close to the door as possible, her eyes taking in his outfit and settling on his legs.

"Oh, yes," he said, "this is Dr. Cummings calling. Please tell Mr. Gregory I'll be late. Another hour. Is everything under control?" Gregory was the pro's last name. What

the hell was his first name? Of course everything was under control. How could things get out of control at a tennis club? Well, he couldn't very well let Miss MacIntyre
know that the emergency was his tennis lesson with the
club pro.

"Now," he said, hanging up. He turned his swivel chair
to face his patient.

"I can't believe it," she said.

"What's the matter?" he said. Miss MacIntyre was a
chronically depressed thirty-five-year-old telephone supervisor who still lived at home with her parents.

"I always wondered if you had legs," she said. It was
the first time he'd ever heard her laugh. The sound reminded
him of a toy tea set he'd gotten for Ellen years ago. His
outfit apparently had some therapeutic value. The session
with Miss MacIntyre was fruitful. Since he'd let down his
guard and worn his "real" clothes, she was able to open
up to him and use the time beneficially. She wasn't a virgin,
after all, she told him. She'd had a child and given it up
for adoption. No one knew about it. Even her parents. She'd
gone away for a year's study at the University of Colorado.
That's what she told everyone. They had teased her about
becoming a ski bum.

"Imagine me on skis," she said.

Indeed, it was difficult to think of Miss MacIntyre on
skis. She was so awkward she rarely made it to her chair
without stumbling.

"The baby was a girl," she said. "The father never knew."

George hated to stop a productive session like this one
as much as the patient did. More often than not, a patient
retreated at their next meeting. Sometimes the patient
would go so far as not even to show up. But the hour
was over, and he really had to get to the tennis club.

He would cancel the rest of his appointments. But, he

thought, the effect of his new garb on his patients was worth exploring. He might even write a paper on it: "The Effects of Nontraditional Clothing by Therapists in Psychotherapy." No. That would leave the door open for a transvestite therapist. How about "The Effects of Therapists' Clothes on Patients?" No. It still wasn't right.

As he swung his tennis bag into the car, he saw Harriet Michaels strut up the walk. "Oh, Mrs. Michaels," he said, "I've got an emergency. See you next week." He threw his rackets into the backseat. Of course, he realized, as he started the engine, he would not see her next week. He would be on Nantucket next week. He saw Mrs. Michaels dab a handkerchief to her nose as he drove by her car. Well, what could he do? He backed up to where she was parked and spoke to her through the open windows.

"How about tonight at seven?" he said. "I think I've had a cancellation." He generally never saw patients in the evening, particularly during the summer. So those hours were nearly always open.

She looked up. She was crying. "Oh, I'd appreciate that so much, Doctor. I really would," she whispered. She got out of her car, opened his passenger door, and got in. She wore a heavy engulfing perfume. Now what? You could just never let your guard down for one minute, could you? She grabbed his hand.

"Mrs. Michaels." He heard his own stern voice. Why did he always have to be the one to be stern? And what was he doing anyway sitting in this car with a patient in the middle of the morning? An attractive patient, he noticed for the first time. She was blond and energetic. Newly divorced, he remembered. The palm she was holding began to sweat. The scent of her perfume was going to make him sneeze. "Mrs. Michaels," he repeated, more gently this time. "I have an emergency."

"Oh, yes," she said, patting his bare knee. "Oh, yes, I'm sorry. Of course you do. Was it seven tonight you said? See you then."

He knew that she came from Melrose. It must have taken her forty minutes just to get here. It would be a shame for her to drive all the way back again tonight. Well, maybe he would take her to the club. No. No. What was he thinking of? He did not stop her as she got out of his car.

He backed up and parked in front of his own house. He ought to let Kate know where he was going. But she was out. He called his answering service with the names and phone numbers of the patients he was canceling and information about rescheduling.

The courts at the club were filled with children and women. Some of those women were better than he was. He was glad that women were more openly competitive. And some of the kids were unbelievable. All that top spin.

He found Gregory. It was Bob Gregory, he remembered now. The young pro sat in the clubhouse with a coffee mug and the morning paper in front of him. "Those Red Sox have a death wish," he said.

"Sorry to keep you waiting," George said. He was more than two hours late. Well, he'd hired him for the day. So it was his nickel. He'd pay anyway.

"It's OK, Doctor," he said. "I understand." Was he rippling his muscles on purpose? "To tell the truth, I had a late night last night and was glad for the extra time."

When had George stopped having late nights? "Call me George," he said. "Otherwise, I feel old."

Gregory smiled. He had one of those wide-open faces that made you think of a cornfield. It wouldn't matter what the pro called George; he'd feel old anyway, just looking at him.

"Let's go," said Gregory, carrying two baskets of tennis balls. "How's your arm?" he asked.

"No problem," George said. He put on the arm brace he hoped would deaden the vibration when his racket hit the ball.

The pro stood at the net and fed him balls. George hit each one as hard as he could directly at Gregory, who volleyed the balls back with ease. Forehands. Backhands. Cross-courts. Down the line. It was exhilarating: the windup, the swing, the hit. And most of all, not worrying about Gregory. Not worrying about anybody. Just concentrating on the ball. The center of the racket and the ball. He would learn top-spin shots yet. It was all a matter of timing. And preparation. You had to line the ball up, take it early, and stroke it from low to high. And then follow through. George was good at following through. What was tough was taking the ball on the rise.

"Attack the ball, Doctor Cummings," Gregory said on each shot. "Attack. Attack. Don't let the ball play you. Go after it."

"George," George said. "Call me George." He had forgotten to bring sweatbands, and the perspiration stung his eyes.

"Attack," said Gregory. "Turn those shoulders and attack."

"It's alien to my nature," George said, when they stopped later for a break.

Gregory looked puzzled.

"Attacking, I mean," George said. "It's not my style. I've always been a retriever, a counterpuncher." His clothes were soaked through. The water tasted good. Gregory had only a few beads of sweat gathering on the gold chain around his neck.

"When I played Little League," the pro said, "my dad

120

told me to go after the ball, whether I was in the field or at bat. He was a little weird about it, you know?" Gregory looked at his feet. "He said I'd never get ahead in this world by waiting for the ball to come to me. He still says it. He's a stockbroker, you know."

Another lousy broker. "Let's go back to the court," George said. "You ready?" He didn't want to play father to this youngster. He wanted to attack the ball. Anyway, the kid's father was right. Waiting around, hoping for the best wasn't good strategy—on or off the tennis court. Why hadn't he seen it before? He had waited for Kate his whole life, waited until she decided she loved him. He was still waiting. He had even hired that detective to snoop around while he waited. And now, where was Kate? Off with that Murdoch bastard again? Well, he was a person, too, wasn't he? He was going to change things. It was going to be different from now on. He was going to take charge of himself. He would learn to take the ball on the rise. He would not let the ball play him. Kate would have to grow up, cancer or no cancer. He wanted her. He wanted her all to himself. And if that was smothering her or cutting off her freedom, or if he was being old-fashioned, that was too bad. From now on, they were going to play by the same rules. His shoulder began to ache as he practiced overhead smashes.

Gregory sailed one lob after another into the blazing sun. "Reach for it," he called across the net. "Reach for it. And snap that wrist."

Was there anything more satisfying than hitting a perfect overhead smash?

"Reach. Reach," said the pro. "And grunt. You'll feel better if you let it out."

Yup, George decided, Kate would have to grow up and learn the rules. But, he thought, as he hit a ball on the

121

frame of his racket and it flew over the fence, she could die. And then where would he be with his rules?

It was after six when he got home. He must have hit thousands of tennis balls. He was icing his arm when Kate came in with a pizza.

"Hi, darling," she said, kicking off her shoes. "I gave Mother the night off."

She was recovering nicely, he thought. He knew the surgeon was right: The chances of more malignancy were very slight. Besides, he couldn't treat her as if she were dying. How would he do that?

"I want you to stop seeing Murdoch," he said.

Kate stopped slicing the pizza.

"I can't take it anymore," he said and felt his mouth dry up as if the dentist had just filled it with sticks of cotton. "I've got to feel more in control of my life." He told her about attacking the ball, taking it on the rise, while she stood poised with the knife over the pizza. Afterward, he recalled that he gave her no opportunity to respond. He told her about Gregory, about top spin, about Gregory's father. He didn't mention that the elder Gregory was a stockbroker.

The pizza got cold. The doorbell rang. It was Harriet Michaels for her seven o'clock appointment.

"I've got to take a shower," he told Kate. "You talk to her." Kate was good at making patients feel comfortable.

By the time he came downstairs, ten minutes later, there were five other people in his office besides Mrs. Michaels. From the explanations, he realized the answering service had changed all his canceled appointments to this hour. He wished he had eaten the pizza. He wished he had videotapes of himself on the tennis court. But he knew he would make the best of this present circumstance. He always did.

122

Sometimes his patients actually benefited from the unforeseen; it got them out of their usual patterns, showed them they were more adaptable than they thought.

"I don't like groups," said one.

"What's the charge for this?" said another.

"No charge," said George. He knew it was his own fault.

Mrs. Michaels said nothing. She sat in one corner of the room picking at her fingernail polish. She wore a too-tight pink top of some sort. George was embarrassed by her ample bosom and his inability to keep his eyes from wandering toward it.

The group began. In short order, they found the similarities and differences among them. They were alternately shy and overbearing, frightened and confident. They laughed as they shared their adventures with George in therapy. They assailed him for his imperfections and declared their affection for him. They were glad it had turned out this way, they said when they left. Even Mrs. Michaels. They all seemed to feel better than he did.

"Have a nice vacation," they said.

"See you in September," they said.

They might all go out together for a drink, they said.

"Maybe you'd like to come see me on Nantucket," George said.

But they didn't hear him. They were deciding where to go. Maybe they would even meet while George was away.

He wanted to go with them. He didn't want to go back into the kitchen to talk with Kate. What if she said she wouldn't stop seeing Murdoch?

It was getting dark. As he walked through the living room, he saw he had put his sneakers on after his shower. And his sweat pants and a polo shirt. Maybe it *was* his clothing that had facilitated such joviality among his patients. Well, why shouldn't he wear what he wanted?

The greenhouse was colorless in the fading light. He entered it on tiptoe, knowing the pebbles on the floor would make their usual crunch anyway. The air was heavy and tropical. The mixture of fragrances was one he liked, and he breathed deeply, as if it were food instead of air. He turned on the hose and sprayed the few plants that were still inside. He walked by each plant touching the soil, humming "I'm Looking Over a Four Leaf Clover." Singing always cheered him up.

It was really dark now. He didn't bother to turn on the lights. Would Kate come if she knew where he was? He wasn't ready for that test yet.

He sat on a stool at the far end of the greenhouse and pressed his forehead on the windowpane. The glass was cool. The surface would have squeaked if he had run his finger across it. He picked up a small cultivator. A patient had given him a whole set of indoor gardening tools from Hammacher-Schlemmer. He turned the cultivator over in his hands, testing its sharp points on his fingernails. What was he so afraid of? He was a success, wasn't he? Second in his class at Boston College. Third at Tufts Medical School. He had more patients in his practice than he could handle. He liked his work.

The cultivator made a sharp wincing sound against the glass. He pressed harder. The glass cracked just a bit in the corner of the pane. He put the cultivator in another corner, and there too the glass made tiny cracks, like the wall of an old tire. The other two corners were easy. And still the pane did not fall out. He knocked it with his knuckles. It held fast. But the cracks were spreading now, like delicate lace, the kind his grandmother used to crochet. This time, when he pressed his hand against it, the pane shattered. He picked its jagged edges from the frame and dropped them on the floor. Then he started on the next pane.

124

· TWELVE ·

Charlie agreed with his mother that sooner or later he would have to make some decisions. Soon, she said, the boys would be going back to school. What was he going to do then? And what were his plans for the house? Would he stay in Newton? He could afford to get a housekeeper, couldn't he? Why didn't he start looking? There was no time like the present. That's what she always said. Unless, of course, he wanted to move back home with the family in Winchester. He could always do that. And she would love taking care of the children. What exactly were his plans?

It was Friday afternoon. Charlie was picking up the kids for the weekend. In the two weeks since Janet had left, they had stayed with their grandparents. That, in and of itself, was not unusual; they often stayed there. Today, Charlie had quit work early. Nothing much ever happened on Friday afternoons anyway. Besides, he was anxious to see the kids, even though he had dinner with them nearly every night at his parents' house.

They were sitting outside in the sloping backyard drinking iced tea and watching the kids play in a small pool their grandparents had bought for them. Charlie was dying for a beer. But the folks would have claimed it was too early in the day for liquor. His father would have said something about a healthy mind and a healthy body. And Charlie didn't want to create any more problems than there were already.

"Well, where did Janet go?" his mother asked. "You never told us where she is. And you'd think that after two whole weeks she'd want to see her children, wouldn't you? I never left you kids overnight until after you were out of high school."

Charlie knew his mother was genuinely concerned. She was the kind of person who liked to get things straight. But he felt oddly defensive about Janet. "She's entitled to her own life, Mom," he said, although he wasn't really sure what that meant.

"Her own life?" his mother echoed. She sat up in her chair to get a better look at Janie. Hers was a world of families: of mothers and children, husbands and wives, fathers and sons. She was puzzled by both Betty Friedan and that Anita Bryant. Once she had even asked him if he'd heard of oral sex.

His father didn't have much to say about Janet, now or ever. She was family, and that was good enough for him. He was glad to have the kids around, he said. Maybe he could make real athletes out of his grandchildren. He'd sure tried with his own kids. "Imagine," he said, "an athletic director with three left-footed kids." But Charlie knew his father was proud of him. He was at the finish line of the marathon each year with his camera when Charlie crossed. And each year he tried to get the photo published in *The Winchester Star*. Charlie was always relieved it never got in; he couldn't get his time down under four hours. Maybe if he'd train year-round instead of two months before the event, he'd do better.

During the summer, his father still directed the park and recreation program he had started in Winchester over thirty years ago. Everyone knew him. They'd even named a ball field after him. It was one of the reasons Charlie had decided not to settle in Winchester. He could never live up to the straight-arrow reputation of his father, although his brother and sister hadn't seemed to mind. But the two years he and Janet had lived with his folks when they were first married had convinced him. The move to Newton was an escape.

Charlie looked at his father. His hair was still dark, and his face was as free of lines as the kids'. It was hard to believe he was sixty years old.

"Listen, Beth," his father said. "Things are different now. Women want to do their own thing. Don't you remember *Kramer versus Kramer*?

"Well," his mother said, "I could never see why that pretty Meryl Streep married Dustin Hoffman in the first place. He's only five feet tall, you know." She pulled a handkerchief out of the front of her blouse and blew her nose.

"The point is," his father went on, "that fathers are getting custody these days. Things aren't the same."

Charlie felt his mouth make an O. He hadn't expected such statements from his father. Had his father ever thought of being married to someone else? No. It couldn't be. Not old Straight Arrow.

"Well," his mother said, clearing her throat, "someday soon I'm going to do my own thing." She laughed and winked at Charlie. "When I find out what that is," she finished.

Little Janie was trying to float hunks of grass on top of the pool water. Her arms and legs were layered with mud. The boys were sitting in the pool spitting mouthfuls of water at each other. They were keeping score. Even the smaller Murdochs liked games.

Charlie wondered how he'd manage with these three kids on his hands. He would probably never have time for a beer. Well, he'd have to teach them to play gin. That was all. And hearts. The boys were old enough. Or crazy eights. But what would he do with Janie? He would just figure it out. He'd made a bundle of money all by himself. And built a whole house. He could certainly figure out what to do with a baby.

"OK, kids, time to go," he said. "Dry off. Get your shoes on. And we'll get this show on the road."

There was the usual resistance as he emptied the pool. "Just five more minutes," Mike and Jimmy said in unison. Although they were more than a year apart, they were the same size and often taken for twins—which bothered Jimmy, who valued his role as big brother.

"Shoes," Janie said. "I want my shoes." She went over and sat in the puddle made from the pool water.

"I'd better change her diaper before you go," his mother said. He'd forgotten about her diaper. He let his mother do it, emptied his iced-tea glass, and chewed on the ice cubes. He hoped his mother would wash the mud off Janie. Of course she would. But he supposed if the kids were going to ride in his car now, he'd have to get used to the mud. Nope, he decided. He never would.

"Can we stop at Friendly's on the way home?" Mike said.

"Please," said Jimmy.

"We'll see," Charlie said.

"Please," they said again. His father had joined their chorus. No wonder he was the King of the Kids, as he liked to call himself.

"OK," Charlie said.

"I really hoped you'd stay for dinner," his mother said when she brought a fresh, clean Janie outside. "We're having hot dogs on the grill." Janie was running toward the pool's mud puddle again. Charlie caught her just in time. The water seeped through his right shoe.

"Oh, no, you don't," he said and swung the baby into his arms. She giggled.

"Splash," she said.

"We'll be fine, Mom. We really will," he said. "You're a lifesaver, you know that?" He hugged her. Janie squirmed free. Jimmy cut her off.

"Oh, no, you don't," he said, mimicking his father.

They walked around the side of the house to the front. The kids' suitcase was on the porch. He knew all the clothes would be clean.

As they made their way out of town toward Route 128, he almost went past Friendly's.

"Stop. Stop," the boys yelled.

"Stop. Stop," said their sister. Her car seat was still in Janet's VW. He would have to get a car seat.

"Ice cream only," he said.

They filed into the nearly empty store. He could see that the boys' bathing suits were still wet. He should have made them sit on towels. He should have made them change their clothes.

"Vanilla with a sugar cone," said Mike.

"Mocha almond with a plain cone," said Jimmy. Both boys were barefoot.

"Chocolate," said Janie.

"I'll pass," said Charlie.

The waitress didn't smile. She was a teenager, a high-school kid probably. His father said the kids today took themselves too seriously. Charlie was anxious to get home. If worse came to worse, he was sure he could anesthetize the kids with the TV. Janet limited their viewing to one hour a day. Maybe it was two hours.

On Route 128, the southbound traffic was unusually heavy for midafternoon on a Friday. Janie and Mike were slurping their ice cream in the backseat. Jimmy took charge from the front. "Use your napkins," he told them, "or Daddy will yell at you."

"No, he won't," said Mike. "Will you, Dad?"

A few months ago, even one month ago, things had been fine. Until Kate had her operation. Now she was going off to Nantucket with that shrink husband. Charlie knew he loved her. But he loved Janet, too. She was his wife, wasn't she? He slipped the car into cruise control at sixty-five and took his foot off the gas pedal. Could Janet have known about Kate? Probably she did know, but didn't care. His father was right: It was a different world now. Janet wasn't anything like his mother. He was weaving in and out of the cars on the four-lane highway. He loved the cruise-control feature of his car more than any other. It was like skiing a slalom course on flat ground.

"Daddy," Jimmy said, pulling on his father's shirt sleeve. "You're going too fast. I feel sick. I'm going to throw up."

"Oh, no, you're not," Charlie said. "You're fine. You're just fine. We're all fine. Now sit back and take a deep breath. We're almost home."

"I can't help it, Daddy," Jimmy said, as he vomited all over the dashboard.

"Oh, shit," said Charlie. "I told you you'd be OK. What happened?" He slowed the car down and pulled over to the breakdown lane.

"I'm sorry," Jimmy said and began to cry. "I didn't mean to. I didn't do it on purpose."

"Oh, shit," said Janie.

"It stinks," said Mike from the backseat.

"Oh, Christ," Charlie said. 'It's OK. It's OK. We'll clean it up when we get home. You all right now?"

"I guess so," the boy said, the tears still coming in separate drops, making his eyes bluer than they were.

"I don't see how anyone can eat mocha almond," Mike said.

Jimmy moved over on the seat next to Charlie. "I'm really sorry," he said.

"It's OK," Charlie said once more and started up the car.

"Dad?" said Jimmy.

"Yes, son," Charlie said.

Jimmy put his arms around him. Charlie felt the wet bathing suit. The little body felt good in his arms.

"You're a terrific kid, Jim Murdoch," he said. "What's a little throw-up? I was driving too fast anyway. I should be the one apologizing."

"Throw-up," said Janie from the back seat.

"Upchuck," said Mike. "Puke."

"That's enough," said Charlie.

It started to drizzle as they turned down their street. By the time they got to the driveway, the rain was pounding the pavement, and long streaks of lightning cracked the sky apart.

Janie screamed. "Boom. Boom," she said.

"OK, you guys," Charlie said. "Here we go." He grabbed Janie in his arms and headed for the back door. Mike and Jimmy ran beside him.

"We could get struck by lightning, Dad," said Mike. "There's a kid in my class who got struck by lightning. It fried his brains."

"It did not," said Jimmy.

Inside, the house was quiet. It had been a tomb for Charlie these two weeks while the kids were at his parents'. He left the TV on all the time. Now maybe some real voices would change all that. Maybe he would get a housekeeper, like his mother said. Then at least he'd have somebody to come home to.

The boys went upstairs to change out of their bathing suits, and Charlie put on an old pair of Bermuda shorts. The baby got her blanket. They would all have to stop calling her that.

"Potty," she said.

"Oh, good, honey," he said, jumping at the signal and carrying her downstairs into the bathroom with her little chair in it. "What a good girl." He tried to remember the exact pitch of Janet's voice. When he got the baby's sunsuit and diaper off, he saw it was too late.

"Potty," she said and went and sat on her chair with the plastic cup underneath.

"Does Mommy have diapers down here?" he said.

"Blankie," Janie said, traipsing off into the hallway, as he searched through the cabinets for a diaper. When he turned around, she was back again sitting on her potty chair, a ragged piece of pink cloth in tow.

"I'll be right back," he said. "I'm going upstairs for your diaper. Jimmy, Mike," he called. "Come on down here and watch your sister." He passed them on the stairway. "She's in the bathroom," he told them.

He stood in the doorway of Janie's room for a moment, suddenly caught by the memory of redoing the room when Janet was last pregnant. That last pregnancy when she had been so miserable. He'd picked out the wallpaper himself— pink with angels on it—and papered the room one weekend while Janet had been away. He'd painted the woodwork, sanded the floor, and got their old baby equipment down from the attic. He knew it would cheer her up.

But she cried when she saw the room. She said it looked

like a Christmas card with all those angels. And besides, how did he know it would be a girl? And what would they do with a boy in a pink room?

She was right, he said. He had only been trying to help. Maybe he could do it over. But at least, didn't she like the floor? Oh, yes, she said, she liked the whole room; he'd been thoughtful. She didn't know what was wrong with her. It was perfect.

He found the stack of disposable diapers under the changing table and took the stairs two at a time going down. He heard the TV and Jim and Mike in the family room. Janet thought the kids' shows were awful, but those he had watched didn't seem so terrible—except that Mr. Rogers program. You could fall asleep watching that guy. Janet said it was the best children's program on the air, that it had a calming effect.

In the bathroom, he found Janie washing her blanket in the toilet, singing quietly to herself. There was water on the floor.

"Clean," she said.

"Messy," he said.

A thin layer of yellow liquid covered the bottom of her potty-chair cup. Maybe they were making some progress after all. The phone rang as he diapered her.

"It's Mom," Mike called. He made it his business to get to the phone ahead of his older brother.

Maybe she was coming home. That was it. Of course she was coming home. She had called every day she'd been away and talked to the kids at his folks' house, but she was abrupt with him if he answered the phone. And now she wanted to talk with him. "Hi," he said.

She wasn't coming home. She wanted to see the kids. Could she come over after dinner? Would that be all right with him? They had told the kids simply that Mommy would be away for a while. And the kids had taken it in and made no comment. Well, if it went on much longer, if he had to hire a housekeeper, there would have to be more than a simple statement.

"Blankie," said Janie, squirming in Charlie's arms.

"Her blanket's in the toilet," he explained to Janet. "By mistake."

She would be over at seven, she said.

He hung up. Were they going to start this awful visitation stuff? Most of his friends at the office—in fact, virtually all the brokers he knew—had been married more than once. Weekend exchanges with the various children were nightmares.

The rain had stopped. He put the baby in her playyard outside. She really was a great baby—always so content to play with whatever she had. She rolled a striped ball across the wet grass. The air was warm and smelled good. Was it nitrogen in the atmosphere after a thunderstorm? Janet would know.

Jimmy and Mike came out with their baseball gloves, and within seconds it seemed as if all the kids in the neighborhood were there. They organized themselves, choosing up sides. "We get Mr. Murdoch," Danny from next door yelled. He was missing two front teeth.

"I'm going to sit this one out, fellas," he said. "And ladies," he added, seeing there were several girls in the group.

"Aw, come on," they all said. "Just for a while."

"Well," he said. It was nice to be wanted. "OK. Just for a few minutes. Then I've got to clean up a mess in my car." Charlie's eyes met Jimmy's, and he realized he had nearly betrayed him. Jim wouldn't want the other kids to know he'd thrown up in the car. Only babies did that. Even Mike knew enough to keep quiet about it.

They set up bases in the yard and began their game.
The kids were nice to each other, giving the younger ones
five strikes instead of three before they were out. Would
they have thought of that themselves? It had to be Janet's
idea. Charlie would have bet on it. Janet liked games where
everybody won.

When Charlie came to bat, both sides cheered and yelled.
"Yastrzemski at the plate," they said. The old man of the
Red Sox, the Captain, was retiring this year at forty-two.
It was a good-natured ribbing. Everyone knew that Yaz
was still the best player the Sox had.

When Louella, the neighborhood's teenage baby-sitter,
wandered into the yard, Charlie pressed her into action.
She had just gotten braces on her teeth and was learning
to talk with her mouth closed. She agreed to fill in. Charlie
was thinking about his car. Between the water from the
kids' wet bathing suits and the mess from Jimmy he was
sure the upholstery was ruined.

He could see the kids from the driveway. The sun was
out now and put rainbows into the oil and grease spots
in Janet's empty space. He wondered where she parked
her Volkswagen now. He gagged as he opened the door
of the Mercedes. Because of the thunderstorm, he'd had
to close up the car. Now he opened all four doors and
went to get a bucket and some rags from the garage. The
leather upholstery was stained, as he suspected it would
be, and the carpeting in the front passenger side would
have to be cleaned. He did the best he could with the carpeting and the dashboard. If Janet were here, she'd say the
water stains gave the leather seat some character. She hated
new things. They were all alike. She used to love the mole
on his back. And her chipped antique china. She even
seemed to appreciate rings on the coffee table and gouges
the kids made in the furniture. She often told him she

couldn't wait to have lines on her face. Imperfections made things more real, she said.

He decided to wash the outside of the car, although the rain hadn't really penetrated the waxing he'd done last week. He was still pleased with the maroon he'd chosen even though the car was two years old. He had agonized over the color as well as the other optional features. Even Janet's lack of enthusiasm and his parents' disapproval of such luxury didn't alter his pleasure. He sat beside the left rear wheel polishing the hubcap. He had grass stains on his knees from sliding into third.

He gave the kids Dinty Moore stew for dinner from a can. Mike and Jimmy took turns feeding the baby in her high chair, trying to keep her hands out of the gravy, while Charlie cut up radishes and carrots.

"Did you see me hit my home run, Dad?" Mike said.

"It was not a home run," said Jimmy.

Charlie poured milk for the kids and got a beer for himself. He'd waited all afternoon for this. He took such a big swig from the bottle the beer went up his nose.

"Bottle," said Janie. "My bottle."

"You have your cup," Jimmy said, pushing the covered container toward her.

"No," she screamed. "No cup."

You had to brace yourself for the dinner hour, Janet had said after Jimmy was born and had repeated when Mike came along. "Norman Rockwell lied," she said.

Charlie sat at the kitchen table in Janet's chair. After all, he was the mother now, wasn't he? "Here," he said, taking Janie's spoon. "Nice stew. Meat," he said.

"I want that radish," Jimmy said. "Mike took my radish."

"Come on, you guys," Charlie said.

"I can drink my milk faster than you," said Jimmy.

"No, you can't," Mike said. The boys raced to the bottom of their glasses.

"Tied," said Charlie. He took another swallow of beer. He'd poured it into a glass, so Janie would forget about her bottle. She was chewing on a piece of raw carrot now. He liked this stew even in summer. He and Janet had lived on canned food like this when they were first married. She had never enjoyed cooking. It surprised him. He thought all women liked to cook.

"How about dessert, Dad?" Jimmy said. He had a moustache of milk and a beard of brown gravy.

"How about wiping your mouth, pal?" he said.

"What's the capital of Michigan?" asked Mike. He'd recently been given a jigsaw puzzle of the United States and was eager to show what he knew.

"Minnesota?" said Charlie

"Oh, Dad," said Mike.

"Chicago?" Charlie said.

"That's in Illinois," said Jimmy

Janie threw her carrot on the floor.

"Michigan. Michigan," said Mike. "The capital of Michigan is Lansing," he said.

"How about apples for dessert?" said Charlie. But the apples turned out to be bad. They'd been there a long time, since before Janet left. He hadn't done any shopping since then, except to buy milk every day.

As if on cue, the VW put-putted into its old space over the oil marks. The door slammed. Forgetting about dessert, the boys ran to the door.

"Mama," Janie yelled from her chair. Charlie lifted her out, and watched her turn to her mother.

"We've just finished eating," he said.

"Yes," she said. "I can see that." Her features were heightened, as if an artist had shaded here and underscored there.

She wore shorts and a halter. She probably weighed less than a hundred pounds.

"Come on in," he said. "Can I get you something?" That was stupid. It was her house, too, wasn't it?

"No, thanks," she said, kissing the baby and kneeling down to hug the boys. "I just want to slobber all over these sweet creatures."

Charlie was too big for the room. At his height, he often felt too big. But this was different. He was in the way here. He began to clear the table as the boys pulled their mother into the family room.

"What've you guys been up to?" she said.

"I threw up in Daddy's car," said Jimmy.

Charlie turned on the faucet in the kitchen sink. He didn't want to hear any more. He rinsed the dishes and put them in the dishwasher. He popped the cap off another beer and washed the stew pan. He ate the rest of the radishes. Janet sometimes fixed them so they looked like flowers. He remembered the baby's blanket in the toilet. She wouldn't go to sleep without it. He squeezed the water out of it and took it to the basement. He put the washer on a short cycle, but even with the noise of the appliance, he could still hear the pounding of little Janie's feet on the floor upstairs.

The basement was clean. His skis and the kids' sleds were lined up against the far wall, as well as various projects Janet had undertaken after the kids were born. There was an old chair she had reupholstered and some oil paintings from an art class she'd taken. There was a Gro-Lite on its end that he'd bought her the year she grew plants from seed. But as with all her hobbies, she had lost interest after a short time. He had encouraged her to try photography. He would build her a darkroom, he said. She said she already had a dark room, and he hadn't understood. As the washer

spun to the end of its cycle, he knew there had been warn-
ings. Jesus. She'd even seen a shrink and taken antidepressants. He'd hoped she'd get over it; he never thought it
had anything to do with him. He put the blanket in the
dryer and went upstairs.

They were all in the kitchen now. Janet was fixing chocolate milk for everyone. The baby was in her pajamas.

"I washed her blanket," he said.

"Oh, great," Janet said. "Thanks." It was as if she'd just
swooped into the house and taken over. Why should she
thank him? He was the one in charge, wasn't he?

"Blankie," Janie crooned.

"I'll just read everybody a story," Janet said, "and then
tuck you all in." She still wore her wedding ring. He stood
in the kitchen doorway while they drank their milk. She
didn't offer him any.

"Why did the moron drink chocolate milk?" Jimmy said.

"Why?" said Mike.

"To grow as big and strong as the Murdoch kids," said
Janet.

"Chocolate," said the baby.

They all laughed, even Charlie, who felt as if he were
in the last row of the theater. "Why *did* the moron drink
chocolate milk?" he said.

"Because," Jimmy said, cackling, "because he liked it."

Charlie was in the family room watching TV when Janet
came downstairs. *Dallas* was on. It was some kind of soap
opera. Someone was drunk, and everyone seemed to be
sleeping with the wrong person. The only things he really
liked on TV were the sporting events, but in the past few
weeks, he had watched nearly everything. Next year was
an Olympic year; the coverage would be terrific. Why
couldn't Janet have waited until February? The winter

games were in Sarajevo. He and Kate had joked about going there. She knew everything about Yugoslavia: the history, the various languages, the currency. She read books about Tito.

"So," Janet sighed, "they're all asleep. The boys could hardly stay awake in the tub. I only got halfway through their story."

He turned off the TV. All those people in ridiculous cowboy outfits were making fools of themselves. "Thanks for coming," he said. Why was he treating her like a guest again?

"Oh, don't turn it off," she said, pointing to the TV. "They were probably just getting to the good part."

"There are no good parts," he said. "Are you OK?" Of course she was OK. All you had to do was look at her to know that.

"Sure," she said. Her job was wonderful. She'd forgotten how good working made her feel. And the hospital staff was friendly and supportive. She had always liked that word *supportive.* She said she had just the right balance of inpatient and outpatient work. Soon she'd begin supervision of social-work students. She was looking forward to that.

And what about her apartment? he asked her. How was it working out? She was still standing by the door, leaning back against one side. Her jawline had an angle he remembered from a long time ago. He knew how it would feel if he ran his fingers over it.

Wonderful, she told him. Just one room, of course. It was all she could afford. But it was close to everything.

He was at a disadvantage sitting down. "You can always come home," he said, sounding to himself like his mother.

She frowned. "I'd better be going," she said.

He saw that his legs were jiggling. He stopped, stretching them out in front of him. "I guess I'd better take a bath, too," he said, pointing to his grass-stained knees.

"Yes," she said, turning and walking toward the kitchen and the back door.

He remembered the car seat, but didn't want to ask for it. He would buy his own car seat. He followed her. "How about staying for another chocolate milk?" he said.

"All right," she said.

Getting her to stay was easier than he'd expected. Maybe she had only been waiting to be asked.

They sat at the table. She wanted a beer, she said. So she had her beer. And he had the milk. She wanted to work out a schedule for seeing the kids, she told him. Did she think she'd be back? he asked. He loved her, he said. He hoped she'd come back. She acted as if she hardly heard him, as she spoke of one patient or another at the hospital. And how this psychiatrist was terrific and that one was a jerk. She had signed up for a graduate social-work seminar for the fall, she said. She was thinking of getting her doctorate.

He got her another beer and put a can of salted peanuts on the table. She ate them all. Her enthusiasm was contagious. He got a hard-on under the table and smiled as he felt his face get red. He shifted his legs and they touched hers. She stopped talking for a moment, as if she suddenly realized where she was, but then went on to finish her story. There was a patient just admitted to the hospital who ate newspapers, she said. Entire newspapers. She'd watched him while he ate *The Boston Globe* in five minutes.

At the door, Charlie looked down at her and took her hand. She didn't pull it away. "I'm dying to hold you," he said.

"Me too," she said, looking past his eyes.

They sneaked upstairs like two teenagers.

Her body was so small he'd always been afraid of hurting

her. But she felt strong as they lay together. "I've missed you," he said.

She didn't say anything. Afterward, she went right to sleep and he lay wide awake, too relieved she was home again to sleep right away.

It was Janie's morning singing that awakened him. He remembered it was Saturday. Janet was gone. From the window, he saw that the VW was not in the driveway. Probably she'd gone to get her things from the apartment. But as the day wore on and she did not come back, he got worried and decided to call her.

No, she said, she did not plan to come back. She was busy just now. Could she call him later? She wanted to see the children Sunday afternoon. Would that be all right?

No, he said. She did not have to bother to call back. Besides, he and the kids had plans for tomorrow. He hung up.

What was happening? Did she hate him? Love him? Probably it was both, he decided, and went outside to mow the lawn.

CHAPTER
· THIRTEEN ·

Kate carefully extended one leg forward and back—and then the other. She was standing on her head on the bedroom floor. What was happening to George anyway? He'd forgotten his appointments; she'd found his appointment book in the laundry hamper. And why were his patients so understanding? They waited, came back, phoned to see if he was OK. It was not dissimilar to Kate's spring semester, when she had allowed the students basically to teach themselves. But predictable George, constant George, knew what time it was to the minute. He would never forget a commitment. Something was wrong. And what was all this tennis nonsense about? She knew his shoulder problem was chronic and was causing him trouble. Her feet hung over now and rested on the wall. The blood rushed to her head; her cheeks burned. Why run around a tennis court when you could get your body pumped up this way?

"I'm worried about you," she'd said to George the previous night when he finally came upstairs after his last appointment. She moved over toward him in the big bed. The dog went into the bathroom for a drink from the toilet.

"I'm OK," George said. "I'm just fine."

"I'm sorry about Charlie," she said.

"Sorry that I found out? Or just sorry in general?" She was surprised to hear him snap at her.

"Oh, George," she said and tried to hold his hand. He pulled away.

"I'm tired," he said. "I'm going to sleep."

"It's going to be fine, George," she heard herself saying. "You'll see. It was the malignancy. I was frightened. But that's all over now, isn't it?" There was a faint scratching at the screen in the window. She imagined a bug caught in a hole the dog had clawed. "I'm sure they got it all," she continued. "Why would they lie? You want to see the incision?" She had not yet shown him the wound. She was still self-conscious about it.

George didn't answer. It was unlike him. Whenever they had differences, his was always the voice of moderation. He took charge in times of adversity, and she let him.

"I'm sorry, George. Really I am," she said. "I've behaved like a teenager, haven't I? I was just so sure I'd die. And then it wouldn't matter anyway." Her nose was running. The dog was digging at the rug in the corner by Kate's side of the bed; she never stopped hoping good things were buried under the carpet.

"Do you want to talk about Charlie?" she said. She realized she would have to say something about the affair, but what was there to say? That she could hardly wait to get her hands on Charlie again? "I won't see him again," she said, knowing she was lying. She reached for a Kleenex and blew her nose. It was the right thing to say. "I love you, George. I always have, you know. George?" she said. But he was asleep. How much of her apology had he heard? She lowered her feet to the floor now and raised her head from the pillow. George could stand on his head if he would only try.

This morning, he had left the house early, wearing his tennis things again. "Have you canceled your appointments?" she called to him from the driveway.

"They're meeting me at the club," he said.

"At the club?" she repeated. But before she could get any answers he was gone. She imagined him with his patients at courtside. Was he teaching them tennis? A new form of therapy. Tennis therapy would probably be as good as any other. She'd heard that on the West Coast psychiatrists were getting seventy-five dollars an hour for jogging with their patients. Maybe at this very moment George was sitting under a tree with each patient between sets. Maybe his patients even wore tennis clothes: the new uniform for therapy. She fingered the green trim of the white pillowcase and tried to imagine Mr. Brader with a tennis racket. The whole business was odd. Maybe she should go to the club and see for herself. But, she reconsidered, that would be spying. And she and George had never spied on each other.

She got up from the floor and went into the bathroom where she turned on the shower. As she took her clothes off, she saw marks around her waist from the elastic of her shorts. The dog lay on the cool tiles of the floor. As Kate had resumed her morning routine, Clancy had got used to it all over again, sometimes even leading the way. The dog knew it was time to shower.

Kate let the water run over her body. Even in the summer, she liked the water scalding. She adjusted the shower head so it sent little bullets of water at her. As she soaped herself, she was careful to wash around the incision; she'd already decided she would never touch the scar. She squeezed hot water in and out of the washcloth. What was she going to do about George? Well, soon they'd be away together for their month on the island. They could straighten things

145

out then. They always got along well on vacations, particularly in the years they'd spent on Nantucket. George had never been a workaholic; he relaxed easily. They rented the same house every August and enjoyed tending the garden and socializing with the same vacationers. Their pattern consisted of riding their bikes to a different beach each day and eating their packed lunch after a swim. Afternoons, they'd read. George needed a vacation. That was it. And he missed Ellen. She had never been away a whole summer before this. But she'd be home soon. They'd go to Nantucket. Ellen would come home. Kate would go back to work. And everything would be OK.

The phone rang in the bedroom as she was toweling off. People just seemed to know when you were in the shower or on the toilet and waited to call when you were in the middle of something. On the other hand, she supposed she was always in the middle of something, one way or another.

"Hello," she said, the steam from the shower still in her throat.

"Hello yourself," said Charlie. "Lunch at one?" He spoke in short phrases when he called her at home.

"I'm in the shower," she said.

"It's a come-as-you-are party," he said.

"We have to talk," she said. It was a line from an old movie, probably from a lot of old movies. She was remembering her promise to George. But George had been asleep. He hadn't heard her. So the promise didn't really count then, did it? It hadn't been a contract. It was more like giving up something for Lent—like candy—and then reneging after the first week.

They made their date. Kate decided it would be their last meeting. A promise to herself was just as important as one to George. Besides, neither she nor Charlie had intended any permanence to their fling. A fling was never

146

permanent, was it? That was the trouble. People tried to make flings into marriages. And marriages built only on chemistry were in deep trouble. Everyone knew that. Passion was an illness, a craziness, which had a short season. She walked into her closet to choose her clothes for the day.

The sun was everywhere. This summer's heat was never going to end. The old stone house retained the previous evening's coolness, and as Kate stepped outside, she thought about Sister Perpetua's purgatory. Kate knew, even in the first grade, that she would never be bad enough to go to hell. But she also knew she would never be good enough to go to heaven without first serving her time in purgatory. Sister had drawn pictures for them on the blackboard in colored chalk: the red-orange flames enveloping the little souls. Kate had singed her eyebrows playing with matches that year.

At the garage door, there were at least twenty cartons blocking the way. Was it possible? The publisher of her anatomy textbook had delivered them here instead of to the college. It was the new edition of the book she had co-authored with a colleague. She'd spent much of last winter going over the proofs and making numerous corrections in the sloppy editing job. There was a thick file of correspondence about the book on her desk upstairs. The publishers wanted it ready by the fall semester. Kate wanted the book accurate. They said she was too picky. "The adrenal glands are over the kidneys, not the larynx," she said. "What difference does it make?" they said.

Clancy was sniffing the cartons with suspicion. Sometimes she lifted a leg on invaders of her territory. After she was spayed, she appeared to be confused about the proper way to urinate.

Were the publishers getting back at her? Were they having the final word by delivering the books here? She didn't have time to call United Parcel Service now. But she couldn't just leave the cartons outside like that. If it rained, she would probably be charged for the damaged books. She opened the garage door and backed her car out and parked it in the driveway. The cartons were heavy, but she was able to lift some and drag the rest inside the garage.

She was really late now. She would have to call Charlie. As she walked across the lawn toward the house, she realized she was dripping. Her legs were rubbery. She lowered herself to the grass. It had to be at least a hundred degrees. George would surely kill himself if he kept playing tennis in this heat. She put her head between her knees to get rid of the dizziness. When she looked up, Joe Lewis, their gardener, was standing over her, his new-looking but old-sounding pickup truck behind him at the curb.

"Morning, miss," he said. He'd been cutting Kate's parents' grass for years. He had always called her miss and didn't change after she and George were married.

"Hi, Mr. Lewis," she said. Everyone always joked about Mr. Lewis and the Brown Bomber, the prizefighter. But Kate had never understood it. Names were sometimes such handicaps.

"Hot enough for you?" he said, walking back to his truck and turning off the engine.

"I'll say," she said, getting up. Her legs were still wobbly. There was an awful odor coming from somewhere. "Oh, no," she said, realizing the truth. "I sat in dog shit. I mean dog mess. Sorry, Mr. Lewis. That just slipped out."

"It's OK, dear," he said, walking to her, his white moustache framing his upper lip. "I've heard that word before. I won't tell your folks you know it." He chuckled. "Let me help you."

· Divorcing Your Grandmother ·

The mess was all over her skirt. She would have to change and shower again. She would never get to see Charlie.

"You know, miss," Mr. Lewis said, "if you'd only waited ten more minutes, I'd have had the manure cleaned up."

"Or if I'd only learn to look where I'm going," Kate said.

"Or if that dog of yours would learn to do its business invisibly," Mr. Lewis said, laughing at his own clever idea. He took Kate's hand and walked her to the back door of the house.

Where did all these fairy godfathers come from anyway? First Mr. Hansell in the lab. And now Mr. Lewis. Ellen would not approve. Ellen would say that women could rescue themselves. The dog sniffed Kate as she came into the kitchen, and left the room, her tail between her legs.

"Some friend you are," Kate called after her.

Mr. Lewis got himself a glass of water from the tap. "You OK now?" he said, looking around. "Where's that cute baby of yours?"

"That cute baby is twenty-two years old, Mr. Lewis. She has her own apartment now."

"Not living with a boy, is she?" he said. Kate couldn't tell if he was kidding or not. But he was on his way out the door, so there was no more conversation about Ellen.

She called Charlie first. "I'm full of dog manure," she said, using Mr. Lewis's word. "I'll be late."

They decided to skip lunch and meet at three at the Ramada Inn parking lot on the Southeast Expressway. Charlie could finish up at work, and Kate could shower and change. She might even have time to deal with the book cartons in the garage.

She phoned her editor collect at the New York office of the publishing company. He had put his hand on her knee when they negotiated the book contract.

"Peter," she said.

"What's doing?" he said. His voice had an odd hitch in it, not a native New Yorker pattern.

"What's doing, Peter, is that I'm standing here covered with shit. I'm surrounded by four hundred textbooks, which your distributor delivered to my house." She was yelling now.

"So call United Parcel and they'll redeliver," he said, as if it were the most reasonable thing in the world. "Nothing to it."

"Peter," she said, "did you do this on purpose?"

"Listen, kid," he said. He was thirty. "Listen, I've got another call. Have UPS call my office if there's a problem. Catch you later." He clicked off.

Well, it really wasn't such a big deal. She didn't need to yell. She would call UPS herself. Writing a textbook had turned out to be more trouble than it was worth. It had given her tenure at the college. That was one good thing, she supposed. But things had never been the same between Carol and her after they had argued about the balance of vertebrates and nonvertebrates. Imagine losing a friend because you liked animals with spines and she didn't. And the publisher—well, they just never seemed to get things right. They put the diagrams for the frog with the shark. Furthermore, the income generated from the sale of the book was less than the minimum wage; she had figured it out. The students paid forty dollars for each text; she and Carol split their dollar-per-book commission. The publisher got the rest. Her next book would not be a textbook. Nor would she attempt to negotiate the contract herself.

She poured herself some orange juice before going upstairs to shower. She still felt queasy. She took off her skirt and rinsed it in the sink. Upstairs, back in the shower, she

150

wondered what Charlie would say when she told him she couldn't see him anymore. He had literally swept her off her feet. He'd made her feel young and perfect. George could never do that. George could only make her feel safe. Was it so wrong to want both men? She was dizzy again. She turned on the cold water. Cold water would perk her up. The dog was sticking her head around the side of the shower curtain. "Oh, baby," Kate said, "I forgive you, dog mess and all." She bent down to kiss her. Encouraged, the dog jumped into the shower. Kate was suddenly tired. She was more tired than she'd ever been. She probably shouldn't have moved all those cartons. She leaned her back against the cool tile and slid down the side of the wall until she was sitting on the floor of the shower, her knees against her chest. The water ran over her head and back. Clancy was standing with her mouth open, the way Kate had done to catch the summer rain when she was little.

"OK, snookle," she said to the dog, rising and rinsing off again. "Let's go." She turned off the water. The dog always responded with a leap to the word *go*. She stood on the bath mat and shook herself dry.

Kate was just about ready to leave the house when she noticed a water stain on the front of her light-blue skirt. Well, no matter. It would dry. Mr. Lewis was pruning some shrubbery in the back of the house. George was still not in his office. The sight of the books in the garage riled her all over again. She had been so enthusiastic about developing her textbook when she first undertook the project. How could she have been so naïve?

The car was hotter than anywhere in the world, although she'd left the windows open. As she sat in the front seat and put the key in the ignition, she felt a wetness on her abdomen. The water stain was spreading. She was a few minutes ahead of schedule; she could go back and change into something less likely to show moisture. She wasn't used to perspiring so freely. But somewhere between the car and the house, she knew the problem wasn't sweat. The incision was "weeping." It had been stupid to lift the books; it had been too much. In the hospital they'd reminded her again and again not to do any lifting for several months. Well, it wasn't the end of the world. It just meant she'd further delayed the healing process. The scar would be an inch wide instead of a sixteenth of an inch. That was all.

This time, she put on a print dress. A stain would be less likely to show. She put a gauze pad over the incision. Well now, what else could happen? Whatever it was, she was not going to change her clothes again.

When she got to the parking lot at the Ramada Inn, Charlie was waiting for her. He was so glad to see her, he said, helping her out of the car, folding her into his arms against his solid chest. She was happier to see him than she'd expected to be. She pressed her cheek against the pocket of his shirt and reached her hands up around his neck. They said that today's women could have it all. Was she really thinking of ending this?

They drove south in his car. "I've got a terrific surprise for you," he said. "Sorry about the seat. The kids spilled ice cream on it. I've been rubbing the leather every day with mink oil."

The seat was a combination of slippery and sticky. Clancy would go crazy with the scent of mink when Kate got home. She found it hard to imagine having children small enough to spill ice cream. They'd never talked much about their kids. Too much reality was detrimental to the excesses of passion. "How are they taking your wife's absence?" she said.

"Oh, Christ," he said, exhaling. "They're fine. That is, they seem to be fine. They've been staying with my parents during the week," he said.

"I never thought of you as having parents," she said. "Dopey of me, isn't it? It must be nice to have them close by."

"I guess eventually I'll have to hire a housekeeper," he said, "or so my mother tells me." They were speeding down the expressway now. She loved the way Charlie drove, as if his were the only car on the road.

"I love the way you are," she said. She leaned over and kissed his neck. What was she doing? This was not her design at all.

"I don't suppose you'd consider motherhood again," he said. "They don't slop ice cream all the time."

"Oh, Charlie," she said. This was impossible. He couldn't really think she would divorce George and marry him. "What about George?" she said.

"George?" he said. "George who?" Was he serious? No, of course not. He couldn't be serious. "We could fix up old George with Janet. We don't even have to introduce them." They were both laughing now. It was too funny: George and Janet. What was it about Charlie that made life so easy?

"It's all going to be fine," he said. "It always is, isn't it?"

Rose-colored glasses, she thought. No matter what happened, his world would be rosy. Self-fulfilling prophecy. Think gloom and you get gloom. Think like Charlie and you get fine. Things could never be other than fine for Charlie. Kate felt the wetness of her incision. She thought about herself in the dog mess. Losing her uterus wasn't such a disaster. It was her humor she'd really lost. Why else would she have yelled at Peter in New York about the books? "What's the surprise?" she said. "Let me guess where we're going."

"I'll give you a clue," he said. "It has nothing to do with cards."

"Yugoslavia!" she said. "We're going to spend the afternoon in Yugoslavia!"

"Close," he said. "But not quite. We need special clothes for this trip." He pointed to the backseat.

"I can't possibly change my clothes again today," she said. She looked behind her. There were ski parkas and pants on the seat. "Siberia," she said.

He didn't answer. He was humming "You Are My Sunshine." Was it a clue? He was driving faster.

"Well," she said. "I'll put my money on Siberia. We're going to Siberia, like Lara and Zhivago."

"Nope," he said.

She continued guessing: the North Pole, the South Pole, Australia. She sang "Winter Wonderland" to get in the mood. She began to wonder again what Charlie's wife was really like. She wondered what had propelled her out of a comfortable existence, away from her children. She'd come back. Kate was sure she'd be back.

They were almost at the Cape now. The terrain was flat. Kate hadn't even got things ready for Nantucket yet. She hadn't even made the list. She sat silently with Charlie, as comfortable as an old married couple. Suddenly, there they were—wherever "there" was. Charlie stopped the car and pulled up beside the coastline and what looked to be an open field. There was a sign: BALLOON ADVENTURES. She imagined a contest to see who could blow up the most balloons in a minute, two minutes, five minutes. It would be fun. She had once run such a contest at a birthday party for Ellen. The children had been too young and couldn't keep the air in the balloons.

"Here we are," Charlie said. "Everybody out."

The front of her dress felt heavy with moisture as she got out of the car, and the heat assaulted her. She'd adjusted to the air conditioning without even realizing it. But the heat from the gravel felt good as it moved up through the soles of her sandals. Why were her feet always so cold?

Charlie was watching her, waiting for a reaction. He was swinging his arms back and forth, clapping his hands together.

"So," she said. "A balloon contest. Right? But then why do we need warm clothes?" And then she saw it: a hot-air balloon on the horizon. It was not far away, but seemed so because of the distortion in depth as the sea met the land. Her eyes must have widened.

Charlie was pleased and laughed. "We're off to see the wizard," he sang and clicked his heels.

"Oh, Charlie," she said. "It's a marvelous surprise."

From a small house Kate hadn't noticed came a young man in cutoff jeans. His raspy voice preceded him. "Jesus, Murdoch," he said, "I've been waiting for you guys the whole day. What the hell happened to you?" He appeared not even to notice Kate. He was tall, nearly as tall as Charlie but much broader in the shoulders, and had the wholesome good looks and perfect teeth of a movie star. "This time of day's not so good, you know. Tail winds. Fog. Not so good."

Charlie introduced them. "Larry Hendricks, Kate Cummings," he said. "Larry went to school with me," he explained. How had he explained Kate to Larry?

"OK, kids, follow me," Larry said, heading back toward the house. "You got warm clothes?"

"Sure we do, Larry," said Charlie. "You got the champagne?" He gathered the clothing from the back seat and followed Larry.

155

Kate inhaled the sea air deeply into her lungs. A balloon ride. What would Charlie think of next?

Behind the house, a deflated hot-air balloon lay on its side, large as a whale. "Put your clothes on," said Larry, as he began filling the balloon from a long hose. "You sure you want to do this? The air's not good today. Too hot down here. Too cold up there." He pointed to the sky. "Dawn," he said. "Where were you at dawn?"

Kate was adjusting the buckle on the navy pants Charlie had given her. Whose ski pants were these? Janet's? Once her mother had given her a dress of a relative who'd died. A second cousin. She hadn't felt right about wearing it. A pink dress. A lovely dress. She had tried it on once, but could never bring herself to wear it. And now, here she was about to go up in a balloon in someone else's clothes, with someone else's husband. If the balloon crashed, they would probably identify her as Janet Jerome, Charlie's wife.

"Hurry up, Larry," Charlie was saying. "These clothes are killing me." The sweat was pouring down Charlie's face. There was a crisp sea breeze now, but the air was still hot. She wondered when Larry would put on his warm clothes.

She zipped up her parka. "What if I have to go to the bathroom up there?" she said. It was a remark George would have made. What was the temperature inside her thermal clothing? The one-dimensional background of sea and sand combined with the shooshing of air into the balloon made her feel off balance, as if she were in a strange place. Like driving through a blizzard, she thought, searching for the right analogy. She smiled. Well, at least she was dressed for it.

The balloon was still on its side but fully inflated now. The sky had darkened. "I'm going to call the weather station one more time," said Larry. "Safe's better than sorry."

Charlie put his arms around Kate. Their parkas rustled together as he pressed her to him. "I adore you," he said.

"Mutual," she said. "Very mutual."

Larry took a long time coming back. Kate and Charlie decided to get into the basket under the balloon and wait for him. "He's getting the champagne," Charlie said. "They always have champagne on these things."

"He's going to the bathroom," Kate said. Maybe Charlie had done this before. With Janet. Or his kids. She supposed it was all right if he'd done it before. They'd both learned not to ask questions about the past. It was a tacit agreement, as if their lives had only begun that day they met in the drugstore. She sat down on the floor of the basket, leaning her back up against the side, as she'd done in the shower only a few hours ago. There was no air moving inside the enclosure.

"I don't think Dorothy wore a ski parka on the way back to Kansas," she said.

"Who?" said Charlie.

"We can't go," said Larry. He was peering over the side of the basket.

"Can't go?" said Charlie. "Can't go? What do you mean we can't go?" His face was red either from the heat or the disappointment.

"Hail storm," said Larry. "Could pop the balloon up there."

"Oh, shit, Larry," Charlie said. "This is important. We have to go." He sounded like a little boy. "A little hail won't bother us, will it?" He turned to Kate.

"It's OK," she said. "We don't want to ruin Larry's equipment, do we?" She had wanted to go, had loved the idea of going, but was relieved that she wouldn't have to die in another woman's ski jacket. "We'll have the champagne anyway. Right, Larry?"

"Sure," Larry said. "Why not?"

They got themselves over the side of the basket and made their way toward Larry's house. They didn't bother to take off their ski things. The house would certainly be air conditioned, wouldn't it? It wasn't. The house was empty except for a telephone and a refrigerator. Larry had just moved in, he said. His wife had kicked him out. Hadn't Charlie told her the story? His wife told him if he wanted to persist with this balloon madness he could do it alone. She had not put him through Harvard Business School so he could take people up in balloons.

No, Kate said, Charlie hadn't told her the story.

They uncorked the champagne, peeled off their winter clothes, and sat outside on the porch steps. By the time Larry let the air out of their balloon, the rain had begun, so lightly at first that they hadn't minded sitting in it. From far away, thunder rumbled.

Inside, the three of them sat on the floor, drinking champagne from paper cups, feeling like survivors. This place had been a real find, Larry said. He'd been cleaning it up all summer. And business was great. Everybody wanted to go up in a balloon, he told them.

Hail pellets pattered at the windows. Charlie uncorked another bottle. In the bathroom, Kate found that the gauze over her stomach was stained a pale pink.

Larry opened a can of baked beans and a box of Ritz crackers. He hadn't had time to connect a stove yet, he said. They ate the cold beans and crackers and drank more champagne. The room grew dark. They would have to come back another time, Larry said. Actually, the predawn hours were the best. They could stay over tonight if they wanted, he told them. The only thing was that he had no beds; there were a couple of sleeping bags upstairs they could use.

Charlie looked at Kate with a question in his eyes. He would stay.

"We really should be getting back," she told Larry. She had never stayed out all night with Charlie.

"September and October are the best months," said Larry. "Much better than the summer. Why don't we make a date for September?"

On the way home, Kate tried to imagine the autumn months. Would she and Charlie ever come back here? Would she like being up in a balloon? "I often dream I'm a bird," she told Charlie, thinking how George had described her as an eagle.

Charlie was weaving along the road. "I shouldn't be driving," he said. "Too much grape cider."

She would drive, she told him. She was fine, just fine. It was better to play it safe.

He pulled over. The rain had stopped now. Charlie said he thought he'd lie down for a minute in the backseat.

Kate adjusted the driver's seat so that her feet touched the pedals. She started the engine. Charlie was asleep before she got back on the road.

"Oh, my," she said aloud. "Balloons and baked beans." Larry's wife hadn't counted on balloons and cold beans. And Charlie's wife had also been disillusioned. Would George ever go up in a balloon? The Mercedes seemed to drive itself. Charlie had worried that the hailstones would dent the body of the car. And the salt air wasn't good for it, he'd said. She was glad she'd moved the book cartons into the garage. They'd have been soaked by now, unless, of course, it hadn't rained in Boston.

CHAPTER

· FOURTEEN ·

George sat against the thick trunk of a pine tree in Charlie's backyard. All the lights were off in the house. He'd come directly from the tennis club. The sweat had dried on his skin and made it feel taut. His shoulder ached. Charlie Murdoch lived only two miles from his own house.

It was dark when he got there. Probably Murdoch's wife and the children had gone out for ice cream. Or had she already left him? George couldn't remember. She had missed her last appointment. Yes, now that he thought about it, she had left him. Gone to Cambridge and resumed her social-work career. She was a fine girl. Charlie ought to have been satisfied with what he had.

From next door a woman called out. "Robin," she said. "Rob-in." Her child was out past his bedtime. Or her dog. Robin could be a dog's name.

He wished he had some ice for his arm. Why hadn't he showered at the club? He knew the answer: He wore his sweat like a badge of some sort. He liked it. And his patients liked it. They'd all agreed to have their appointments at the tennis club. Even the grumpy Mr. Brader. And all these years George had chained himself to stuffy offices and business suits. He should have thought of this new arrangement sooner.

He wasn't able to give his patients as much time as they'd had before. He did have to get on with his own lessons after all. But it had seemed to take some pressure off them. Contrary to popular opinion, it wasn't easy for most people to spend a whole hour talking about themselves. George gave each patient about fifteen minutes. The rest of the hour they watched him practice. When they sat together on the bench by the side of the court, George was eager for the interaction. He was able to make the transition from forehand to psychic pain in seconds. His insights were keener than ever.

His patients responded not so much to what he said. It was watching him play tennis that made such a difference, they told him. They never knew people actually worked so hard. They had always thought life was easier for others than for them. They liked seeing him lose his breath; they loved it when he went for broke on a shot. They brought him ice water and offered to pick up the balls so he could conserve his energy. This was the longest heat wave in history, they reminded him. He should be careful. "It's like I've said all along," Mr. Brader intoned. "Actions speak louder than words."

Unfortunately, George's body was paying the price, he realized, as he sat under Charlie's tree, on Charlie's lawn, outside Charlie's house. Where was the gallant Mr. Murdoch anyway? Silly question. Of course, he was with Kate. That's where he was. Well, George could wait. He was a patient man. A firefly dotted the night with a brief spark, and George tried to catch it in his hand. He missed.

He was going to tell Charlie to stay away from his wife. And that would be that. Hadn't he already told Kate not to see her lover again? This confrontation with Charlie was

long overdue. What had he been so afraid of? He hadn't
wanted to interfere with Kate's life. He hadn't wanted to
lose her by holding on too tightly. He had never really
doubted her loyalty to him. He knew she expected more
from life than he did and was prepared to take more risks.
She had to try everything, and her intensity had drawn
him to her. But things were different now. Maybe it was
her illness, the surgery, her recovery that had jolted him.
But he was no longer so complacent. He was angry. His
doormat days were over.

The car hummed into the driveway and Charlie got out.
George sat in his place under the tree and watched. He'd
taken off his sneakers and socks, and the grass and pine
needles were kind to his tired feet. A locker-room odor
made its way to his nostrils; it was not entirely unpleasant.
Charlie got a rag out of the trunk and vigorously rubbed
the body of the car. He spat on the headlights and wiped
them off. George picked a piece of grass and put it in his
mouth. It had no flavor.

Charlie patted the top of the car and turned toward the
house. George said, "Nice car you've got."

"Yeah," Charlie said absentmindedly, as if he were used
to voices coming out of the dark.

"Hello, Murdoch." George was standing now. He felt a
corner of his mouth quiver as he walked toward the driveway. His knees throbbed. Even clay courts damaged old
knees.

Charlie was squinting. "Who's there?" he said, looking
down at George.

He doesn't know who I am, George realized. He doesn't
even know me. It wasn't the way he'd fantasized at all.
There were small stones under his feet now. Ellen always
built up calluses on her feet in the summer and could walk

barefoot anywhere. "It's George Cummings," he said.

"Oh, yes," Charlie said, offering his hand but wobbling backward.

"Nice car," said George again.

"Mercedes," said Charlie.

"I can see that," said George.

There was a long silence. The blade of grass was caught between two of George's front teeth. That same firefly went by him again.

"Robin," the woman from next door called. "Robin."

"That's her cat," Charlie said. "Robin Hood."

"I thought so," said George. Was Charlie trying to be glib? Well, he wasn't going to get out of this. "Listen," George said. Charlie was jiggling his leg again, the way he had that night in the hospital. "Listen. I want to talk with you about Kate."

"Sure," said Murdoch. He glanced back toward the car. "Let me take this stuff out, and we'll go inside and sit down. OK?"

"OK," said George. He wasn't sure he wanted to go inside the Murdoch house. He wondered if Kate had ever been there.

Charlie opened the back car door and pulled out what looked like a pile of ski clothes. "Let's go," he said.

It was the sort of house that was full of acute angles. The kitchen had all kinds of sharp, shiny gadgets George couldn't even identify. Murdoch's wife was probably a gourmet cook. But she was gone, George remembered, as he took note of the counters strewn with dirty dishes and open boxes of crackers and cereal. He sat at the kitchen table. A child's toy skittered across the floor as he moved his feet.

Murdoch was standing over him. His eyes were red. "Look, George," he said, smiling. "I'm afraid I'm just a bit loaded. I'm going to put on some coffee. What'll you have?"

"Coffee's fine," George said. Who was he kidding? Coffee would keep him awake all night.

Charlie put the kettle on the stove and excused himself to the bathroom. It was cold in the house. George felt his body stiffen defensively. The goddamn house must be centrally air conditioned.

"Nice and cool in here, eh?" said Charlie when he came back. The kettle was starting to whistle. A rack of knives hung on the wall over the stove.

"It's a deep freeze," said George. "Let's open a few windows." He would drink coffee, but he'd be damned if he'd ruin his joints in canned air.

"Yeah," said Charlie, pouring the water into the mugs of instant coffee. "The thing Janet hates most about this house is that the windows don't open. You want cream and sugar?"

"No, thanks," said George. How could anybody live in a house with the windows glued down?

"Here," said Charlie. "Why don't you put on this ski parka?" He went to the pile of clothes he'd dumped in a corner of the kitchen.

George took a ski jacket. No doubt Murdoch was also an expert on the slopes. "There's something weird about this," he said, putting the parka over his shoulders. "Like Nixon and his roaring fires in the White House in the summers he was there."

"You know that Janet's left me, don't you?" Charlie surprised George by saying.

"Yes," said George. He slipped his arms into the parka and zipped it up.

"Was it your idea?" Charlie said.

"What do you mean?" George said.

"She's moved out. That's what I mean," said Charlie. "It sure as hell wasn't my idea."

"Why don't you give your wife credit for having some ideas of her own?" said George. This Murdoch could be abusive. Surely he couldn't be blaming George for his wife's departure.

"That sounds like something Janet would say," Charlie said.

"Look, Murdoch," George said. "I came here to talk about my wife, not yours." He paused, expecting some acknowledgment of what he'd said.

But Charlie drank his coffee and jiggled his leg under the table. He said nothing. His eyes wandered around the room.

"You've got to leave my wife alone," said George.

Charlie got up and circled around the table behind George. He shuffled across the room, where he picked up a package of Fig Newtons and brought it back to the table. George had never liked Fig Newtons. "You want me to stop seeing Kate?" Charlie said.

He was playing for time, George realized, as Charlie walked behind him once again. This time he went to the refrigerator and carried two bottles of beer back to where he'd been sitting. He twisted off the caps and handed a bottle to George. "Want a glass?" he said.

"No, thanks," George said. It had been wrong to meet Murdoch on his own turf. The element of surprise had gained him nothing. He took the bottle and set it in front of him. Although he'd never been much of a drinker, he took a long swallow from the bottle. The beer exploded in his throat. He liked it.

"I'm in love with Kate," Charlie said. The words seemed strung out longer than a minute. He guzzled his beer and chomped on a Fig Newton.

166

"I thought you were in love with your own wife," said George.

"I thought you didn't want to talk about Janet," said Charlie.

"Well, how can you be in love with two women at once?" said George. This was not going the way he'd planned. He was playing straight man to Charlie. He needed to take the offensive. He needed to charge the net, the way he'd been practicing at the club. He needed to hit a powerful, deep shot, a deadly shot, run to the net, and put the ball away. He drank the last of his beer. He stood up in his parka and his bare feet. "Murdoch," he said, "I didn't come here for a discussion. I'm here to tell you to stay away from my wife."

Charlie stood on his side of the table. He was a huge man. He smiled and caught George's eyes. "We're at an impasse, friend," he said.

"I'm not your goddamn friend," said George. The blade of grass was still wedged between his teeth.

Charlie sat down and scratched his mass of red hair. "How about this?" he said. "I get out of Kate's life when you stop seeing Janet."

"It's not the same," said George. Was this guy for real? This was the man Kate found so irresistible? What was George so worried about? Kate was too mature, too smart to stick with Murdoch, wasn't she?

Charlie threw his bottle toward the wastebasket across the room. He missed, and it rolled across the linoleum and stopped by the pile of winter clothing Charlie had brought in from the car. "I need more practice," he said. "Hook shot. My best." He began throwing Fig Newtons, arching his arm over his head until one finally went in. "You a Celtic fan?" said Charlie.

"I'm leaving," said George. "You think about what I've

said." That was stupid. He sounded like somebody's father. Besides, how could you have a conversation with a drunk? He'd been too agitated himself to take in just how drunk Charlie was.

He slammed the door as he left. It was childish, but he didn't care. It felt good. He wished he'd slammed it hard enough for the whole house to collapse.

As he walked across the driveway back to his tree, he realized he hadn't accomplished anything by coming here. He sat down and leaned back. Imagine it. Charlie actually felt that he was the wronged party. That bastard just sat there eating cookies and accusing George of interfering in his life. Of course, he was drunk. What could you expect? George pulled his socks on. They were stretched out and hung limply around his ankles like plants needing water. His sneakers felt too tight. He didn't bother to tie them. He was hot now. He was roasting. Hot. Cold. What was wrong with him? He still wore the goddamn ski parka. He unzipped it and threw it on the ground. He got up and stomped on it. He looked around. The lights were off in the house now. He imagined Murdoch stretched out across a bed fully clothed. George picked up the jacket and tried to rip it apart, but it held. He took a sleeve in his teeth and pulled. Nothing happened. This was crazy. Charlie would just buy a new parka anyway. George left it on the grass and began walking down the driveway. He felt in his pocket for his car keys and stopped just as he was about to enter the street. He put his fingernail between his front teeth and pulled out the blade of grass.

He thought for a moment and then turned and walked back slowly to Charlie's car. The doors were locked. No matter. George lifted his keys from his pocket and fingered the mother-of-pearl penknife that had belonged to his father. He'd carried it on his key ring since his father's death and used it to clean his fingernails. As he turned it over in the palm of his hand, his keys jangled softly. He pulled out the small blade and tested it on his left index finger. It was still sharp. Crouching down beside the right front fender of the car, he punctured the tire with one jab. It made no noise as the air seeped out. The other tires took even less time. But the fourth time he bent his knees, he felt something give way. He had wrenched himself.

He stood back to admire his work. In the dark, you couldn't really tell anything was wrong with Charlie's beloved Mercedes. Maybe Charlie would get into it in the morning and actually flap down the driveway before he found out he was going nowhere.

George folded the penknife. What would his father have said if he was still alive? Well, he wasn't alive. And George didn't care anymore what people said. Hadn't they ruined his old house? The one he grew up in? Hadn't they painted it gallbladder green? He put his hand on the hood of the car. It was disgusting: twenty-five thousand dollars for one car. Kate probably liked it. It was the old razzle-dazzle business again. His palms were moist on the hood. Fingerprints. He was leaving evidence. He opened the knife and scratched off the marks where his hands had been. The screech of metal on metal was somehow agreeable. At first he didn't see the paint was coming off, so preoccupied was he with the task and the sound of his work. A small brown cat had joined him, purring whenever he made the scraping noise. He supposed it was Robin Hood from next door.

He had no notion of how long he'd been there. His shoulder was aching again, and his left foot hurt. He'd been standing on one leg to ease the pain of his twisted knee. When he saw the first faint traces of light in the sky, he put the knife in his pocket.

He sat in his own car in front of Charlie's house for a long time. His watch said four-thirty. What had he done? He'd ruined a man's car, although, he reminded himself, it wasn't just any man's car. He couldn't help it: At least one part of him felt avenged. But Charlie would surely know who'd done it. He could prosecute and George could go to jail. He imagined his patients coming to the Concord Reformatory for therapy.

He called Kate from the hospital in Wellesley where he'd done his residency. "I'm checking in," he said.

They didn't want to admit him. They asked him what day it was and who the last four presidents of the United States were. They asked if he knew where he was. Did he really want to be in a psychiatric hospital? Didn't he want to go home and get a good night's sleep?

"I'm out of control," he said in his usual calm voice, as he handed over his weapon. "I'm going to murder someone if I'm not protected." They didn't believe him. "I've just killed a car." There. He'd said it. Chips of maroon paint still clung to his hands.

By the time Kate arrived he was in his room. The nurse on the floor was sure she remembered him from somewhere. Had he been a patient at Bayberry before? He lay on his bed and faced the wall. Kate put her hand on his shoulder. He wanted to ask for some ice, but didn't.

"I'm sorry," he said.

"It's going to be all right," Kate said.

He slept so soundly that in the morning he didn't know where he was when he woke up. He felt better. He was going to straighten things out here. He was going to get in touch with himself. This would not be so terrible. It was August anyway, wasn't it? He was supposed to be on vacation.

170

CHAPTER

· FIFTEEN ·

George smiled to himself. If he had only known. If he'd only known they had gardening therapy, he might have come to Bayberry sooner, although he was slightly disappointed when he found the gardens full of vegetables rather than the flowers he'd hoped for. He had tried his hand at vegetables once or twice. But the last time, it had ended with his picking the asparagus fern and rooting it in his greenhouse. The asparagus stalk had rotted.

It was the afternoon of his second or third day in the hospital. Or was it the fourth day? He hadn't been here a week yet, had he? He was weeding in the vegetable beds of the large hospital garden. A hundred years ago, the place had been a big farm. It was part of the hospital folklore that the farmer's wife had thought she was a witch and had danced naked in the cornfields. The farmer had donated the land for a private mental hospital. It wasn't until fifteen years ago, just after George completed his residency, that the name had been changed from asylum to hospital.

It was unbearably hot. At least they'd let him wear his tennis things, although it wasn't easy shuffling along in sneakers with no laces. They didn't really think he was going to hang himself with shoelaces, did they? How long was a shoelace anyway? Sixteen inches? His neck measured fifteen and a half. By the time you knotted the shoelace around your neck and tied it to its mate, would it even be possible? Besides, would shoelaces from his sneakers hold his weight? He dug his hands into the soft earth. It was dry underneath.

Most of the tomatoes were still green, but some were partly orange and nearly ready for picking. He'd always liked the fragrance of tomato plants and thought they must smell like something nice from his childhood, but he was unable to complete the association. Well, that's why he was here, wasn't it? His connections were askew. Why was it so hot? An earthworm tunneled its way through the cavity left by a weed George had just pulled. He picked it up and cradled it in his hands. The worm rolled into a ball in an effort to avoid the light. He could put it in his pocket and take it to his room if he wanted to. He looked up. The attendant was watching him. Well, what would he want with an earthworm? He dropped it back into its hole and buried it.

He wanted to play tennis. He needed to practice every day. He didn't mind the heat when he was working on his backhand. But that was part of his craziness, they told him. It was crazy for a psychiatrist to see his patients at a tennis club. It was crazy for a middle-aged man to play tennis ten hours a day during the longest heat wave in history.

There were courts on the hospital grounds. He had played on them himself when he was a resident. What was wrong with a little exercise? he asked the staff. He hadn't listened to the answer.

His patients. What was he going to do about his patients? Kate had told them he'd decided to leave a few days early for Nantucket. At least, that's what she said. "I could see them here," he'd said. But she began to chew her lip in a way that made him realize she didn't know he was joking. Didn't she know you could feel more than one thing at a time? Did she really think he'd ask his patients to come for therapy while he himself was an inmate of a mental hospital?

His knees were starting to ache again now. He sat down among the vegetable beds and brought his legs up to his chest. He looked around for eggplants. He liked their purple flowers and teardropped fruit. But there were only rows and rows of tomato plants. He rubbed his knees.

"Anything wrong, George?" the attendant said. They all called you by your first name here. George wasn't used to it yet. The attendant was younger than Ellen.

George didn't feel like talking. He reached across the bed and grabbed a hose that was streaming water into the dry ground. He held it to his mouth and then to his cheeks. He could barely feel it, but he knew the water must be cold.

"George?" The attendant was walking over to him. He'd been sitting in the shade.

George put the hose down. Now there was something you could hang yourself with. And they just left it around in the dirt.

The attendant was leaning down. He had a bump on his nose. "It's going to be all right, George," he said, putting his hand on George's shoulder in a friendly grip.

George looked up at him. It hurt his neck. He wondered if the young man played tennis but didn't ask him.

"Do you want to go back to your dorm now?" the attendant said.

A dorm. He was forty-five years old and living in a dorm. He inched himself over to another tomato plant and began weeding. There it was again—that smell. "It's Communion," he said, speaking for the first time to no one in particular. That was it. The tomato plant aroma was identical to the texture of the thin wafer he still remembered.

The attendant registered no reaction. No doubt he was used to his charges' religious revelations.

The wafer had always stuck to the roof of George's mouth, the way the tomato leaves stuck to your fingers and their odor hung in your taste buds. He had not even heard of mental hospitals during his days of Communion.

His parents had grown tomatoes in their Victory garden during the war. They had let him have his own vegetable patch with lettuce, tomatoes, and cucumbers. It must have been about the time of his First Communion.

"Sister Marcella says we aren't a good Catholic family," he'd told his parents. He remembered the cucumber vine had wound itself around the rest of his plants; he'd been surprised by its prickles.

His mother had made a funny noise. His father had said nothing.

"She says good Catholics have more than one child." Even now, he remembered how the nuns had favored Maura Mahoney. There were twelve children in her family.

His father had taken him for a long walk that evening. He'd explained the difference between form and content. What was in the vegetable garden was much more important than the fence they used to keep rabbits out, he'd said. George wasn't sure what that had to do with being a good Catholic, but he remembered the smell of tomato and fertilizer and that his father had carried him on his shoulders when he got tired. Was it the same summer the war ended?

"When was the war over?" he asked the attendant.

As they walked across the grounds, George discovered the attendant's name was Charlie and that he was neither a stockbroker nor a tennis player. He was a black-belt karate expert. His mother had thrown a roller skate at him when he was four years old and had ruined his nose. He was considering plastic surgery. Not for cosmetic reasons. His girlfriend claimed his snoring kept her awake.

"Too bad about Yaz retiring," he was saying. He was a Red Sox fan.

George had a hard time matching the young man's stride. His sneakers got looser and looser. He hadn't been to Fenway Park since he was a boy He wondered how to spell Yastrzemski.

"But you know," Charlie said, "at forty-two, you can't keep running the bases, can you?"

Someday this kid would be forty-two himself, George thought. Or even forty-five. He would have to hang up his black belt.

Approaching his building—he was not going to refer to it as a dorm—he noticed people lying on the sprawling lawn. It was hard to tell if they were patients or staff. When he was a resident, the staff had been required to wear uniforms. He was wondering what had happened to Maura Mahoney and her eleven brothers and sisters. An attractive woman came toward them on the cement walk. She was nearly on top of them before he saw that it was Janet Jerome. He should have remembered she was working here. All of his reactions were delayed.

"Oh, Dr. Cummings," she was saying before he could think how to avoid her. "I didn't know you were on staff here." She was going on, talking very fast. She was saying how thrilled she was with her job, with the hospital, with her new life. She owed it all to him, she was saying.

George looked at his shoes with no laces. He knew his knees were caked with dirt. And the attendant. The attendant was a giveaway.

She was so sorry she hadn't been able to see him at his tennis club, she said. Her schedule was so busy now. How had it worked out? she wanted to know. What a great idea, she told him. Was he going to write a paper about it? She hardly resembled the sad sack of a young woman who'd spent an hour weeping in George's office less than a month ago. He imagined her on a skateboard; she seemed that young, that energetic.

"How are things going?" he said out of habit. But she had already told him. Things couldn't be better.

She looked at the attendant. "I'm Janet Jerome," she said, reaching to shake his hand. Even her voice was confident.

"Charlie Cutt," Charlie said.

Janet met George's eyes with an understanding look. She assumed that Charlie was the patient.

George couldn't think what to do or how he felt. He was frozen in this moment. It wasn't enough that he had dreams that the real Charlie Murdoch was chasing him with his maroon car fender. He had to run into Charlie's wife. He had to have an attendant named Charlie with a black belt in karate. He was beginning to hyperventilate. If only he could just hit a few tennis balls . . .

"Yaz is packing it in," said Charlie, breaking the silence. "I feel awful about it."

Janet gave George another knowing look. Anything could sound crazy if you thought the person was a mental patient.

"Of course you feel awful," said Janet, looking hard into Charlie's eyes.

"It'll never be the same without old Number Eight," said the attendant.

Janet turned her attention to George. Her teeth were straight and even. Her words were crisp. "Maybe we could schedule our meetings here," she was saying.

Why hadn't she noticed his shoes? Or his dirty finger-

176

nails? Or the keys hanging from the attendant's belt? Or the attendant's belt? Patients were never allowed to wear belts.

"Of course," she said, "you're on vacation for August, aren't you? I forgot for a moment. I was just so glad to see you." She moved her face closer to his. "You go to Nantucket. Right?"

George tried to keep eye contact with her, but he blinked and had to look away. He felt Charlie begin to get restless. He heard his keys move like a handful of nickels as Charlie shifted his weight from one foot to the other.

Janet was still talking. She had always wanted to go to Nantucket, she said. She loved the idea of going to an island. But since she had just started working, there would be no vacation this year.

George was thinking about the small yellow flowers on the tomato plants early in summer. He was wondering about the earthworm he'd buried. What was it like to be an earthworm? To swallow the darkness whole?

"I've kept you long enough," Janet's voice almost sang. She was grasping his hand. "You don't know what a treat it was to have seen you," she said, appearing not to notice the dirt on his fingers. "Bye now."

"You're a doctor?" Charlie said.

George hiccuped. It jolted his diaphragm as if someone had punched him from the inside.

Charlie stood squarely in front of him, blocking his path. He put his hands on his hips. "So," he said, "you're a doctor." He was the same height as George, but his shoulders were twice as wide.

George hiccuped again.

"You thought you could fool me, didn't you?" said the attendant. "It's an experiment, isn't it? You're a goddamn phony."

177

If only George could have a drink of water, he'd be all right. His body gave another little leap as he hiccuped once more.

"Big smart doctors," Charlie said. "Always checking up on us little guys, aren't you? Think we fuck around all the time, don't you? Well, let me tell you, Doctor," he spat out the last word, "you never fooled me for a minute."

George stepped off the path into the grass and ran to his building as fast as his flapping sneakers would allow. The attendant followed, shouting at him about cover-ups and sabotage. At the door, George turned to face his assailant. The young man's face was so close George could smell his Dentyne gum.

"I am a patient," George said.

"Bullshit," said Charlie. The bump on his nose was freckled.

George could hardly pull the big door open. He hiccuped again. In the hallway, the attendant signed him in.

"There you go," he said, patting George on the back. "Take good care of him," he said to the nurse. "He's dangerous."

Later, George sat with Kate in a corner of one of the common rooms where patients were allowed to receive visitors. People milled through as if looking for someone or something. Patients were always asking visitors for matches for their cigarettes. Some others were lobbying for nonsmoking areas in the lounges and cafeterias. It was a no-win situation.

George spent much of his time at the hospital thinking of things he would tell Kate when she came to visit him. But while she was there, nothing he could say was quite right. He was glad when she went home.

He thought that today he would tell her about the hiccups and the six glasses of water he drank, recorded by the nurse

178

on his chart. He might tell her about the attendant's discovery that George was a doctor. But once she was sitting opposite him, his ideas seemed trivial. So he said as little as possible and waited for her to leave.

He was still embarrassed about Murdoch's car. Not sorry. Oh, no. He would never be sorry. When Kate told him Charlie had cried that next morning after he saw his Mercedes, George had laughed. Charlie had dialed 911 on the telephone. The Fire Department had arrived within minutes. The neighbors gathered at the end of the driveway. The police found no clues except an old ski parka under a tree in the backyard. They told Charlie it was probably some teenagers. He shouldn't worry. His insurance would cover it.

Kate hadn't laughed. He might have been prosecuted, she told him.

"Crime pays," George said. "The Shadow knows."

He could have lost his license, she said. And then what would he do?

He would do it again if he had the chance, he said. For once in his life, he had let himself go. He liked it, he told her, although he was less sure than he sounded.

Today, she had brought him some licorice. Shoestring licorice. He supposed you might even hang yourself with it. He'd begun to regard the hospital's restrictions as a challenge.

"George," Kate said. "It's all my fault." She fidgeted with the clasp on her handbag, clicking it open and shut. He thought she had never looked so beautiful.

"It's your vacation," she continued. "Come on now. Come on home. I've got everything ready for Nantucket."

"It's going to be all right," he patted her hand. "You'll see." He wondered if any of his tomato plants would be taller tomorrow.

CHAPTER

· SIXTEEN ·

Kate's hair blew out of control around her face. It was always windy on the ferry, no matter what the temperature on shore. She loved being on deck; she knew the salt air had recuperative powers.

George had told her to go to Nantucket without him. It would be good for her, he said. After all, she had to remember she was still recovering from her surgery. And he was going to be fine. If he could just stay another week or so in the hospital he knew he'd be fine

She believed him. She realized that one of the things that had sustained their marriage was that she had always been able to believe him. Even seeing him at Bayberry had not destroyed that. He had been able to convince her that August was the right time for a psychiatrist to be in a mental hospital. It made perfect sense.

But she still had a hard time accepting the notion that George was responsible for wrecking Charlie's car. She couldn't remember ever seeing him lose his temper. She had never before considered it. Maybe his patients did all his craziness for him. Maybe he even needed her unpredictability as a balance.

She pulled her windbreaker around her. The dog flapped her tail back and forth on the deck floor. George was right: There was no point in staying home when they'd already paid for the house rental. They'd wasted two weeks as it was. Besides, she was only able to visit him a half hour each day. Still, even though he told her the best thing she could do was to go, it felt wrong to be leaving him. In the hospital she would ask about his tomato plants in the garden. He would pretend he hadn't heard her. She would repeat her questions. And then he would ask when she was leaving for Nantucket. Sometimes she actually spent more time talking to other patients than to him.

Driving her car out of the boat and down the gangplank, Kate remembered the first time she and George had come to Nantucket. Then the islanders had had a tough time making a living. Now the narrow streets were crowded with tourists, bicyclers, and determined shoppers. The dog was panting at the window. She'd chase a moving bike if she could.

One year when Ellen was a teenager, they'd rented a house in town, to be where "the action" was. But after that they'd gone back to the Dinsmore place near Madaket at the far end of the island. It was a hundred yards from the beach, and the surf there was challenging, just the way they liked it.

Joanna Dinsmore was waiting for Kate in a rocker on the front porch, as if she hadn't left since last August. She was a tall, reedy woman, past seventy, who had looked exactly the same for twenty years.

"Lots of commotion," she said, without bothering to say hello. Her eyes had that same faded-denim look that was always so striking.

Clancy ran around the outside of the house sniffing her old haunts.

182

"Bird watchers," Mrs. Dinsmore said. "Come all the way from Canada, the Midwest just to see one damn bird."

There were warm currents of air coming in from the roaring sea. George loved it here. He had never wanted to go anywhere else on his vacation. Oh, once she had persuaded him to go to the Caribbean in the middle of winter. And there'd been that trip to the Grand Canyon. But as far as he was concerned, Nantucket was better than heaven.

"It's got yellow feet," Mrs. Dinsmore said. "Supposed to be in West Africa. Got lost. Looks like an ordinary heron to me."

"You saw it?" Kate said. Her father had once been interested in bird watching until her mother told him it was a silly thing for a grown man to do.

"Down near Quaise Marsh. Four thousand miles from home," Mrs. Dinsmore said. "You ever been four thousand miles from home?"

Yes, that was just about how she felt, Kate thought. "Let's go," she said. "I'll drive."

They left the dog sitting in front of the house, as if she'd lived there for years. Kate wasn't ready to go inside just yet. In the car, Kate realized Mrs. Dinsmore had not asked about George. Well, she had always seemed the kind of woman who took things as they were and never looked for either more or less.

At the marsh, there were hundreds of people of all ages spread out with telescopes, binoculars, and cameras. It was silent except for the usual sounds of nature: a medley of bird calls, the rippling of water, the tall grass brushing against itself. Away from the shore, the air was close.

Kate wondered if George was weeding in the hospital garden now. He had said another week would do it. Then what? The light was beginning to fade now as a large cloud moved across the sun. The colors and sounds of the marsh became muted. She cleared her throat. People around her turned and stared. "Sorry," she said.

"There it is," someone said in a stage whisper.

Everyone's head bobbed in the direction of the pointed finger. Binoculars went up. People gasped.

"That's it," they said. "The heron."

Its color was the gray of a mourning dove, and its shape was that of an elegant egret. As the bird rose in flight, Kate saw the feet, yellow as a rain slicker. Cameras clicked. Mrs. Dinsmore elbowed her. "See. See," she said.

"Ssh," said someone else.

The bird seemed to hang in the air as it made a slow ascent.

"What's going to happen to it?" said Kate.

"Probably just stay here until it dies or somebody captures it and sends it back to Africa," a bespeckled man said.

What would George say about all this fuss over a lost bird? If Ellen were here, they'd have made up a story together about the lost heron with the yellow feet. She heard someone say the bird stirred the water with its feet as a way of attracting fish. Once upon a time, she caught herself beginning the story, a bird with yellow feet stirred the frog pond to attract fish, and up came a beautiful princess. . . . For heaven's sake, she couldn't still be in the fairy-tale stage, could she?

On the way home, Mrs. Dinsmore told her the bird spread its wings as it peered into the water, probably to cast a shadow and cut surface reflection. Of course, having studied animals all her life, Kate knew they were smarter than humans. If she had only looked beyond those first easy, dazzling moments with Charlie, she wouldn't be alone here now.

She unpacked the car and fed Clancy. She'd brought

George's clothes just in case, although she was almost certain she was going to spend this time here without him. She hung his things in the closet anyway. He had a few pairs of old khakis that he never wore anywhere except Nantucket. Maybe their best summer had been the first one they spent here. What she remembered most about it was that George had fallen asleep in the sun and had gotten a blistering burn. When she peeled the skin from his back, she knew she had never been so intimate with anyone. His skin was lighter than air, and there had been more layers than she could count.

As she walked through the house now, assuring herself that nothing had changed, the dog padded after her. The place was always clean and airy. The Dinsmores had replaced the small old windows with large panes of glass, so that the ocean was everywhere. There were pots of wild flowers spread throughout the rooms. Kate inspected each bathroom, each closet. As she sat on the edge of the old claw-footed bathtub, she wondered what she was looking for. She thought about the young graduate student at the college who was doing his thesis on bathroom privacy. Did she keep the door opened or closed? he wanted to know. And was it different if someone was in the house? If she was taking a shower? Using the toilet? Open or closed? She had thought him attractive until he'd asked her to participate in the study. He'd gotten a government grant to do his research.

There was still enough of the day left to walk by the ocean. She and George always watched the sunset their first night here. Except for a few gulls the beach was empty. Because of the strong undertow it was not a place that ever got too crowded. Kate's calves stretched as her feet sank into the coarse brown sand. The dog made her way directly to the water's edge and ran in and out like a child. She swam only when Kate was in the water with her.

Would Ellen still call this sky pink cotton candy? Perhaps she was too grown-up for that. Kate dunked her toe in the water. It was always colder than she hoped. George said cold water was good for you. What was wrong with her anyway? Couldn't she just see the sunset with her own eyes? Feel the water with her own foot? Why did she have to bring Ellen into it? Or George? Why did she always have to think how they would see things?

The dog was digging in the sand. Kate sat down beside her. She thought about the gray heron with the yellow feet casting its shadow on a pond. Your eyes would take a few seconds to adapt if you wanted to look through a shadow. And how long, she wondered, could you hover over your own darkness?

The tide was going out now. Kate felt the beach's moisture on her bottom. The dog was playing with a crab. Kate dug her fingers into the sand. Would she be all right? She had never been alone like this. She would make a castle, she decided. So she thought in terms of fairy tales. Was that so terrible? There were worse things. She didn't think she was really afraid to be alone. She patted the sand around what looked more like an enormous breast than a castle. Well, it would be a feminist castle, she thought, digging a moat around it. She wished Rhoda were here. The idea of a castle made in the shape of breasts and fallopian tubes was too good to keep to herself. She laughed out loud.

Clancy abandoned the crab and licked Kate's face, putting her paws on Kate's shoulders. Kate leaned backward and crushed the castle as she lay on the sand. The dog leaped around to the side still licking Kate's cheeks. Kate rolled over and got up on her hands and knees and panted. The dog wasn't fooled. Kate sniffed Clancy's ear and licked the dog's nose. The dog got down on her front paws, her rear up in the air. Kate did the same. Clancy barked. Kate lay down on her back atop her castle and laughed. She rolled over and over. The sand had no smell, but its grit made small dots on her arms and legs. She lifted her hands up toward the night. The incision didn't hurt. The incision. The incision. It had been like carrying a sick child around with her. She sighed. The dog danced around her in the darkness.

Kate lay there for a long time lifting up one leg, then the other. Where was that runaway bird now with its yellow feet? She took handfuls of sand and dropped them on her abdomen. Mosquitoes buzzed The dog's collar jangled.

In the morning, she called Bayberry and caught George in the cafeteria. Oh yes, he told her, he was wonderful. Was she having a good time? Was everything OK? And was that coffee he heard perking in the background. He was going horseback riding this morning.

It was coffee. She had put it on for George without thinking while she heated the water for her tea. She told him about the African heron. She said she'd watched the sunset and had missed him.

He was more talkative than he'd been face to face. How was Mrs. Dinsmore? Was she still wearing those old sneakers? Had Kate been swimming yet? Was the island crowded? And actually, he said, didn't she think watching the sunset was a little corny?

"I hung your clothes in the closet," she said. People were already on the windy beach, anchoring their blankets with shoes or picnic baskets in each corner. She had just eaten a fresh pear. She was still in her nightgown.

"Don't count on me," he said. It was the same matter-of-fact tone he used when dealing with difficult patients on the phone.

"OK, George," she said, remembering how much she

liked saying his name. Had he meant to hurt her with his remark about the sunset?

She unplugged the coffeepot and took her tea out on the deck. How would she manage without George? She was so self-sufficient, everyone always told her. So independent. Had such a mind of her own. Well, it would be only two weeks. She could survive.

She began to plan her day. There was too much sugar in the tea. Swimming. Would her suit still fit her? It would feel soothing to be swept back and forth by the current. Reading. Something mindless. She had not brought *Ulysses*. Cooking. She would make herself an elegant dinner. Maybe she would even invite someone. She knew everyone on the beach. What would it be like to entertain without George? And what was he doing now? You could die falling off a horse. Or be paralyzed. Her tea was cold. Some kids on the beach looked up and waved at her. She waved back and then remembered she was in her nightgown. Maybe at dusk she'd go back to the marsh and look for the lost bird.

She changed. Her suit was comfortable. She found a spy story George had read last summer. The sun was so bright in the glassed-in house she put on her dark glasses as she collected a blanket, a towel, an apple. The back hallway where they kept their bikes was empty. Well, maybe there was one good thing about being here alone. George was so enthusiastic about bicycling that she had never wanted to complain about the tedium of pedaling from one beach to another. Their bikes were at home in the garage leaning next to one another. Still, she thought, leaving the house, squinting behind her sunglasses at the sparkling ocean, still, she'd prefer George on a bike to his being on a horse.

CHAPTER

· SEVENTEEN ·

Kate was half dozing on her blanket, her feet just grazing the water, when Charlie appeared without warning in the middle of the second week. He'd been phoning her each night. Sometimes she answered. Sometimes she didn't. They had never spoken of his coming to Nantucket. She felt the color rise to her cheeks as he stood on the sand, his shadow over her. He'd already changed to a bathing suit. She put down her latest spy intrigue.

"I adore you," he said.

"George has taken up horseback riding," she said. Whenever she called, George was either coming from or going to the stable.

Charlie sat beside her. "Don't be angry," he said. "I had to see you." The hair on his legs stood on end.

"Oh, Charlie," she said. She wasn't going to look at him. She had told him on the phone that their relationship was over, that the pain exceeded the pleasure. He didn't know what that meant, he said. He continued to call her anyway. He was sure she'd change her mind. No, she told him, she wouldn't. Maybe they could be friends, he said. No. She had tried that before, she told him. It never worked.

"You shouldn't have come," she said now.

"I know," he said. He took her hand. "You look terrific."

She knew she looked terrific. And why shouldn't she? This was her vacation. She was tanned and relaxed and had no one to think about but herself. Except for George who was probably killing himself on a horse right this minute. Or Ellen, poisoned or lost in the Maine woods. She stood up. "I was just going for a swim," she said.

He walked with her to the water. His skin was pale. He was going to burn.

"Great surf here," she said, realizing she'd grown unused to conversation in the past ten days. She dived in, the cold water less of a jolt than the sight of Charlie standing there at the water's edge. His hair gleamed redder here than at home, and his legs looked longer from this vantage point. Floating on her back, allowing the current to sweep her offshore, she wondered if Charlie would be interested in the displaced bird at the marsh. Well, maybe it would be OK to have him here. Maybe she could make him see that you just can't love two people at once. The undertow pulled more strongly now as she rode a wave in toward shore. The salt water stung her eyes; she dived for the bottom and used her hands to crawl along the sand through the algae. When she came up for air, she was able to stand. She looked around for Charlie but couldn't find him. She knew her lips were purple, but she languished in the rush of oxygen in her blood. Her toes picked up shells from the ocean floor.

When she saw Charlie's arms flailing about, she thought at first he was kidding. He was out only a few yards beyond her. There was no one else close by.

She used the cross-chest carry. He knew enough to relax and let her do the work. She should have warned him about the undertow.

"Oh, shit," he said, when they got to the beach and he coughed up water.

"It's OK," she said. She was breathing hard. Her rib cage couldn't hold her lungs.

"Are you all right?" He looked at her stomach.

She had forgotten about her stomach. It still bulged unnaturally but hadn't bothered her in a long time. "Are you OK?" she said.

"Oh, I'm a real he-man," he said. Even after drowning, his grin was disarming.

"They've never had a guard on this beach," she said. She thought it odd that no one had noticed them. You could go down out there and not even be missed. The water came in around them now. Charlie was shivering. "Oh, my," she said. "Let's get a drink for ourselves." She could already taste the bourbon on her tongue. A kindergarten-aged kid ran by, splashing them.

"Oh, shit," said Charlie. His face was white.

They had their bourbon straight up and sat on the porch wrapped in old beach towels. Kate knew they both should have hot showers, but she was too exhausted to do the right thing. She could still feel the weight of Charlie's body against hers as she dragged him to shore. Clancy sniffed him, and finding him acceptable, settled herself in the shade.

After the second drink, the color came back to Charlie's face. "I wouldn't want to end it all in the water," he said.

"No?" she said.

"No. On the ski slope maybe," he said. "Or on Heartbreak Hill in the marathon." He smirked. "Or in bed," he said. "With you. Like Rockefeller."

"Look, Charlie," she said. She'd drunk the liquor too quickly. "No talk about bed. OK?" Her fingers tingled. She had the urge to reach over and touch him, as if they were playing tag.

"You got a deck of cards here?" he said.

"Check in the hall closet," she said. "I'm going to start dinner." What was he doing here? Where was his wife? What if he'd drowned?

In the kitchen, she took out the fresh swordfish the man from Finney's had delivered. She poured herself another drink and turned on the oven. She heard Charlie going upstairs and seconds later the shower running. She cut up onions and anchovies to stuff the mushrooms and put them under the broiler. The timer ticked too loudly. She sat down and waited. The red fender of the moped she'd rented poked out of the back hallway. She had tried to imagine George on his horse at Bayberry while she rode her moped as fast as it would go from one end of the island to the other. The timer went off.

When Charlie came downstairs, she was on the porch with a fresh drink. The mushrooms, flanked by raw vegetables, were on an aluminum tray on the table.

"Gorgeous," he said. "Too good to eat." He paused. "Almost," he added, eating one mushroom whole.

"Would you rather ride a horse or a moped?" she said.

"How about a helicopter?" he said.

"Or a balloon?" she said. Would she ever go up in a balloon?

"A raft or a canoe?" he said.

Maybe they could be friends after all. She had never had a relationship like this. "I'm trying to understand horses," she said, finishing her drink.

"Well, I'd choose a moped over a horse." He got up and sat on the wooden floor by her chair. "How fast does a moped go anyway?" He held her foot in his warm hand.

"Is Janet coming back?" she said.

"I hope so," he said without missing a beat. He ran his fingers across her instep.

"I'm getting very drunk," she said. Was it the liquor or just his presence that was doing this? She jiggled her foot free.

He fed her a piece of raw cauliflower. "I can see that," he said.

The swordfish burned. Even the dog refused to eat it. Charlie made coffee. He had not been able to find any playing cards. He brought out a jigsaw puzzle, which he set up on the kitchen table. It was a map of the city of Boston. "Easy," he said. "Duck soup."

Kate was still wearing her bathing suit. "I burned the swordfish," she said. She was beginning to see double.

"Help me turn the pieces over," he said. "I'll take Beacon Hill. You take the North End."

"No sir," she said. "You have to start with the edges first, not the inside." She and George always began with the edges.

"You do the edges," Charlie said. "I'm doing Beacon Hill. Here's Cedar Street."

"I'm very quick at putting things together," she said.

"Not as quick as I am," he challenged.

The sun was just rising when they finished. They had not talked much while they worked on the puzzle. And at the end, they had not even argued over the last piece.

Charlie made more coffee. Kate took a shower, and they drove off to Quaise Marsh to see the bird, who did not make an appearance that day. Some watchers speculated that the bird was dead. Others claimed it had tried to get back on course. Charlie told everyone it would be back tomorrow, as if he knew. But he spoke with such authority that people nodded their heads and agreed with him.

Back at the house, Charlie went upstairs to sleep and Kate made her usual morning call to George. They had trouble locating him. Maybe he had left the hospital. Maybe he had decided to come here to surprise her. A metallic taste covered her tongue. She could picture George getting off the ferry at this instant and hailing a cab. Or riding his horse down Main Street. Her head ached.

"Kate?" His voice finally came on the wire.

"Oh, George. Thank God," she said.

"What's the matter?" he said. "Are you all right?"

"Yes. Yes," she said. "I was worried when you didn't come to the phone right away."

"Sorry," he said. "I was jogging around the building to warm up. Today's the big day."

Had she been right? Was he checking out of the hospital today? She began to think of what flight she could catch from Nantucket to Boston.

"Imagine," George was saying. "They're finally going to let me play tennis. First time in a month. Imagine."

"Tennis," she said. She was safe. Tennis, gardening, horses. Somehow that was not the sort of stuff that ended up in psychiatric journals. "Who are you playing with?" she said, wondering if they had a pro at the hospital.

He told her the name. He couldn't talk long, he said. He'd never felt better. Things were perfect. He'd see her soon. He hung up without asking how she was. She hadn't told him about the moped.

Yes. It would be only a few more days until she saw him. She was glad he was better. She wished she could be there when he hit the first few tennis balls. Maybe it would have been more loyal to rent a bike instead of a moped.

Upstairs, she watched Charlie sleeping on her bed. He lay on his side facing the edge, as if he didn't want to

take up too much room. His feet hung over the end. She
had never seen him asleep before. There had never been
time for that.

She took off her sneakers and lay down next to him on
the flowered sheet, fitting her body to his. The hairs that
grew on the back of his neck were bright red. As she ran
her finger across them, she felt uncontrollably sad. What
if the heron was dead? She timed her breathing to match
Charlie's and nestled her head against him. When they woke
up, it was dark and they were in the same position. They
were both dying of thirst, they said at once. There was
no question of their making love.

Kate squeezed fresh orange juice and made a ham-and-
cheese omelet. She used ten eggs. They ate everything.
Charlie agreed to leave in the morning.

They went back upstairs with a Chinese checkerboard
and its marbles, but they were too tired from their sleep
and big meal to play. They collapsed on the bed and propped
themselves up with pillows, sighing as if they'd just finished
a long race.

"You're a lovely man," Kate said, touching Charlie's bare
foot with hers.

"King me," he said.

"I mean it," she said. She wished he would lean over
her face and lick the tears that dripped down her cheeks.
She dug her nails into the palms of her hands. There was
no point in wishing.

"It's all going to be OK," he said. "We're all going to
live happily ever after. You'll see. Your textbook will become an international best seller. George will win the U.S.
Open. Janet will save the world from itself."

"And what about you?"

"I'll own the greatest car of all time," he said. "Faster
than a speeding bullet."

She was smiling now. How was it that he always knew exactly the right thing to say?

They slept with their clothes on. When she drove him to the airport in the morning, she knew they would not meet again.

After Kate had made the analogy for herself that her relationship with Charlie had been like a trip to an exotic and marvelous place, she felt better, as if she finally had things straight. It was a cliché—that there are some places you visit with relish but don't want to live—and she knew she could never really dismiss her feelings for Charlie as quickly as that. But she was like Dorothy coming home from Oz. There was her fairy-tale mentality again. Well, what did you do when Prince Charming wasn't your husband and your husband was your best friend? You went home to Kansas. That's what you did.

She spent her last day in the marsh with the birders. The yellow-footed heron still did not appear. Some of the watchers talked about going home.

That evening, she took the jigsaw puzzle apart and put it away in the closet. She got out the vacuum cleaner and tried to pick up the sand she'd traipsed in. She dusted the tops of furniture carefully, although she was certain Joanna Dinsmore would go over everything again within an hour after she left.

Upstairs, she cleaned her bedroom and bath. She was already thinking about the stack of mail at home. In her zeal, she knocked over the nightstand with the Chinese checkers on it. The marbles rolled everywhere.

"Jesus," she said. "Jesus, Mary, and Joseph." She sat on the floor fingering first a green marble, then a blue one. She put them both in her mouth and spit them across the room.

• • •

In the morning, she decided not to go back to the marsh. It would be better to believe the bird was safe. You could never know for sure anyway.

She packed the car, stopping at the dump on the way to the ferry with her two weeks' worth of trash. As she drove through the busy center of town, she realized she would have to gear up for life at home. She had almost become introspective during these two weeks. She had not made even one list.

As she rolled the car down the ramp into the belly of the ferry, the dog looked this way and that, trying to catch everything. George always said that Clancy looked like Johnny Carson when she sat in the car.

CHAPTER
· EIGHTEEN ·

Kate made it home from Woods Hole in two hours. Fortunately, all the traffic on the Bourne Bridge was headed toward the Cape, away from Boston. Even Route 3 was backed up for miles. You couldn't expect anything else at the start of the Labor Day weekend, everyone's last gasp for the summer.

Although it was dark when she reached Newton and she still had the sea in her ears, the old house had its own comforting noises. Hearing the floorboards make their protest as she walked across them, she felt pleased to be home. She turned the lights on, opened some windows, poured a Sprite, and settled herself in George's office, where her mother had neatly stacked the two weeks of mail.

The office was the same as she'd left it. Ellen's high-school graduation photograph stared up at her from its silver frame. She remembered that George kept their senior-prom picture in the front drawer of his desk. Whenever she saw it, she thought about how these pointy shoes had pinched her feet. Well, there was life after high school, wasn't there? She began sorting the mail. One pile for her. One for George. A smaller one for Ellen. A fourth pile for junk. A fifth for magazines. There was more junk than anything. She looked at her own mail. There were notices of faculty meetings at the college. Postcards from friends on vacation. A letter from her publisher. The new edition of her textbook had been ordered by several major universities for their comparative anatomy courses. There would be a second printing.

She moved George's mail to the right side of his desk. Tomorrow he'd be home, she thought, as she tried to get comfortable in his swivel chair. They had never been separated for so long. She closed her eyes and tried to imagine him sitting here with her now. She got up and moved to the patient's chair and leaned her head back.

Labor Day weekend. She had always been glad when it came. Not that she didn't like the summer. She did. But she liked getting back to work. Even as a kid, she had been anxious for school to resume. She liked endings when there were new beginnings and was usually impatient to get on with whatever came next once she had squeezed the most from the present. Besides, she thought, slipping off her sandals, Ellen would be home tomorrow night. She was staying here until the summer sublet vacated her apartment at the end of the weekend. They would all be home. They could all get back to work, back to normal.

She returned to George's chair, took up a pencil and paper, and began making the menu for the weekend. Lobster for George. Fresh vegetables for Ellen. Bean sprouts. Spinach. She was halfway through her shopping list when the doorbell rang. It was five minutes of ten. The dog was barking. The bell rang again.

She stubbed her toe on the threshold as she went to the hallway. Oh damn, she mouthed. There was nothing worse than a stubbed toe. When she opened the door, Kate found a squat, broad-shouldered woman in a business suit. Humid air pushed its way inside.

"Are you the lady of the house?" the woman said.

Oh, really. Could it be a salesperson at this hour? "Yes," Kate said. "But I don't want anything. Thank you." She pushed the door closed.

The doorbell rang right away.

She opened the door so angrily that the dog ran to a corner of the hallway. "Look," she began. She leaned down to rub her toe and found blood oozing from the nail.

"Mrs. Cummings," the woman said. "I'm not selling anything. I'm Marabel Greenleaf." She paused, as if the name were supposed to mean something.

Kate realized at once that this must be one of George's patients. Greenleaf. The name wasn't familiar. "I'm sorry," she said. "Dr. Cummings isn't at home."

The woman nodded.

"He's away on vacation," Kate said.

The woman laughed. "I'll say he is," she said.

"He'll call you when he gets home," Kate tried to reassure her. "I'll be sure to make a note of it." The darkness surrounding the woman gave her a two-dimensional quality.

"Mrs. Cummings," she said. This time she inhaled as if she were about to go off a high diving board. "I'm from the Star Detective Agency." She produced a card with her name on it.

This woman was crazier than Kate had first thought. Imagine. A detective. Kate turned the card over in her hand; the printing was raised. She had to get rid of her.

"Your husband hired me," the Greenleaf woman said. "To keep tabs on you," she continued. "And your boyfriend." Was she sneering? "That Murdoch fellow." She *was* sneering.

"I can't believe it," said Kate. She closed her eyes. Her head was light. She made a small tear in the woman's calling card and looked again at her throbbing toe.

"Now then," the woman said, all business. "He pays me every week, you know."

No, Kate did not know. How could she know? Her head might float right off her body if she stood here much longer.

"Sorry if I put you off with my 'lady of the house' routine. I was making a little joke." She twisted her upper lip into an odd smile.

"A joke," said Kate.

"Well," said the woman, "the truth is I've had no money from him for a month now. Your husband, that is. Of course, I know he's in the nut house. And I wouldn't want to bug him there. But I really need my money. You know how it is. Overhead."

Kate heard herself sigh. She felt as if she'd been underwater for a long time where the sounds were muted, where things were only one color. She stepped back from the door. "You might as well come inside," she said and led the way to George's office.

The woman's body puffed out like a ruffled grouse as she sat in the patient's chair crossing and uncrossing her short legs. It was *Mrs.* Greenleaf, she told Kate, although she was divorced. She knew a lot about divorce, she said, both personally and professionally. What did Kate want to know? She'd be glad to help her out.

Kate wondered how much detectives charged. She couldn't believe George would do this. Her weekend menu with its nine careful squares—one for each meal—seemed larger than any piece of furniture in the room. She was making a conscious effort to ignore her toe. "OK," she said, as she let herself sink into George's chair, "you've been working for my husband now for how long?" She held on to the arms of the chair, waiting for the answer. The woman wore heavy orthopedic shoes and thick stockings. Her own bare feet blended into the Oriental pattern of the rug. Her toe might be broken. She would probably lose the nail.

"Several months anyway," said the Greenleaf woman. "At two fifty a week. Plus expenses."

Kate turned the sheets of her menu over. "And what did you do for two hundred and fifty dollars a week, Mrs. Greenleaf?" Divorced or not, the woman still wore her wedding ring.

"Confidential," Mrs. Greenleaf said.

Kate's throat was dry. She'd forgotten to put drinks on the shopping list. What kind of woman would snoop on someone for money? Well, she was not going to offer her a drink. George had spied on his own wife. George had known about Charlie all along. And he had said nothing. He was paying this woman two hundred and fifty dollars a week to spy on her and Charlie. And then he said nothing. "I can't believe it," she said.

"It's more than a thousand he owes me now," said Mrs. Greenleaf.

Maybe the woman even took photographs. Maybe George was planning to divorce her and produce pictures for evidence. She thought again of the prom picture in the desk drawer. "Tell me exactly what he paid you for," she said.

"I really can't, Mrs. Cummings. You understand, don't you? My clients pay for discretion, you know."

Kate stood up. She couldn't bear one more minute of this woman's presence. Her brown eyes were too sincere. She was too reasonable. She was just doing her job, she said. And what did Kate see in that Murdoch guy in the first place? Especially with a husband like Dr. Cummings. That Dr. Cummings was a gem, a real gem.

"Mrs. Greenleaf," Kate said. "If you'll just leave your bill, I'll see that my husband gets it."

The woman pulled a small packet of papers from her handbag and handed it over. On top, Kate saw a receipt for air fare from Boston to Nantucket.

When Kate went to pick George up at the hospital the next day, he hugged her so hard she lost her breath. He looked different, she thought. His jaw was firmer, more square, more determined. And his hair was over his ears. He was tan and looked as healthy as if he'd been at the beach. He smelled of horses. He'd been riding that morning, he told her.

At home, she watched as he rolled on the floor with the dog. He had really missed the dog, he said. And what time would Ellen be here? Was her room ready? Where was his mail? And had she checked his plants? He was going to the greenhouse to see what his plants were up to.

Kate went to the kitchen to begin the preparations for George's homecoming dinner. Her toe still hurt. She washed potatoes for the salad and put them on the stove to boil. She got the other ingredients from the refrigerator and lined them up on the counter: green pepper, celery, cucumber. She got out a pan to boil the eggs. She had no idea how to bring up the Greenleaf issue. Was she the same person who had stood on her head every morning all these years telling herself how in touch she was? Well, George had not stood on *his* head. Why had she assumed they were attuned to each other? She began chopping the green pepper. She'd been fooling herself. Now George was going to divorce her. She glanced across the room at her straw purse on the chair by the back door. The packet of itemized bills Mrs. Greenleaf gave her last night didn't take up that much room in her bag, but they certainly told the whole story: times, dates, places. She heard George on the staircase now.

She looked down at the green pepper, at its vibrant color.
Well, she could just pay Marabel Greenleaf the thousand
dollars herself. She wouldn't even tell George. She took
the eggs off the stove to cool. George loved eggs in his
potato salad. Ellen didn't. She would make one batch with,
and one without. That was it. She would get a cashier's
check for a thousand dollars and send it to the Star Detective
Agency. The account would be closed. She put a piece of
green pepper on her tongue.

She was chopping the onions when George came into
the room in his tennis shorts. He poured himself a glass
of milk and sat down at the table. He was talking quietly
about his backhand. He had finally learned to watch the
ball, he said. Another patient, a world champion from
Czechoslovakia, had helped him. "Think of it," he was saying, "Boris choked on every big point and ended up in
Bayberry for treatment after the U.S. Pro Tournament at
Longwood. I even saw him play there when you were in
the hospital. Whoever thought I'd be friends with Boris
Orlov?"

"George," she said, turning around to look at him. He
was supposed to have recovered from this tennis craze. Her
eyes were tearing from the onion.

"Boris and I are collaborating on a paper about tennis
and psychotherapy," he said. "Maybe it'll even be a book."
He downed his milk in one gulp.

Kate was lining up the tomatoes George had brought
home from the hospital. First, she arranged them from larg-
est to smallest, as George went on talking about his project
with Boris Orlov. Then she ordered them from ripest to
least ripe. What would she do with thirty-five tomatoes?
Imagine. He had actually hired a detective to follow her.
The ripest tomato squished in her hands.

"So," George was saying, "I'll just be a few hours." He

laced up his sneakers. "They took the laces out of our shoes as soon as we came off the court," he said. "Think of it. They took the laces out of Boris Orlov's sneakers. That man earned a million dollars on the tennis court last year. I'll bet you even his shoelaces are custom made."

Kate washed her hands and watched what was left of the tomato slip down the drain. She went across the room and stood in front of George. "Don't be late for dinner," she said. She put her hand on his shoulder. "And don't hurt yourself."

As soon as he left, she went to the phone and dialed Charlie's number. It rang once, and she hung up. He ought to know about the Greenleaf woman. She looked at the potatoes cooling on the counter, still steaming. She was calling Charlie less to protect him than to tell somebody. She called Rhoda. There was no answer.

Just yesterday she had been on Nantucket. The most important thing in her life had been getting a last glimpse of the rare black heron with the yellow feet. She began to think about the lemon-meringue pie she'd planned for dessert; it was too hot to turn on the oven. She dialed Charlie's number again without picking up the receiver.

Well, she was not going to stand here and think about it. She would go pick up the lobsters. Maybe she'd even go to the club and watch George play. Or go to her parents' house. Her father's roses were in their third bloom now. Maybe she could drive into town to the college and find Howard Hansell. He would not understand about the detective, but he would hold her hand and tell her not to worry. She picked up her car keys. Their jangle made the dog appear instantly; she was always ready to go. "Can you believe it, Clancy?" Kate said. "Your father is a spy." The dog tilted her head to one side. "A secret agent," Kate said.

She didn't really feel as glib as she sounded to herself. The dog barked.

"Well," Kate said as they got into the car together, "there's no reason why I should cover up for him." The dog sat in the front seat, her head out the side window. "A thousand dollars. Plus expenses." The dog stood up and looked behind them at a German shepherd. On the radio, Tip O'Neill was being interviewed about the slaughter of more than two hundred marines in Lebanon. Once again she reminded herself how glad she was that Ellen was a girl. It would be impossible for the parents of those young men to live with that kind of death for their children.

In the fish store, she chose the female lobsters that George liked. George. How could he have done this to her? "Espionage," she said, as she put the packages in the car. The dog jumped into the backseat and sniffed at the cardboard box holding the lobsters.

"Two wrongs don't make a right," Kate said. She drove straight home, forgetting her father's rose garden. "Who does George Cummings think he is?" She drove through a red light. She would serve the itemized bills from the Star Detective Agency on George's dinner plate. "Happy homecoming," she would say. She would invite Mrs. Greenleaf for dinner. She could even invite Charlie. She would stuff the bills inside their lobsters like fortune cookies. One thing for sure, she thought, pulling into the driveway, she was not going to keep quiet about the detective. "You, Clancy," she said, nose to nose with the dog, "you are my best friend." The dog bounded out of the car after a squirrel on the back lawn.

Kate was still talking aloud when she entered the kitchen. George was already home and had the TV on. He was watching the preliminary rounds of the U.S. Open. "I can't figure out why they ever called it Flushing Meadow," he said, taking her packages. "Sounds like a toilet, doesn't it?" It was his usual joke about the Open, ever since it had been moved from Forest Hills. Maybe some things about George hadn't changed after all.

They waited as long as they could for dinner, hoping Ellen would appear, although she told them she'd be late. At nine o'clock, they sat down in the dining room with their lobsters and potato salad. Kate had opened a bottle of Riesling, but George said he was drinking only bottled water or milk now. Just like Boris Orlov.

"It's really not good for you, Kate," George said. "Dehydrating."

He hadn't the slightest idea of what was good for her. She cracked one lobster claw open. She felt the Greenleaf papers against her chest where she'd tucked them inside her bra. "What do you think about espionage?" she said.

"Where did that come from?" he asked. "Speaking of intrigue, did you know there have been death threats against some of the players at the Open?" he said.

She admired her arrangement of daisies against the dark mahogany of the table. She imagined picking the petals off a flower one at a time: Tell him now. Tell him later. Now. Later. "Death threats?" she said.

"There are a lot of crazy people in this world," he said, dipping a piece of lobster into his pot of melted butter.

At the bottom of Greenleaf's hotel bill on Nantucket, she had written, "Murdoch on island 8/30, 8/31. Stayed at beach house with K.C. for 2 days (& nights)." The detective had followed them all this time, using her expense account. The hotel bill itself was enormous. She had even charged George for a sweater and wool socks. She hadn't known the nights were so cold, she wrote at the bottom of the bill. "Crazy?" Kate said now.

"You know what I mean," he said.

"How would you feel about a death threat?" she said.

She was going to enjoy this. She felt the corner of one bill poking her breast. It had been stupid to put the bills over her heart.

"Well, I've had patients threaten me, of course," he said.

"Of course," she said. The wine tasted rusty. She looked at the glass for sediment.

"And you've had students threaten you over grades, haven't you?" he asked.

"Of course," she said. In fact, she had never been threatened by a student. "But no death threats."

"Nobody's safe anymore," he said, beginning his second lobster.

They had just gone to bed when they heard Ellen come up the stairs two at a time. The dog leaped over the corner of the bed to meet her. The hall light they'd left on for their daughter framed her blond head as she poked it into their room.

"You up?" she said. "I'm home." She came into the room and hugged them both. "I'm dead," she said, flopping on the bed between them. "On the road for six hours from Maine. Took each kid home in the city. Door to door. Two more hours. Gotta go to bed. We all cried all the way home. Great kids." Her energy pierced the night like a tonic.

Kate wanted to turn the light on and see her features. She grabbed her hand. It was calloused. "Come here, you," she said, pulling her closer, running her hand over the thick, curly angel-hair. "I'm so glad to see you," she said.

"Me, too," said Ellen. "You finish *Ulysses?*" She laughed, kissed them again and was gone. The dog trotted out of the room after her.

"She looks wonderful," said George.

"How could you tell?" said Kate, remembering that George's eyes always accommodated the darkness before hers did.

"It's perfect, isn't it?" he said. "Everyone's home." He moved over toward Kate on the big bed and put his arms around her. "Lobster, the U.S. Open, Ellen and you," he said. "What else is there?"

"Spying," she said. Ellen's presence had given her the strength she needed. Now was the time. It was going to be easier in the dark.

"What?" he said. He was kissing her cheek.

"Greenleaf," she said. She had the papers in the drawer of her night table. She was ready now.

"What?" he said.

"Greenleaf, George," she said. "Marabel Greenleaf. The Star Detective Agency. Spying." She felt his body stiffen. "The jig's up, George," she said, sounding incredibly silly to herself. Maybe in ten years she would think this was silly.

He moved away from her and sat up in bed. He was silent. Was he going to change the subject? Now was the time to produce the evidence. She opened the drawer and gave George the packet of bills.

"What's this?" he said.

"Proof, George," she said. "Proof that you're a spy."

He turned the light on and began to look through the papers. "I can't believe it," he said.

"She came here last night," Kate said. "She wanted money. A thousand dollars."

George looked toward the door. He dropped the papers on his lap. "I'd forgotten about old Marabel," he said, chuckling. The papers separated as his laugh accelerated into a cackle and the bed shook.

"You'll wake Ellen," she said. But she knew that wasn't true. Ellen was a sound sleeper; even alarm clocks didn't rouse her. Kate's fingers tightened on the bottom sheet of the bed. Maybe she really didn't know George at all. The old, predictable George she knew had destroyed a car, hired a detective, obsessed about hitting a yellow ball with a racket, and had taken his August vacation in a mental hospital.

"It's too much," George gasped, holding his sides, as he rocked back and forth on the bed. Tears streamed down his cheeks onto his yellow pajama top.

"I don't see what's so funny," she said. One of her fingernails broke off and shot across the room, as she let go of the sheet. "A thousand dollars. Plus all those expenses. She even followed me to Nantucket."

"I see that," he said, rummaging through the papers. "She had to buy wool socks to keep up with you." He reached for the handkerchief he kept under his pillow and blew his nose.

"How can you laugh?" she said. She was whining. Hot tears swarmed across her eyes. Was that how she'd gotten away with her antics? By playing the little girl when things got difficult? After all, no one could ever really blame a little girl. Was that why she clung to fairy tales? Had her mother been right all this time? Had she never grown up?

"I can't help it," George said. "It's funny."

"You spied on me, George," she said.

He looked at her straight on, his eyelashes glistening from the moisture. His jaw was firm. "Yup," he said. "I did."

"You knew about Charlie all along?"

"Yes," he said.

Her kneecaps were rattling. "And you let me go on with it?"

"Let?" he said. "Let?"

He was right. Had she been expecting him to set the limits for her? She *was* a child.

"I was afraid," he said.

"Me too," she said. She was thinking back to the time

211

before her surgery when she and Charlie had started their affair. She wondered now what George's fear had been about. Probably it was different from hers. "I was frantic," she said.

"I thought you might die," he said. "So I hired Greenleaf to watch over you. It was crazy." He laughed and threw his hands up in the air.

"Like a guardian angel?" she said.

"Oh yes," he said. "Saint Marabel. How does it sound?"

"Oh, George," she said. "I thought you were going to divorce me." He might still want to divorce her. She lay back on her pillow and looked at the ceiling. Maybe she'd go downstairs and make the lemon-meringue pie now.

But George's face was over hers, too close to read his expression. He said nothing. He kissed her. It was a long kiss. His eyes were closed. He began to chew on her lower lip, gently at first, then harder. The taste of blood was sweet in her mouth.

CHAPTER

· NINETEEN ·

On Labor Day morning Charlie was sitting in his car half a block from the Cummings house. Janet had taken the kids for the weekend. He was due at his parents' house in the afternoon for the annual family picnic. The street was empty. He could wait. Sooner or later. George Cummings would come out of his house and drive off to play tennis. And then he would surprise Kate.

Bits of yellow pollen from the leafy trees lining the street fell on his hood. He rubbed his hand over the car seat. He would never feel the same about his car again. Sure, the insurance had covered the new paint job, and the car was the same maroon color he had loved. But he would never be able to forget the sight of his Mercedes that morning, that awful morning. Chunks of rubber from the gouged tires lay everywhere, and the car itself had looked like a molting dinosaur, a dead dinosaur. He ought to have prosecuted that son of a bitch Cummings, although he couldn't prove anything for sure. Even the cops were baffled that the inside hadn't been gutted. He should have had George Cummings put away at Walpole Prison. Instead, the jerk went and locked himself up in a loony bin. The very shrink who'd been treating his own wife.

Well, Charlie still couldn't stay away from Kate. His father always told him there was more to life than having a good time. But if that was true, Kate certainly didn't know about it. That was what he liked: She never took herself seriously. There was no talk about the meaning of life or the consequences of actions. Everyone else was always so worried: his clients, his mother, his wife. Kate rolled with the punches. Whatever happened, she liked it, loved it, saw something worth doing in it. His freshman year in college, he'd had a philosophy professor who'd asked them if the glass was half empty or half full. It had taken Charlie nearly the whole semester to understand the question. For Kate, the glass was ninety-five percent full. She was the least ambivalent person he knew. But would she leave her husband? That was the question now. Probably not. That fruitcake. Besides, she wouldn't want to begin again with three little kids. He knew that. He pressed his foot on the gas pedal. It didn't matter. He would work it out. He could talk her into it. He was a supersalesman. He wasn't going to give up just because of what she'd said on Nantucket.

He was counting on Cummings to leave the house to play tennis. He was a fanatic. Where the hell was he? It was nearly nine. Maybe he could even whisk Kate away for the day before she knew what hit her. Even if he could just get her to agree to meet him later, he was going to consider it a victory.

They expected him in Winchester at noon. His parents. His brother and wife. His sister and husband. Seven nieces and nephews. He didn't want to go. They would all feel sorry for him. Could they get him another beer? they would ask. Or another hot dog? They would not want to ask about Janet. They would tell him that. But they wouldn't be able to help themselves. They would pat him on the back and get him to play touch football.

Good. There was Cummings getting into that midget of a car, that Toyota, in his tennis gear. He drove up the street, away from Charlie. Now was his chance. He locked his car and ran on the uneven sidewalk toward the house. He decided to go to the back door, the one George had come out of. He knocked. The barking inside made him rise out of his shoes. Oh, sure, the dog. That damn dog with all the white hair. How could anyone stand it?

Kate opened the door with her back to it. "What did you forget, darling?" she said. When there was no answer, she turned.

Darling. She had called George "darling." She had never called him anything but Charlie. "Here I am," he said, walking into the kitchen. Not a very modern kitchen. Not like Janet's. Or his. Or whoever's kitchen it was now.

"Charlie," she said. "What are you doing here?" She was tanner than she'd been only a few days ago. Her eyes sparkled, and her collarbone jutted out like an invitation. She wore a pink sundress that made her look like a teenager. There was a dish towel in her hands.

He went to her and picked her up around the waist. The dog growled. She would want to bring the dog when she came to live with him. Maybe he could get used to a dog. The kids would love it.

"Put me down," Kate said. "George hired a detective."

"I love you," Charlie said. He felt her ribs under the thin fabric.

"A detective," she said. "To follow us. To report to George. She followed us to Nantucket."

"She?" said Charlie. This George was certifiable. Nuts. He was goddamn nuts.

"The Star Detective Agency," said Kate.

"Let's get out of here," said Charlie. Cummings had already wrecked his car and told his wife to leave him. He had put a tail on him. For all Charlie knew, he could even have a gun. He could be out there right now with a gun.

"Don't worry," said Kate. "It's all right. I've forgiven him; we've made it up. I just had to tell someone. I still can't believe it." She twisted her wedding ring as she spoke. Her bottom lip was swollen.

Made it up. They'd made it up? She was still standing there with the dish towel over her arm twisting her wedding ring. "Then if he's not going to shoot me, I might as well sit down," he said. He smelled coffee. The table and chair were made of heavy oak, a carbon copy of the stuff at his parents' house. The table was round; Janet would like that. The chair creaked under him.

"You've got to go, Charlie. This is crazy," Kate said. She wasn't wearing his earrings.

"Just one game of slapjack," he said.

There it was: that infectious laugh of hers. "Oh, Charlie," she said. "Another time. I promise. Another time." She took his hand and tried to pull him from the chair. Her body strained against the thin pink of her dress. He thought about kissing each of her fingernails as she pulled again. "You've got to go," she said, sucking on her lip. "I'll call you soon. This week. I promise."

"We're going to have that balloon ride," he said. But the idea had lost its power for him. He would have to think of something else. He stood up to go. The coffee smelled better than anything in the world.

"I won't forget, Charlie," Kate was saying. "I'll call. I will."

The opening of the back door startled them. Kate gave a little gasp; they looked at each other. There was no way out of this now. He'd been stupid to come here. Now he was only going to cause trouble for Kate. And then she would never want to see him. What would George Cummings do this time? The tap water was running slowly. Kate sat down at the table.

It was the mother, Kate's mother, her arms full of bundles. "I've got all the pies, dear," she said to the stove. "Oh," she said, turning her head arthritically, "there you are." She placed her packages carefully on the table. "Apple. Two apple. A cherry. And a lemon meringue for George. And how are you?" she said, looking up at Charlie for the first time. "We've met, haven't we?" She held out her hand. "I'm Mary Logan, Kate's mother."

"Charlie Murdoch," said Charlie. She looked much the same as she had that other time he'd seen her, the time he'd brought Kate the balloons. He wanted to glance at Kate but didn't dare. It was only a question of time before she remembered him.

"Murdoch. Murdoch," Mrs. Logan said. "Oh, yes, you must be a friend of Ellen's. Graduated ahead of her, did you? Glad she's home after that wilderness business in Maine, I'll bet. How nice. You staying for the picnic?" That woman sure did know how to fill in the blanks. All he had to do was nod and she would probably tell him his life's story.

"Sit down," she said, pushing him into his chair. "Have some coffee. Kate, why didn't you offer Charlie some coffee? Sugar or cream? A man your size likely takes both. Am I right?"

She was right. Kate stepped on his foot under the table. "Thanks very much," he said. "But I do have to be going." He got up and backed toward the door. "Nice meeting you, ma'am," he said.

"I know we've met before," Mrs. Logan went on.

He wondered if Kate would ever have blue hair like her mother's. He had to get out of here. Kate was tapping her fingers on the table. The faucet was still running.

A swinging door at the end of the room opened and a young girl, a college-age girl, came in. The daughter. She wore cutoff jeans and a green T-shirt that said ERA NOW. She was blond and muscular. "Hi, everyone," she said. "What's doing?"

Kate stood up and walked toward her daughter. "Hi, darling," she said, enveloping her in her arms. The girl nestled next to Kate like a small child.

"Mmm," she said. "You feel good, just like my mom." Kate held her face in both hands and kissed her nose.

"I was just leaving," he said.

"Sweetheart," said the grandmother. "Come here and let me see you. And for goodness' sakes, say hello to your friend Charlie here. Try to get him to stay for breakfast. Oh dear, I see you're still biting your fingernails."

"Hi," said the girl, approaching Charlie. "I'm Ellen." She took his hand and shook it firmly. She was taller than her mother, and her hair was as light as Kate's was dark.

"Hi," said Charlie.

Mrs. Logan looked from Charlie to Ellen to Kate. "But," she said, "I thought you knew each other."

"You assumed, Mother. You assumed," said Kate.

Would he never get out of here? He looked at his watch. It was only nine-thirty. Ellen was pouring herself some orange juice. She carefully squeezed a lime into it.

Mrs. Logan gave him a long look up and down. He thought she might make him turn around or walk across the room. He was glad he didn't bite his fingernails. "I've got it," she said. "You're the balloon man."

Ellen had her head in the refrigerator.

"Mother, please," said Kate.

"Please what?" Mrs. Logan said.

Charlie's back was against the door now. He felt the knob

pressing his hip. Probably the doorknob would fall off and roll across the floor and he'd never get out.

Kate's mother looked at him again. Then she looked at Kate. "Oh, no," she said. "Honestly, Kate." Her look changed from confusion to knowledge. She cleared her throat. "Well," she said, glancing over her shoulder at Ellen, who was stirring a raw egg into her juice, "if you're not Ellen's friend, then you must be George's patient. That's all. Am I right?"

"Oh, yes, Mother," Kate said. "You are absolutely right. You've absolutely hit the jackpot, haven't you?"

"Where is Daddy?" said Ellen.

"Playing tennis. Where else?" said Kate.

Charlie could think of plenty of other places George might be. He might be out there right now breaking the windows of Charlie's car with a baseball bat. He might be inside Charlie's house with a bomb. Maybe it was a good thing Janet had the kids.

Ellen drank her concoction and moved toward Charlie. "Excuse me," she said. "I'm going for a run." Her voice was throaty for an angel. She kissed her grandmother. "I missed you," she said.

"I'm leaving, too," he said. Finally, he could go. He opened the door for her. The knob did not come off in his hand. "Tell Dr. Cummings I'll call about my next appointment," he said to Kate.

Mrs. Logan winked with her eye at him but scowled with her mouth. Kate was in for it.

"My grandmother's a little nosy," Ellen said, "but she means well. Don't let her bother you."

Charlie let out a long sigh as he followed Ellen to the street. He looked to his left toward his car. It was still there.

Ellen was stretching out her legs. "Did my father know

you were coming?" she said. She was doing deep knee bends.

"Oh, no," he said. He wondered if his knees would crack if he tried a knee bend.

"An emergency?" she said. Her voice cracked on words of more than one syllable.

"More or less. You a feminist?" he said, looking at her jersey.

"Aren't you?" she said. "Isn't everybody?" She was running up and down in place. She stopped. "You OK?" she said, touching his sleeve.

The gesture moved him. He didn't want to be alone. He didn't want to go to his parents' so early. He couldn't go back inside to Kate. She was probably getting chewed out by her mother. He wished he could do something with Janet and the kids, but he didn't even know where they were. "How about having a cup of coffee with me?" he said.

She had Kate's green eyes, but the lashes were blond, not black, and the skin around them was freckled. This Ellen was a woman who had her own charms. "Going for a run," she said. "Besides"—she massaged her calves—"I don't use caffeine. And neither should you."

"It's because I'm a psychiatric patient, isn't it?" he said. "You're afraid of me. Is that it?"

"What did my grandmother mean about balloons?"

"Who knows?" he said. "Come on. Let's go." He began walking toward the car. She would come. She would feel sorry for him. She would have to come.

She leaned over to tie her shoe. The muscles in her long legs were pronounced, as if carved into her frame.

"I run the marathon every year," he said.

"I don't believe you," she said. Her eyebrows were so light you could hardly see them.

"Why not?"

"Because you're a patient of Dad's," she said. She laughed. It gurgled up deep from her throat. She was teasing him. She brushed her hair behind her ears. They were too large for her head. He was glad to see she had at least one imperfection. He didn't count her fingernails.

She made no comment about the car as he drove through Newton Center. Everything was closed. She was telling him about her summer in the woods. She'd spent a whole summer with juvenile delinquents in the Maine wilderness. It had really helped the kids, turned their lives around. They proved they could overcome obstacles and rely on themselves to make the most of what they had. They had written poetry. She didn't really go for her father's brand of therapy, she said. She believed in action. Doing was more important than talking. Didn't he think so?

"Tell that to Janet," he said.

"What?" she said.

"Listen," he said, "how about if we go home and get my running shoes and go for a jog by the river?"

"What about your coffee?" she said. "You'll die if you don't have your coffee." She was teasing him again.

"I don't use caffeine," he mimicked her. "At least not today."

She waited in the car while he went inside to change.

"Nice house," she said when he came out.

"All set," he said. "I don't suppose you eat sugar." He handed her a Fig Newton.

"Who else lives here?" she said.

"My three kids," he said. "They're with their mother today. In Cambridge. A born-again social worker."

"Divorced?" Ellen said.

"Not yet." Was it really going to happen? Janet hadn't said anything yet about a divorce.

"You have custody," Ellen said. It was a statement.

"Have you ever been married?" he said.

"Don't believe in it," she said.

They were on Storrow Drive now, where there was almost no traffic. It was getting hot. He rolled up the windows and put on the air conditioning. She was eating the Fig Newtons.

They parked on Bay State Road and walked the block to the river and began running west toward Boston University. Ellen had a shorter stride than his, but she had a spring in her gait that gave her power.

"Be nice to me," he said. "I'm out of shape."

"Besides," she said, "you're a mental patient. Right?"

Was she telling him by her teasing that she knew the truth about him? That he was no mental patient at all? As they crossed the B.U. bridge, he found himself wishing Janet were a runner. If he ran like this all year round, he'd have a terrific marathon time. His feet pounded the black-top. He looked up. The Hyatt Regency crowded his vision, as if it were moving toward him, instead of the other way around. Kate. The Hyatt Regency. The grapes. The Brie. The soft blue carpet. As he made the turn onto Memorial Drive, he began panting.

"Let's stop for a bit," Ellen said. They sat on the grass in front of MIT. She wasn't even breathing heavily, but there were circles of sweat under her arms and around the neck of her T-shirt.

"I'm a has-been," he said.

"What are you really?" she said, shoving a finger into her mouth and chewing on a nail.

"You mean other than famous marathon runner?" He was trying to manufacture some spit in his mouth to quench his thirst.

222

She was stretching her legs out again, this time behind her as she sat on the grass, making a Z with her body. First one leg and then the other. She had to be double-jointed.

"Let's go," he said. He didn't want to tell her he was a broker. He didn't want to think about working. The day after a holiday was always a zoo. All his clients would be after him to make a killing. And what did it matter if pork bellies were up or down a few points? Right now, all he wanted to do was keep moving.

They ran back across the river at Charles Street. He was breathing in gasps again. He had a pain in his side. What were Janet and the kids doing now? He imagined them picnicking at Walden Pond, the four of them. And a man. There had to be another man.

"Want to stop?" Ellen said.

"No," he said. He tried to kick his feet behind him, but they were barely off the ground. This girl was in fantastic shape.

They passed the Mass General, where Kate had been for her operation. There was a water fountain by a fenced-in playground along the river. It didn't work. There was a wad of pink bubble gum in it.

"My mother was in there this summer," said Ellen, indicating the hospital with a flick of her head.

"Is that so?" he said. One foot in front of the other. Pounding. Pounding.

"I worried about her," she said. "She acts like she's a tough bird. Stiff lip and all. But my theory is that Chicken Little lives somewhere in each of us. Even my mom."

"Chicken Little?" he said.

"You know," she said. "Chicken Little. The sky is falling. Foxy Loxy. Turkey Lurkey. Henny Penny."

How could Ellen talk and run at the same time? He tried to think of sitting behind the wheel of his car. He couldn't.

His legs hurt; he was going to have shin splints. Why was he trying to impress this girl?

"Did you have much chance to talk with her?" Ellen said.

"Who?"

"Mom."

"No," he said. "I didn't." So she didn't know about him and her mother.

"How long have you been seeing Dad?" she said.

"Just twice," he said. That much was true. He had only met George two times. Once at the hospital when he'd found out Janet was in therapy with George. And the other time when George came to the house and told him to stay away from Kate. The night George wrecked his car. "What's he like?"

"Dad?" she said. "Mr. Nice Guy. That's Dad. One of the good guys. He and Mom adore each other."

The pain in his side was getting worse. It was spreading up to his rib cage. It was silly not to stop. But they had passed Berkeley Street now. Oh sure, George Cummings was a good guy. He'd only screwed up Charlie's entire life. Maybe kids never saw their parents the way they really were. They were passing the Esplanade. He had not been to one Pops concert all summer.

"Almost there," said Ellen. "I figure about five miles. Think so?"

"A hundred and five," he whispered.

"I heard you," she said.

They stopped. They had come full circle. Charlie lay face down on the grass and felt his temples throb.

"You all right?" Ellen said. He felt her cool hand on the back of his neck.

Right now, his father was probably lighting the charcoal for the barbecue. Charlie rolled over on his back. The sun gave Ellen a halo. "You want to come to a picnic with me?" he said. The family wouldn't bother him if he brought a girl home.

"Can't," she said. "Parents having people over. Have to be there."

"Why do you talk in shorthand?" he said. He was beginning to feel better now. The pain had gone away. They were walking to the car.

"Obnoxious, isn't it?" she said. "I guess I'm in a rush. There's just never enough time to do everything, is there?"

Everybody was in such a goddamn hurry. This girl. Even Charlie himself. Suddenly, he saw his car as she must see it and was ashamed of himself. She'd been in the woods all summer without even a bike taking care of teenagers and all he could do was worry about his precious car. He was off the track, his father would tell him, if he knew how Charlie had been living.

"Good run," Ellen said, when he stopped in front of her house. Kate's house. "Let's do it again." She patted him on the shoulder.

"Sure, sure," said Charlie.

"You want to come in for a cold drink?" she said. "You can see Dad now. He's here."

Oh, no. Nobody was going to get him to go into that house. "I've got to run," he said. "Well, not really run," he said, when she laughed at his choice of words. "My folks are expecting me."

She got out and jogged around the side of the house to the back door. The dog came out from the bushes and leaped up beside her. Charlie took one long look at George's Toyota in the driveway. Baby blue. What kind of man would buy a baby-blue car?

CHAPTER
· TWENTY ·

George adjusted the color on the TV in the living room. "It's time," he called out.

There was a slight glare on the screen from the west window. He closed the curtain across it, but not before looking outside and catching sight of the purple asters he had planted from flats last spring. Priests wore the same purple vestments during Lent. obviously unaware it was a fall color. Kate and Ellen were somewhere in the house. What did they care about the U.S. Open anyway? It was just going to be the greatest tennis match of all time. That was all. Jimmy Connors versus Ivan Lendl. American versus Czech. East versus West. Experience versus power. Sensational tennis.

George surveyed the room of worn yet comfortable furniture. Brown stuffing showed through the arms of his rose chair. It was a hand-me-down, like everything in the room, except for the TV. He couldn't remember where it all came from.

The paintings on the walls were Ellen's. There was one of blue flowers he particularly liked. In high school she'd decided to become an artist. Of course, all that changed in college when she opted for a literary career. And now she claimed her commitment was to inner-city kids. She had plans to edit a book of their wilderness journals. He had hoped she'd become a psychiatrist.

In the week he'd been home from Bayberry he'd taken it easy. He brought his plants in from the garden and repaired his greenhouse with new panes of glass. He enjoyed the smoothness of the putty in his hands, on his fingertips, as he fitted in each new pane. He still remembered the feel of the sharp edges of glass as they had fallen to the pebbled floor. There were only six panes broken, although in his mind he'd destroyed the entire structure. He thought about people in glass houses throwing stones; he ought to be able to draw some parallel for himself.

He'd spoken to all of his patients by phone and scheduled appointments for the coming week. At his office, he told them. Not at the tennis club. Most of them, it turned out, had hoped for the club. They liked it there. They liked watching him play. Well, he would have to see how it went, he said. He had missed them.

Pat Summerall and Brent Musburger were jabbering on about the big match. Neither of them was a tennis player. Summerall had been a place kicker in the National Football League. And Musburger. Who knew where he came from? The players were on the court now warming up. George resisted the urge to swing his arm with each stroke.

"Ladies. Ladies," he called again. "It's time." Where were they? Nothing could be more important than this match.

"Here we are, George," said Kate. She came in carrying a cut-glass bowl of whole strawberries and a small plate of confectioner's sugar.

Ellen brought a wooden board with cheese and crackers on it. "The cheese stands alone," she sang, kissing her father's forehead. "Who's playing?" she asked. George hadn't seen her since Labor Day when she'd moved back to her apartment in town.

"Connors and Lendl. Connors and Lendl. Terrific match. Look. There they are."

"Which one is Connors?" said Kate.

"Come on, you two. Let an old man have his fun," said George. They knew more about tennis than they were saying.

"Have a strawberry, Dad." Ellen popped one into his mouth.

The match was just beginning. It was a hot day at Flushing Meadow. Even a week after Labor Day the summer continued. Would it ever be over? Planes flew over the stadium. The tournament should never have been moved from Forest Hills. The strawberry was huge in his mouth. His tongue ran over its texture. Kate still hadn't apologized for her behavior with Charlie. She said she forgave George for hiring a detective, but never really acknowledged why he had done it in the first place. Of course, he should have handled himself better. He hadn't had to wreck Murdoch's car or hire Marabel Greenleaf. But you'd think Kate would admit her part and apologize just a little. He looked across the room at her where she sat next to Ellen on the lumpy couch. She rolled a strawberry in the powdered sugar and carefully placed it on her tongue. There had to be more on her mind than the taste of a strawberry.

"I'll bet you could take either one of them, Dad," said Ellen. "But my money's on Lendl."

It was unbelievable how hard the two men hit the ball. Connors went for the line on every shot. Even if George was five years old and just starting to play tennis, even if he worked at it for twenty years, he could never be that good.

"El's got a new boyfriend," said Kate.

"Not a boyfriend," said Ellen. "Just a friend."

"So far," said Kate.

"Come on," said Ellen.

"She won't say who it is," said Kate. "A mystery man."

Well, Kate should know about mystery men. "Look at that shot," he said. It would be nice if El found a young man. George had never liked the idea of her living alone in that apartment in the Back Bay. A beer commercial blared. No one ever seemed to object to the combination of athletics and Lite beer. "I'll bet Jimmy Connors isn't a beer drinker," he said.

"Did you tell Gram everything when you were my age?" asked Ellen.

"Oh, sure," said Kate. "Right, George?"

Were they watching the match at all? A lethargic Lendl was losing the first set badly. "When we were Ellen's age," he said to Kate, "we were married." He was going to say they had been newlyweds, but the word no longer appealed to him.

"Nobody gets married so young anymore, Dad," Ellen said.

"How about you and your new friend?" said Kate. "How old is he?"

"Enough, Mom. OK?" said Ellen. Kate was never able to see in what ways she was like her own mother.

The first set was over. Connors had won it with ease, six games to three. Lendl actually seemed depressed. Millions of people were watching; he made more money on the pro tour than anyone else; he had nothing to be depressed about. The beer commercial came on again.

"I'll get some drinks," said Kate. "Iced tea?"

"Spring water," said George. "No ice." Kate was as energetic as she'd been before her surgery. And maybe even more attractive. When she spoke, her eyes grew large and

dominated her face until that's all you thought there was—
just those green, green eyes with the long dark lashes. He
could never figure out how she did it. It only happened
when she talked, not when she listened.

"Iced tea is fine," said Ellen.

The second set was starting. "It's more fun when it's
close," George said, as Kate left the room.

"Dad," said Ellen in a low voice. "The man I've been
seeing . . ."

"The mystery man?" he said. "What a smash." Connors
had leapt up for a fantastic shot. "Did you see that?"

But Ellen was looking right at him. She had moved up
on the edge of the sofa. "He's a patient of yours," she
said.

"A patient?" he said. Kate was rattling ice cubes in the
kitchen. If she put ice cubes in his bottled water, it would
defeat the whole purpose.

"Met him here last weekend. Labor Day," she said.

"Uh-huh," he said.

"Just friends. Jogging partners. That's all. No big deal,"
she said. "Nice guy. Just thought you should know."

"Who is it?" he said. This match was terrific. Lendl had
finally come alive. He turned to Ellen. "Tell me the truth,"
he said. "Why didn't you ever want to learn to play tennis?"

"Charlie Murdoch," she said.

He couldn't have heard her right. "Who?" he said.

"You've only seen him twice," she said. "Big, tall guy.
Thirty or so. Red hair. Wife left him. Three kids. Nice guy.
Charlie Murdoch. Remember him now?"

George sank deep into the pink chair. Kate came in with
the drinks on a tray. She had put ice cubes in his water.
A fat old football coach was drinking a mug of beer on
the television. George stood up, walked to the window,

and pulled back the curtain. The purple asters were tall in the late afternoon sun.

"Goddamn it, Kate," he said. "What the hell good is it to have ice cubes from the tap in spring water?" He picked up the glass and squeezed it and then set it down on the tray, the water spilling over the sides in a tidal wave. Brent Musburger announced the match was dead even in the second set.

Ellen's mouth opened. She looked from one parent to the other. "It's only a glass of water, Dad."

"Not exactly," he said, glaring at Kate. He would kill her. He would stuff her mouth full of those damn strawberries until her cheeks burst, until her whole body turned red, until she became so fat and so red people would laugh at her. No one would want a fat red liar around. What was she cooking up this time? Had she actually decided to give Murdoch to her own daughter?

"I'll get you some more water," Kate said. "No problem. Sit down. Relax. No ice this time."

"Are you OK, Dad?" said Ellen. "You're not mad at me for seeing your patient, are you?"

"Everything's fine, honey," he said. He started to go to the kitchen where he and Kate could have this out once and for all. But she was back with a fresh glass of water already.

"Here you go," she said. "Can I at least put a strawberry in it?"

Oh, she was so cute, wasn't she? That was her trouble. She had always been so damned cute. "Ellen was worried," George said.

"Worried?" said Kate. "What about?"

"I never said I was worried," said Ellen.

"She was worried," George said, "that I'd be angry."

"Angry?" said Kate. She put her glass of iced tea down on his latest issue of the *National Geographic* and began

232

to listen carefully. Sometimes her lips moved when he talked.

"Must you always make rings on my magazines?" he said. "You never make rings on your own damn magazines."

"What were you saying about Ellen?" said Kate. She did not move her drink. She sat down and put her arm around her daughter.

"Don't talk about me like I'm not here," said Ellen.

"Ellen was worried I'd be angry that her new friend is one of my patients," said George.

"What do you mean?" said Kate.

"A patient. A patient." George was going to keep control of himself. He was. He sipped his water. "El's friend told her he was one of my patients."

"He is, isn't he?" said Ellen. "That's what Gram said."

"Oh, your grandmother was here, too, was she?" he said. Applause from the TV filled the room.

Kate was getting impatient. "Well, are you worried or not?" she said to both of them.

"Of course, I'm worried," said George. "The patient is Charlie Murdoch."

Kate dropped the piece of cheese she was about to eat. She tightened her grip on Ellen's shoulders.

"What's wrong, Dad?" said Ellen. "He's a nice guy. We've gone jogging together every day this week. He doesn't seem weird or anything. Not to me anyway. Actually, I was thinking of helping him out with his kids. They're darlings."

"You've met his children?" said Kate.

"The man," said George, "is a homicidal maniac."

"I can't believe it," said Ellen. "He seems so normal. Gram even thought he was an old friend of mine from high school at first. Right, Mom?"

"Oh," said George. "You were there, too?" He looked at Kate, but her eyes were on the piece of cheese on the

233

floor by her feet. "Where the hell was I?"

"Playing tennis, Dad," said Ellen.

He had actually forgotten all about tennis. He began to hear the TV commentary in the background. Lendl had won the second set in a tie breaker and was leading in the third.

Kate moved the piece of cheese closer to her with her foot, picked it up, and put it on a napkin. "What happened, George," she said in her teacherly voice, "was that Mr. Martin came looking for you."

"Murdoch. Murdoch's his name," said George. "Get his goddamn name right."

"Yes," she said. "Murdoch. Anyway, he came to see you. It was some sort of emergency, he said. You were playing tennis. I told him he could wait for you. He decided not to. And he left. That's it." Did she think she could wash it all over by talking to him as if he were one of her students?

"I was just going for a run," said Ellen. "He came with me. He's a pretty good runner, but out of shape. Nice guy. I'm telling you he's a nice guy."

Imagine. Murdoch had the nerve to come to George's own house. The guy was incredible. "Sweetheart," George said to Ellen, "I know you want to believe the best about everybody. I know that. But the truth is that this fellow Murdoch is a psychopath. Oh, he's a charmer. I'll grant you that. But the man is dangerous. I wouldn't say so if it weren't true."

"I just spent the morning with him," Ellen said. "Running. And breakfast."

"Listen to your father," said Kate. "He knows what he's talking about. Has he ever lied to you?"

Oh. So Kate didn't like this any better than he did. She was even eating the cheese that had been on the floor. She was upset, too. Was it because she'd finally seen through

Murdoch? Or because she didn't want to lose her precious boyfriend to her own daughter? He glanced over at the TV. He had completely lost track of the tennis match, the greatest match of all time. There was no action on the court. Maybe it was all over. It was supposed to be three out of five sets. Kate was still talking to Ellen. Pat Summerall was explaining the delay in the tennis. Connors had a case of diarrhea and had to leave the court. The officials were allowing him only one interruption.

"Look, you two," said Ellen. "Don't get so excited. It'll be all right. Besides, if he's so dangerous, how come he's got his kids with him?"

"That's one of the issues," said George. "The state's trying to get custody. It's a very complicated case. I shouldn't even be discussing it. You know that. Promise me you won't see him again."

"I can't promise," Ellen said. "I feel sorry for him. His wife's gone. Left him with three little kids. He needs help."

"Please, El," said Kate. How could she have let that creep into the house with her own daughter there? And her own mother? No wonder Mary Logan had been so nice to him lately. She was no dummy.

"What would you have done, Mom, if Gram had told you whom you could see and not see?" said Ellen.

"This is different," said George. "This guy is a mental patient. He's dangerous. Furthermore, it's totally out of line for a patient to date the therapist's daughter."

"Not date," said Ellen. "Just run together. No big dates. Nothing like that. Next you'll have us married. Honestly."

Kate opened her mouth to say something, but George was going to make his point. "Ellen," he said. "Dear, there are more than a million people in this city you can befriend. You can even run with several thousand of them, I'll bet. Why complicate your life and my life and Mr. Murdoch's

235

life by seeing him?" Again, there was applause from the television.

"The man needs a friend," Ellen said. "Now let's watch the tennis. Who's winning? How much did I bet?"

And that was that. Ellen would make up her own mind. "I'm glad you mentioned it to me," George said, "that you'd met Murdoch."

"Well, I'm not," said Ellen. "However," she went on, throwing a berry at him across the room, "I forgive you for loving me too much. You too, Mom." She blew Kate a kiss, as she moved away from her on the couch. "Actually," she said, "Charlie's too old for me."

Kate sat on the edge of her seat, her mouth still open. For the first time all afternoon, her eyes were focused on the television.

The tennis match was in the fourth set. Lendl was ahead in the third when Connors left to go to the bathroom. Imagine having diarrhea on national TV. Apparently, it hadn't bothered him. He came back onto the court and won the set.

Kate was talking about dinner. Trout almondine. Acorn squash. What did he care about dinner? For her, any occasion was reason enough for a special meal.

"I guess Connors is going to win, Dad," said Ellen. "What do I owe you?"

In fact, Lendl had all but thrown in the towel. This last set was a rout. It was interesting: Some people just gave up. George stretched his legs out and went to the window again. The dog was chasing bees. Well, he supposed he could have another talk with Murdoch. His patient. His homicidal patient.

CHAPTER

·TWENTY-ONE·

Kate and Rhoda entered the jewelry shop arm in arm. The dim light inside was soothing compared to the glare of plate-glass windows along Newbury Street. By coincidence, they wore identical yellow sundresses. They were of one mind about many things, they'd discovered.

"How may I help you?" said the young shopgirl. She was alone and had to unlock the door to let them in. She turned the key after them, explaining there had been a rash of robberies on their block recently.

"You can never be too careful," Rhoda said. She was no longer using her cane.

Kate was attracted by the glimmer of gold and silver in the elegant display cases and remembered Charlie's earrings in her purse. She was going to return them. Rhoda had returned her wedding ring here and had gotten more back than she'd paid for it. Not that Kate was out to make a profit. She'd decided to exchange the tiny gold kites for something else, something she chose herself. She'd considered mailing Charlie's hospital gift back to him—or even sending the earrings to his wife. But she'd reconsidered. Why shouldn't she do something nice for herself? Besides, she certainly was in no mood to do anything nice for Charlie. She had phoned him. She had told him never to see Ellen again. He had asked her why. He had said she was getting bent out of shape for no reason. Why was she so excited? And when were the two of them—Kate and Charlie—going to get together? He claimed he had no designs on her daughter. He had told Ellen she could save on rent if she moved in with him and took care of his kids. That was all. But unfortunately, he said, she had refused.

"He'll use anybody to get what he wants," Kate told Rhoda. But in spite of herself, she felt Charlie's presence in this shop. He had been here while she lay moaning at the Mass General, probably where she was standing right now. He had chosen an exquisite gift for her.

"And I thought he was such a sweetheart," said Rhoda.

"A nice guy. That's what Ellen called him," Kate said. She opened her bag. "I'm returning these," she said, plunking the earrings out on the glass counter.

The girl jumped. She was so thin she seemed almost anorectic. "Sorry," she said. "It's just that the last person who opened her purse like that pulled out a gun."

"A robbery?" said Rhoda. "Here?"

"She made me lie on the floor," the girl said.

"She?" said Kate.

"She took only the gold," said the girl.

"What you need," said Rhoda, "is a metal detector at the doorway."

"What I need," said the girl, "is another job. My mother thinks I should work in a bank."

"How safe can that be?" asked Kate.

"What's safe?" said the girl. "My boyfriend went hang gliding last weekend and broke his leg. My sister slipped in the bathroom and broke both arms."

"You can't be too careful," repeated Rhoda.

Kate looked at the handmade pieces: unusual shapes of silver and gold formed into earrings, pins, rings, bracelets. She might have saved the earrings, put them in the box with her baby teeth, looked at them once a year when she cleaned out her bureau. But what good was that? This exchange might not even be the right thing to do, but it was a reasonable compromise. She chose a hammered-gold necklace of nickel-sized circles to exchange for her kites.

"The free spirit chooses connections," said Rhoda.

"Have you ever considered psychiatry as a profession?" said Kate. She ran her fingers over the black velvet cushion on which her necklace lay.

"Not until just now," said Rhoda.

"I don't get it," said the salesgirl.

"That's OK," said Kate. "Neither do I." The velvet was like the fur behind Clancy's ears.

There was some money left over; the salesgirl wrote out a credit slip for Kate in calligraphy. Rhoda had admired an unusual amethyst set into a silver pin. Kate would come back for it later.

The truth was they had only been killing time until the appointment with Doctor Parks. Kate was sure she had another malignancy. For two mornings now, she had felt a lump in her breast. Ever since the Greenleaf encounter, she'd had terrible dreams—that she had lumps all over her body. She dreamed her mother was chastising her for wearing the wrong shoes. Brown instead of black. Or she was lost in a crowd, looking for George who was always walking away from her. She woke in a panic, feeling herself for malignancies. George was gone; he was sleeping in another room. He had to get his life back in order, he said. He was sick of her antics with Murdoch. She felt her legs.

Nothing unusual. Her shoulders. Her neck. But one morning, on her way to the bathroom, she felt the small lump in her left breast. She decided to ignore it.

She spent that day—yesterday—at her office working on materials for the fall semester. On the way home, her hand moved to the breast. No lump. She had imagined it. She knew people recovering from surgery often thought they had other ailments during the postoperative period.

When the lumps grew in her dream that night, she was frightened. Her mother pointed a long finger at her, again telling her she'd worn the wrong shoes. It was the most important thing in the world to wear the correct shoes. Kate could see that. Then why did she wear brown instead of black? What was wrong with her? Why didn't she think clearly? Her mother came closer. The finger grew as long as Sister Perpetua's pointer in the first grade. Kate felt her body growing in disturbing ways. Bubbles popped up from the skin on her arms and legs like huge blisters, the skin getting tighter, tighter, more taut, until it burst and the flesh inside spattered everywhere. People walked away from her, and all she could see was their backs. She woke several times in the night, only to repeat the dream when she went back to sleep.

At daylight, when she again felt the lump in her left breast, she called Rhoda. George was already in his office seeing patients. Besides, she didn't want to ask him to feel her breast. Not after all that had happened. He'd probably tell her she deserved to have cancer. Maybe he was right. She made the appointment with Dr. Parks and met Rhoda at the jeweler's.

The walls of the doctor's waiting room were a light green.

"Peaceful," said Rhoda, pointing to them.

"I feel like Grandma," Kate said. The other patients were young mothers-to-be, their large bellies proclaiming their reason for being here.

Rhoda took Kate's hand and gave it a pat. "The waiting is the worst part," she said. "Not knowing."

Yes, Kate thought, she would definitely go back to Newbury Street after this and buy Rhoda that pin.

In the examining room she put on the paper gown. She wondered if George, or Charlie, or even Dr. Parks had ever sat on the edge of an examining table in a paper gown. She dangled her feet over the edge of the table. Would she have breast implants like Rhoda's? Kate imagined cells in her breast dancing around at this very moment, like Rumpelstiltskin when they hadn't been able to guess his name. Like the Satan described so vividly by the nuns after you committed even the tiniest venial sin.

When the doctor came in, he examined her carefully. The incision from the hysterectomy was healing nicely, he told her. But what had she been doing to widen it so much? He was used to better scars than that. Did she want to blemish his record?

Her feet were cold. They were probably turning blue. The mobile over the table moved in slow motion. Frogs. Dr. Parks had had the same frog mobile over his examining table for years.

She would know when the scar turned white that she was fully recovered, Dr. Parks told her. It would take about a year.

She wondered what Rhoda was doing in the waiting room. Maybe she was thinking about her various surgeries. No. Rhoda looked forward, not backward.

Kate could resume her marital relations, Dr. Parks was saying.

"Oh, great," she said. She looked the doctor straight in

the eyes through his rimless glasses. He had dandruff in his bushy eyebrows.

"Now," he said. "What's this about a lump in your breast?" He opened the front of her hospital gown and felt the wrong breast.

Why had he made her wait so long? Why had he looked at the incision? Talked about marital relations? Worried about the artistry of his scar? She should have made him check her breasts first.

"Everything fine here," he said.

"Wrong breast," she said. She was not going to cry.

He began palpating the left breast. She already thought of it as *the* breast, rather than *her* breast. His fingers were warm and sensitive. They knew what they were seeking. He looked at the wall, as if he were listening for a burglar.

"Exhale," he said.

She hadn't realized she'd been holding her breath. The grip of fear squeezed the tears down her cheeks until they were dripping into her ears.

"I don't feel anything unusual," he said. "No growths. Seems fine." He made no comment about her tears.

"But I felt something," she said.

"Show me," he said.

She sat up on the examining table and felt her breast, as she had done that morning, looking at the wall, as Dr. Parks had done. "Gone," she said. Her nose was running. He handed her a tissue.

"You ever had a car accident?" he said.

She nodded.

"You know how for a time afterward, whenever you drive, you still expect disaster?" he said.

"Yes," she said. She understood exactly what he meant.

"Recovery is more than just a white scar," he said, looking at his watch.

Just when she was about to compliment him on being

human, he looked at his watch. He was behind schedule. The expectant mothers were waiting.

"I can arrange a mammogram for you, if you'd like," he said. "But I feel certain you have nothing to worry about."

Kate looked at her arms and legs where the blisters had mushroomed for two nights. She was all right? She was really all right? Dr. Parks was writing something on her chart. "I'm OK then?" She didn't recognize the weakness in the voice she heard, her own voice.

"Perfect," he said. He shook her hand with both of his. "See you next year."

At home that night, she sat at the kitchen table waiting for George. It was dark now. The sun was setting earlier, and the evenings were slightly cooler. George had resumed his practice with apparent ease. For two days anyway, he had seen his usual schedule of patients in his office. When he was through for the day, he took off for his tennis club.

She was making her list: Things she could do for George. For their marriage. Creamed mussel soup was simmering on the stove. The asparagus was washed and ready for cooking. Plants. She should pay more attention to his greenhouse. She hadn't even known the windows were broken. Maybe they should entertain more. Be more social. The list grew.

George was late. She was hungry. Her hand moved to her breast. Through her cotton blouse she searched for the invaders. Nothing. The phone rang. Her mother. Kate looked at her shoes, waiting for her mother to tell her they were wrong. As if her mother could see through the telephone. As if she even knew about the dream.

"George came by on his way to play tennis," her mother said.

"Oh?" said Kate. After that day in the kitchen when

Charlie was there, her mother had said nothing more on the subject. She had yelled louder than Kate had thought possible. What a mess Kate had made of her life. How it had all begun when she left the Church. That it wasn't too late. God was forgiving. How every day for thirty years she had got down on her knees and prayed that Kate would come to her senses and see that a life without God was not a life at all. Lately she had missed no opportunity to point out how wonderful George was, how attentive, how considerate, what a good father, what a good provider.

"Your father has some aphids on his roses," her mother was saying. "George came over to take a look."

"He's such a perfect son-in-law," said Kate.

"Kate!" her mother said. "Honestly."

"Just kidding, Mother," she said.

"You don't know how lucky you are," her mother went on. It was becoming a litany.

Kate stirred the mussel soup. Maybe she ought to take it off the stove. "Listen, Mother, I have some good news for you."

"You went to the Church," her mother said. "You made your confession." She never gave up.

"Not exactly, Mother."

"Well, what is it? I can hardly wait."

She wanted to tell her mother she didn't have breast cancer. She wanted to say the affair with Charlie was over. "I'm letting my ears grow back," she said.

"What?" said her mother.

"My ear lobes. My pierced ear lobes. I decided you were right." Kate thought about the necklace of gold links in its cottony box on top of her bureau upstairs and remembered what Rhoda had said about connectedness.

"Tell me I'm dreaming," her mother said. "After forty-five years, you finally tell me I've been right. A true moment of glory."

After they hung up, Kate took the soup off the stove and went back to her list. It was a silly list. She would never be a tennis player or a botanist. She could only be herself, her sassy, reckless, independent, irreverent self. In fact, this whole list-making idea presupposed she had more control over things than she actually did. Sure, you could make a grocery list or plan a course outline. But suppose people didn't feel like eating when you planned a meal? Or what if you missed a teaching day for some reason? It threw your whole schedule off. There was no way to control time. Once a distributor had sent two thousand live frogs instead of two hundred fetal pigs. She had lost half a semester trying to straighten out the error.

She put the soup in the refrigerator. George always said she should go ahead and eat without him, but she knew he hated to eat alone. Besides, it was part of her own pleasure in cooking that they taste the food she prepared at the same time. She could go to the tennis club now and watch George play. He would like that. She could finally see the top-spin shots he had mastered this summer. But it was too late. Their cars would probably pass in different directions. Things could never be the same between them, he'd told her after he'd found out Ellen had been seeing Charlie. Maybe he would even want to divorce her after all.

She went to the living room and put on a tape of The Platters' hits. "Twilight Time" was the first selection on the album. She turned the volume up as high as it would go and walked slowly, purposefully to George's office. She began with the top left drawer. If he had seen a lawyer, the evidence would be in here somewhere. Nothing. The second drawer. Unpaid patient bills. "The Great Pretender" resounded through the house so loudly that the dog howled from her post by the back door. The third drawer held George's stationery. She pulled out a sheet and tried to imagine living somewhere besides this house. She slid the sheet back into the drawer and closed it. On the right side of the desk, the top drawer contained notes on yellow tablets for lectures at the medical school or for papers in the idea stages. Nothing about divorce. A file drawer held records of his patients. George never took notes during therapy sessions. He had trained his memory. A colleague of George's at the hospital knit while her patients catalogued their problems. There was often discussion about her clicking needles at staff parties. The Platters were singing "I'm Sorry."

Kate opened the middle drawer. George's checkbook. A pamphlet on growing artichokes. Samples of psychoactive medications in small packets. Letters and postcards from his patients and medical students on their vacations. Single staples loose from their container. The same leaky Sheaffer fountain pen he had used since college. As she was just about to close the drawer she found their old high-school-prom photograph. A black-and-white picture. She couldn't remember the color of her dress. "Only You" boomed from the stereo. The photograph had been torn in two and scotch-taped back together. She looked at the doorway, expecting to see George, but no one was there. Maybe her dress had been blue.

"The Magic Touch" reached her even upstairs. Mercifully, it was the last song on the tape. If George was going to divorce her, she would find out soon enough. There was no point in looking through his bureau. She picked up the box with the new necklace from the top of her own dresser. It had been foolish to make the exchange. She would never wear the necklace. She opened the box and was again drawn by the delicate gold links. She held the piece around her neck, her arms raised, elbows parallel with her ears, and looked in the mirror. The phone rang. She put the necklace in its box and went across the room to pick up the receiver. No one was there. "Hello," she said. "Hello."

Well, she could try it or just this once, she thought, fastening the necklace on herself before the mirror. The gold circles rested gracefully on her collarbones as if sculpted just for her. If she ever decided to wear it, she would need a dress with a low neckline. A green dress. In her closet she found a pair of jade slacks which were just the right color; she draped them around her shoulders. The phone rang again. Only once this time. She felt for the tiny holes in her earlobes, which were probably growing smaller at this very minute.

CHAPTER

· TWENTY-TWO ·

The first day Charlie was late at the day-care center they charged him thirty bucks. A dollar a minute. The center, in the basement of the Lutheran church, had been a great find. The women in charge knew what they were doing. Janie loved being there and even agreed to leave her blanket at home. The only thing was that he had to pick her up before five. They charged you a dollar a minute after five o'clock. It was a problem. How could working people possibly get there in time? But that was the rule, and after that first day, he toed the mark. Somebody should open a chain of child-care centers with reasonable hours and fees. It was costing him more than a hundred a week for Janie.

He had looked for a housekeeper and had interviewed several women. The only one who seemed to like kids had three little ones of her own she would have to bring along with her. The other applicants came with their own demands, as if they were paying him. One said she couldn't care for a child in diapers. Another wanted to make sure he had a color TV. A third said she did only light housework. What the hell was that? It was going to be harder than he had thought to find someone.

Meanwhile, he had Louella, the neighborhood kid with braces, to meet the boys at home after school. She was reliable enough, and Jim and Mike liked her, although they teased her about her headgear. Louella had even agreed to pick Janie up at the church and bring her home in a taxi. But the day-care ladies wouldn't release her into the custody of a minor.

Well, Janie was asleep upstairs now. And the boys had just come down in their pajamas. He'd promised them a card game even though it was a school night and past their bedtime. He hated to be the only one awake in the house, he thought, as he sat cross-legged on the family-room carpet. A thin layer of dust covered all the tabletops and was impossible to avoid from this angle. He shuffled his cards. They had pictures of striped bass on them.

"What are we going to play, Dad?" asked Jim. "War?"

"Too violent," said Mike in his mother's tone of voice. "I vote for slapjack."

"I know," said Jim. "I doubt it. That's the best."

The layer of dust seemed to grow as Charlie sat there with his knees jutting out. The boys' pajamas had orange polka dots on the white cotton. When Janet bought them she'd said they would ward off the chicken pox.

Mike shuffled his cards carefully. He was not as adept as his brother. The kids liked games where they each had a full deck. Charlie leaned back against the sofa and ran his hands through the thick brown shag carpet. Another dust collector. "How about spit?" he said.

"Yay!" said both kids at once. Children were so easy to please. Not like wives. Or women. Or mothers.

The three of them arranged their four rows of cards and were ready to begin. "OK, you guys," said Charlie. "Win, lose, or draw, this is the last game of the night."

"Ready," said Jim.

"On your mark," said Mike.

"Get set," Charlie said.

"Go," they all yelled at once.

"Spit!" said Mike, as each turned up a card in the center of his triangle.

Charlie remembered the card games he used to play with his brother and sister. He was thinking again about how often he had excluded Lois. He would have to make sure the boys were nicer to Janie than he'd been to his own sister. Lois had been especially thoughtful since he and Janet had separated, dropping meals off and calling to see if he was OK, even though she had three small children of her own and a full-time job. He didn't know how she managed it all.

"Put your four on the five, Dad," said Jim. "Come on. You're slowing us down."

"How could I be so dumb?" said Charlie.

"It's OK, Dad," said Mike, giving his brother a knowing look. There was nothing quite like feeling superior to your own father.

"Spit," said Jim.

"Spit," said Charlie. This was one of the few card games he and Kate had never played. Damn. He hadn't wanted things to end with her. When he saw her that day on the beach at Nantucket, that day he had practically drowned, he knew she had already put him out of her mind. She had rescued him; she'd taken him to look for that silly bird; but she was annoyed with him for coming. And now she was really mad at him. She had screamed at him over the telephone. She was right about his seeing Ellen. He had been too lonely to see it.

"Your queen, Dad, your queen," said Mike.

"The queen on the jack," said Jim.

"Sorry," said Charlie.

"Pay attention," said Mike.

"Yeah," said Jim. "Watch what you're doing."

They were terrific kids. Janet had done a great job. They had patiently helped him into the school routine, explaining about the importance of exact change for milk money and clean gym shorts. Most of the kids at school were divorced, they told him. And none of them was any more weird than any other kid. So he shouldn't worry. They were getting divorced, weren't they?

Divorced. Divorced. He didn't know. All he could do was wait and see what happened next.

"Out. I'm out," said Mike.

"Me too," said Jim.

"I was first," Mike said.

"It was a tie," Jim insisted.

"I was last," said Charlie, showing the boys the piles of cards still in front of him.

"Oh, Dad," Mike said.

Charlie's own father had never let him win. It dulled your competitive edge, he said, not to go all out. Well, Charlie didn't need to win everything. Only when it came to dollars and cents. That's when it really counted.

"Chalk up another one for me," said Mike.

"And me," said Jim.

"Hey, Dad," Mike said. "How many cards you got left?"

Charlie made a great to-do about counting them out. "Sixteen, seventeen, twenty-two," he said.

"You need practice, Dad," Jim said.

"Yeah, practice makes perfect," said Mike.

"Are you guys picking on me?" said Charlie, getting to his feet.

"One more game?" said Mike.

"Upstairs you go, you two," said Charlie. They always went for the extra inch.

He read them a short chapter from *Charlie and the Chocolate Factory*. It had been their favorite during the last year. This was the third time they'd been through it Once when he'd tried to skip a part, they'd caught him and made him start over.

Downstairs, back in the family room, he turned on the TV and dumped himself into the brown tweed sofa. He picked up the *The Globe*. Some laid-off firemen in the city had been indicted for arson. There was more of the ongoing debate about whether or not to require fingerprinting of all children. At Disney World, they were making preparations for Donald Duck's fiftieth birthday. On TV there was an ad for Maxi pads. The dust on the glass-topped coffee table invited him to write his name in it. He did. Next to it, he printed J-A-N-E-T. He couldn't stand the dust another minute.

In the kitchen closet he found what he needed: an old T-shirt, now a dust rag, and a bottle of Windex. The blue liquid was the same color as Aqua Velva, the first present Janet had ever given him. He sprayed it on the glass tabletop before he realized he needed paper towels rather than cloth to clean the surface. After his second application and the sound of the squeaking towel on the glass, he knew it was clean. He was wondering what would have happened if he'd used Aqua Velva on the table when Ellen called.

"Run at the usual time tomorrow?" she said. She had a habit of neither saying hello nor identifying herself.

On the TV a man and a woman were climbing into bed together. He turned it off. He and Ellen had been meeting by the river at noon this week. He could no longer run early in the morning because of getting the kids off to school and Janie to day care.

"I'm supposed to take a client to lunch," he said.

253

"So have a late lunch."

The wet paper towel felt like an old diaper in his hand. "I don't know," he said. "I'll need time to shower and change."

"No discussion," she said. "We've got to get you back in shape. Only six months till the marathon, you know. We'll start early. See you at eleven forty-five."

He let himself be convinced. He had become her project, like one of her wayward teenagers. "You win," he said. "Quarter of twelve at the B.U. bridge." Maybe this year would be his best marathon.

He began dusting the other surfaces in the room. He turned on the TV again. A commercial for a laxative. He Windexed the screen. It would be OK to run with Kate's daughter. They hardly even spoke to each other. He found a can of Pledge in the closet when he got the vacuum cleaner out. Just what he needed. He sprayed the tops of the end tables and bookcases. The heavy scent of artificial lemon hung in the room. The cloth got wet and dirty. The surfaces were beginning to shine. Just as he plugged in the vacuum cleaner, the phone rang again. Ten o'clock. It would be his mother.

"Hi, Mom," he said.

"Hello? Is this Mr. Dustin Hoffman Kramer versus Kramer?" Every night she said the same thing.

"You interrupted my vacuuming," he said. She'd get a kick out of that.

"Everything all right?" she said.

"Couldn't be better."

"Any new housekeeper leads?"

"Not yet," he said.

"The children have a good day?"

"Fine," he said. Now she would ask about the day-care center. It was getting to be a comfortable dialogue.

"Is Janie OK at that place?"

"She loves it, Mom. Really."

"And how's the market?"

His mother knew nothing about the stock market. The folks had never had enough money to think about investing. "Up and down, Mom," he said.

"Well, all right, dear," she said. "I was just checking on you."

"When do I get to check on you?" he said.

She laughed. "One of these days," she said.

They hung up. He turned on the vacuum cleaner. It drowned out the TV noise and made the picture snowy. Shag carpeting was a real problem to keep clean. Janet had told him that, but he had insisted. Small objects clattered their way into the machine. Plastic soldiers. Safety pins. You had to be careful they didn't get stuck and break the fan belt or burn out the engine. Back and forth. Back and forth. The motion and the hum of the motor didn't allow him to think of anything except the task at hand. It was like mowing the lawn indoors. He moved the furniture out from the walls, picking up toys and coins before vacuuming. He took off his shirt.

When he had finished, he stood in the doorway and admired his efforts. It was good to have things in order. Of course, he might have done the windows, too. But it was stupid to do windows when the sun wasn't out. The TV weather report was on now. Rain tomorrow. Ellen would expect him to run even in the rain.

He put another load of laundry in the washer. How could only three kids get so many clothes dirty in only one day? The clothes from the dryer were still warm as he folded them in piles on the kitchen table. Maybe he could get Louella to do the laundry. He would pay her extra. Maybe he should talk to her mother first. It would be terrible to lose Louella. She was the neighborhood prize.

He stood in front of the open refrigerator. Maybe he was hungry. Maybe an egg and tomato sandwich would make him feel better. He had the eggs frying in a matter of seconds in the cast-iron pan Janet complained was too heavy. He put slices of raisin bread in the toaster and went back to the refrigerator for the tomatoes. The vegetable bin was a mess—full of squishy, rotting cucumbers, heads of lettuce, and black tomatoes. The toast popped up. He turned off the stove and arranged his snack on a dinner plate, breaking the yolks with his fork. He would have to clean out the refrigerator.

At midnight, he phoned Janet. "Listen," he said, "I know you're asleep."

"No, I'm not," she said.

"But," he continued, "I have to talk to you." The back of the kitchen chair was sticking to his sweating shoulders.

"Yes?" she said. "What's up?"

"Can you come over?" he said.

"Now?"

"Yes," he said. "Right now."

"Are the kids OK?" she said.

"Yes," he said. "Everyone's fine."

"How about tomorrow then?" she said. "Do you know what time it is now?"

"It's important, Janet."

There was no response.

"Everyone's fine," he said. "You're fine. The kids are fine. The market's fine. But I'm lousy. I've got the washer on and the dryer and the TV." He had poured himself a beer before he'd dialed her number. The foam had disappeared now. If he talked any longer the beer would be warm. It was funny how quickly beer got lukewarm.

"Charlie," Janet was saying. She was telling him she had to be at work at seven tomorrow. She said there would be other times they could talk, that it didn't have to be now.

He could take a swig of beer right now and it would taste so good. It would be the best thing he'd ever tasted. But he'd probably burp right in Janet's ear. Then she'd never come back to him. "You should see what happened in the refrigerator," he said.

"I can just imagine."

Had he really phoned her to tell her about carrots with no backbones? "I'm going to sell the Mercedes," he said. Did he mean it? Had he actually said that? He did mean it, he told her. He had had bad luck ever since he got the car.

She'd be right over, she said. He should just stay right where he was. Where was he? In the kitchen? He should just sit down and wait for her.

And where else could he go, for Christ's sake? He drank the whole glass of beer in one gulp and waited for the burp.

He was still sitting at the kitchen table when she arrived. She wore a denim skirt and a green turtleneck jersey. She had taken time to brush her hair. Each strand was in the right place.

"Hi," he said.

She put her keys and wallet on the table next to the black tomatoes and stood with her hands on her hips. "What am I going to do with you, Charlie?"

"Marry me?" he said. He heard the washer downstairs move into its final spin cycle.

"Oh, Charlie," she said, picking up the vegetables one by one and putting them into the garbage disposal.

257

"Not the celery," he yelled over the noise. "The celery gets caught. Too stringy."

She turned the disposal off. "Not this celery," she said. "This stuff is mush. How can you stand it?" She went to the refrigerator and began taking everything out: pickles, eggs, cheese, two grapefruits. "Disgusting," she said. She began opening the cupboards. The washer clunked to a stop. They'd bought it after Jimmy was born.

"I'm getting rid of the car," he said. She was investigating an open box of pancake mix. He ought to put the clothes into the dryer.

"It's almost one o'clock in the morning," she said. "What am I doing here?" She sat down at the table and finally looked straight at him.

He got up as if they were on a seesaw. "And I'm throwing this out, too," he said. He picked up the cast-iron frying pan and dumped it into the plastic wastebasket, which toppled over. "And this." He pointed at the food processor she'd thought was such a waste of money.

She was standing beside him at the counter by the sink. His egg plate sat there with a few raisins on it. Her head barely reached his shoulder. She took his elbow. "Come on and sit down," she said. "How about a round-table discussion?" She laughed. She actually laughed.

Maybe when this whole thing was over—if it ever was—he'd buy a round table. It couldn't be that your wife would leave you because of the shape of the kitchen table, could it? "Janet," he said. "We can work it out." She was still holding his arm. "I know we can work it out."

She moved to the other side of the table. She was silent.

"Is there another man?" he said, holding his breath. Should he tell her about Kate? Did it matter now? His wrist stuck to some jam left on the table from a previous meal.

258

No, she told him. There was no one else. It was just that she didn't think marriage was conducive to women's mental health. "Look at me," she said. "I had a career. I kept my maiden name. And still I felt trapped."

"I love you." His leg hit hers accidentally under the table. "Excuse me," he said.

She was hungry, she told him. Maybe they could order a pizza. She went to the phone.

"We can do anything," he said.

She ordered a large pizza with everything on it. Maybe, she said, he would like to see her apartment.

Oh, sure, he said. He'd love to see it. But wouldn't she rather be here, at home, with him and the kids? And had she noticed how much they'd grown already this fall?

She missed them, she acknowledged. All of them. But she had to have a place that was her own, where all the noises and silences were hers.

His nose was running. He wiped it with the back of his hand, the one with the jelly on it. He had no idea what she was talking about. How could you own silence? Maybe he could build another room onto the house, he said. Her room.

"It wouldn't be the same," she said.

"I guess I'll put the laundry in the dryer," he said. "Last load."

Before he could move, she got up and stood by his chair and rested her hand on his shoulder. "I've been thinking," she said.

He wondered how long you could leave wet laundry before it mildewed.

She was sitting on his lap. She weighed nothing. She thought she might come home on weekends, she was saying. Keep her apartment and spend weekends with him and the kids at home. What did he think?

259

He pulled her close. His nose touched her earlobe. For a split second he thought of Kate's gold earrings. Weekends would be fine, he told Janet. Just fine.

The doorbell rang. There was no pepperoni on the pizza.

It didn't matter. Charlie's mouth was watering. Janet loved him after all.

CHAPTER

· TWENTY-THREE ·

George stood in the garage just after dusk, inflating the bicycle tires with an old hand pump. The dog was sitting under the big oak tree, where all afternoon she'd been stalking a pheasant. The bird perched itself on a low limb just out of reach. You'd think a dog would get a stiff neck looking up like that all the time. George rubbed the back of his own neck and kept pumping. There had to be a better way.

He had persuaded Kate to take a bike ride with him. He knew she disliked biking, but she'd been trying to make up to him. She filled his desk with flowers and packages of sweets. She helped him bring in his plants from outdoors and set them on the pebbled ledges in the repaired greenhouse. She came to watch him play tennis. She was doing her penance, all right. But she would never say out loud that she was sorry. He knew that.

He took off his sweater and laid it on top of an open carton, a relatively new carton for the garage. Inside were eight or ten books. He picked one up. It was the new edition of Kate's anatomy text. She'd told him they'd been delivered here by mistake. United Farcel must have missed this carton.

The smell of newness struck him as he thumbed through the pages, pausing at the numerous color photographs, remembering how much labor the project required. And then, there it was—the dedication staring out at him: *To George whose love makes everything possible.* Below it was the co-author's dedication to her family. They had dedicated the first edition to their former teachers. *Whose love makes everything possible.* He rolled it around in his mind. Why hadn't she told him? Not about the dedication. But that his love made things possible for her. That he mattered to her.

He placed the book back in the carton and put the pump away. The bikes were ready. Kate came out of the house. She was wearing faded jeans and an old T-shirt of Ellen's that said SAVE THE WHALES. A sweater was tied around her hips. The evenings came earlier and chillier now. She'd told him about her breast scare, but to look at her, you'd never know she was afraid of anything. It was something about the way she held her head and the way she walked, as if she were immune to everything but her own pleasure.

"Follow me," he said, straddling the narrow bike seat and pedaling down the driveway.

"We're off," she said.

The dog barked. George would be willing to bet she'd still be under the oak tree when they came back. Maybe you could carry perseverance too far.

By the time they got to Walnut Street, he was enjoying the rhythm of the pedaling motion and the flow of cool air against his body. He looked back. Kate was just behind him. There was not much traffic. It was still the second half of the dinner hour. People had not yet drawn their drapes, although their lights were on. What if she'd really had a malignancy in her breast? It could happen. She could die. He would have to write her obituary the way he'd done for his folks. Why was he thinking about this now?

She wasn't going to die. Was he still angry with her for
her betrayal? Or was it just his usual pattern of rehearsing
the possibilities? Behind him, she was singing and yodeling
without one care about what anyone might think. Maybe
he resented her spirit. The same quality that enabled her
to yodel or fill his desk drawers with flowers had also propelled her away from him into the arms of Charlie Murdoch.
Of course, she now swore never to see Charlie again. Unless
they ended up having him for a son-in-law. There was
no rehearsing that possibility. George pedaled faster over
a potholed place in the road.

A piece of rubber hung loose from his handlebar. He
yanked at it, but it wouldn't budge. He wiped his hand
on his pants. He hadn't changed after work. Probably he
shouldn't be wearing his work trousers for bike riding. He'd
gone back to his usual style of dress, except for sneakers.
When his patients asked about his tennis, he pointed to
his feet, saying he was still at it.

He was always surprised to be faced with so much anger
each September. You'd think his patients would be glad
to see him. He was glad to see them. He was especially
glad this fall. But as usual they let him have it, blaming
him for going away, for having such a good time, when
they were so miserable. They threatened to quit therapy.
They cried. They swore at him. They hated him, they said.
Who did he think he was, leading them on and then dropping them for a whole month? Just look at his tan, they
said. Probably he was lying on the beach while they were
desperate. George crossed over the Mass Turnpike and
turned left on Washington Street. It was dark now and
cars drove with their headlights on.

"Where are we going?" Kate called, interrupting her singing. She broke out into "Wonderful Copenhagen" before
he could answer.

He was perspiring. Most of his patients got rid of their anger that first week, although there were a few who would never be able to forgive him for going away. He thought about how he was going to diffuse his own hard feelings toward Kate. He knew it was a mark of faith in the therapeutic relationship that his patients trusted him with their rage. Could he do that with Kate? He had never been able to do that with anyone. He'd let his anger out by wrecking Murdoch's car. But where had that gotten him? He was still picking at the loose rubber on his handlebar, finally pulling it off. He smiled. He couldn't help it: Charlie had dialed 911. He had been humiliated. That son-of-a-bitch. George was still enjoying his revenge. He threw the chunk from the handlebar onto the street.

He turned down a side street where the houses were closer to the curb. The faces of people were actually visible through the windows. Most of them were watching television. Sometimes, George thought, it was as if the whole world did nothing but watch TV. Who was more real, anyway? Ronald Reagan or The Fall Guy?

Kate was singing "From Lucerne to Weggis Fair." You'd never know that her bike seat wasn't comfortable or that her thighs got tired after the first mile. She followed him with no complaints. That was one of the things that bothered him about her: She just never complained about anything. Right now she was following after him, having a fine time without even knowing where they were going. If she had been leading, George would have wanted to know exactly where they were headed, how long it would take, and the most efficient route. Well, he knew where they were going. He turned up Thompson Street. There were no kids playing this time. It had been no more than two months since he'd been here that night before visiting Kate in the hospital. There were cars parked in front of some

of the old-style frame houses. He rode slowly down the
middle of the street. The light in front of his old house
made it impossible not to notice that awful green on what
should still be a white frame structure. He stopped. Kate's
brakes squealed behind him.

"Oh, George," she said. "I see what you mean. It's a
dreadful color, isn't it?"

The shades had not been pulled. Now was his chance
to see the morons who'd defiled his house. He walked his
bike to the side by the fence and leaned it against a shrub.
The blinking light of a TV made it hard to focus.

"Let's go in," said Kate. "They'd be glad to know a former
resident. It would be fun to go in." That was Kate. Always
ready for a goddamn adventure.

"Ssh," he said. He peered in the window. All the furniture
was empty. It was modern furniture, not at all like his parents' large overstuffed divans and chairs. The walls were
painted white; his folks had always had paper on them.
George's eyes moved around the room. He stood on his
toes to get a good look. There they were. On the floor in
front of the TV were two school-age children in pajamas
and a young man and woman. They played a board game.
Parcheesi. His own mother had played Parcheesi with him
on that very floor. But there'd been no TV then, of course.
And they never had the radio on or the Victrola just for
background. When you listened, you listened, his father
told everybody. George had wanted to hate these people.
But it was hard to hate anyone who played games on the
floor with their kids. The father still had his tie on. At
least he should loosen his tie.

"Come on," he said to Kate. "Let's go." He moved toward
his bike, stumbling on a mound of dirt. Probably the people
had a dog that dug holes. No. A dog would have barked
when George and Kate approached the house.

"Shall we ring the bell and go in?" said Kate. She was putting her sweater on.

George felt dirt in his sneakers. He'd done his own share of digging in the backyard when he lived here. Those kids would be just about the age George had been when he began making maps and burying treasures. "Quiet," he told Kate. He took two wrenches from the tool pouch behind his bicycle seat. "I've got an idea," he said, handing her a wrench.

"Am I allowed to talk now?" she said, poking him in the ribs with her wrench.

"Follow me," he said, taking her hand. "Watch your step," he added. "Hurry up. Be still." He led her to the back of the house.

"How can I walk and be still at the same time, George?" she said. "You're not going to break into this house, are you?"

He laughed. Was she worried about his sanity? Oh, it was fine for her to do something unexpected, wasn't it? But if he ever stepped out of his mold, she overreacted. "Break in?" he said. "No. No. We're going to have ourselves a dig."

"A dig?"

"We're going to recover the chameleon we mummified. And our licorice. Maybe licorice gets better with age. What do you think?"

"I think, George," she paused. "I think you're crazy." She giggled. "Let's do it."

The yard was dark, and there were no lights on in the back of the house. "Should have brought a flashlight," he said. He tugged at her hand. She tugged back.

"Do you remember the spot, George, the exact spot?"

"Sure," he said. "I made the map a hundred times to get it perfect. Don't you remember? It's right under the

266

apple tree on the left." His eyes were getting used to the dark now. And just in time, too. A sandbox in front of him grazed his ankle.

"You're amazing, George," Kate said, appearing to give up her reservations about his mental health. "Once upon a time," she said, "there was . . ."

"Quiet," he said. Of course. She and Ellen would make a funny story out of this to add to their collection. He knew Kate was thinking what fun it would be to tell about this adventure.

"Ellen will never believe it," she said, confirming his intuition.

There was a clatter by the house. Their bikes had fallen.

"Oh, George," Kate said.

"Ssh," he said.

They stood poised, ready for the worst. Nothing happened. Obviously, everyone on Thompson Street was too mesmerized by their televisions to worry about prowlers.

"There it is," he said, spotting the apple tree. His parents had planted the tree on some special occasion. It had been a sort of shrine for his mother over the years.

A light went on in one of the bedrooms. The game inside was over, and the parents were putting the kids to bed. He wondered if they shared a room and if they had to say prayers the way he'd had to. "Hail, Mary," he said aloud.

Kate hadn't heard him, or if she had, she pretended not to. "Come on, George," she said. She had tunnel vision once she'd made up her mind what her focus was. She was saying something about Raiders of the Lost Ark.

They knelt down together by the tree. The ground was heavy with dew, which seeped through his trousers. "Ready?" he said.

"Ready." She held her wrench up as if she were waving a flag.

The earth came up in clumps and splattered their clothing, their hair. The wrenches were better digging tools than he'd thought they'd be. Kate began humming.

"Ssh," he said.

She threw a wad of dirt at him. "Ssh yourself."

He picked up a handful of loose sod and slipped it down her back. She swept her pile of dirt up at him with both hands. Surely the people inside must hear them now. But no one came. George and Kate grunted and giggled as they continued their fight. They were both covered with dirt. They shivered at the same time and stopped. The soil was damp. Without speaking, they resumed their digging.

"Let's face it," he said, after what seemed like a long time, "the treasure's gone."

"Five more minutes," she said.

And then his wrench struck something. He pulled it out. Yes. It was the same old wooden cigar box he'd gotten from his uncle years ago.

"Open it. Open it," said Kate.

The thin string was still tight around the wood, holding the box closed. He rubbed the dirt off it with his fingertips. It might have been yesterday or even this morning that he and Kate had buried this old box. She was fishing around in the hole now and extracted two long red candles. One was broken. The guardian-angel candles, they'd called them.

"Are you going to eat the licorice?" she said. "I'll try it if you will."

The box was heavy in his hands. "I'm not going to open it," he said.

"What? Not open it?"

"Look," he said. "We know it's here. Right? Let's just put it back as it is. I like the idea of the box being here." He put it down between them.

"Candles, too?" she said. She understood. Already, she was making the hole big enough to bury the treasure again. She kissed the broken candle and laid it gently in the soil.

He took the other candle from her, kissed it, and laid it on the other side of the hole. It was the same secret ritual they'd done nearly forty years before. She remembered. So did he. They both held the cigar box and centered it between the two guardian angels. A mixture of dirt and wax clung to his lips.

"Ashes to ashes," she said.

"And dust to dust," he said.

They packed the dirt in with their hands. It didn't take long. *"Dominus vobiscum,"* they said together. When they couldn't find their wrenches, they realized their tools must have been buried, too.

"Two more angels," Kate said.

"Dominus vobiscum," he said again. As an altar boy, he never got to say *Dominus vobiscum;* it was the priest's line. Even now he could never say it enough times to erase that old longing.

They marched as soberly to their bikes as the eight-year-olds they'd been when they'd first interred their treasure. Kate sang "Tantum Ergo."

They were back on Washington Street before he thought to make sense out of their ritual. He hadn't planned any of this. His plan had been to go by his old house and then stop at Kate's parents' place. He wasn't sure what had happened just now in his backyard. Maybe they were renewing their commitment to one another. Maybe she was telling him she loved him, the way she had in the dedication of her new anatomy text. Oh, why couldn't she, just once, acknowledge that he was central to her life?

She was calling him now. He'd been gradually accelerating. "George," she said. "Stop. Stop."

269

He pulled up by the sidewalk and turned. She was filthy. The dirt was caked on her clothes. He must look just as bad. "What is it?" he said.

"Let's go to Albemarle," she said. Her lips were blue, but she was still ready for action. Albemarle was the park where they'd played as kids.

"You're cold," he said.

"Don't be a spoilsport," she said, changing directions. "It's still early."

He looked at his watch. Time didn't really matter. "I'll follow you," he said.

Her bottom spread across the bike seat. He liked following her. But no wonder she didn't enjoy riding bikes. She tried to do it all with her legs, keeping her shoulders stiff. She had stopped singing now. Well, she must be having a good enough time. She didn't want to go home right away. Of course, he thought, as she made a turn, that could be because she didn't want to be alone in the house with him. Oh, God. Would he ever know where he stood with her?

The park was well lit. They sometimes played night baseball here now. When he was a boy, people went home when it got dark. Kate coasted right by the playing field and cut across the grass to the swings and jungle gyms. The grass was bumpy. There wasn't a soul anywhere in sight.

In front of him, Kate leaped off her bike. "We're here because we're here," she sang. Why didn't she tell him? Why didn't she sing him a goddamn love song, for Christ's sake? He got off his bike and let it fall to the ground.

"Sing me a love song," he said.

But she had already launched herself on a swing and hadn't heard him. "Come on," she said. "I bet I can still go higher than you."

He sat in the next swing. The flat seat felt good on his

buttocks after the narrow bike saddle. But he did not rise off the ground. He shuffled his feet in the dry dirt and gravel and wondered how to control his mounting emotions. There was no reason to be so angry. She was only having a good time. "Tell me you love me," he said to his sneakers.

She was standing on the swing now. She actually seemed to have no fear. "Shall I jump off?" she said.

"You're nuts," he said.

Across the way, the bright lights on the empty ball field added an element of expectancy, as if the game were just about to begin. Behind the swings were the woods where he'd had his first cigarette and first drink of hard liquor. The cops knew that's where all the kids hung out and never interfered except in cases of rowdiness. He was glad they'd come here, he and Kate. It reminded him that he'd grown up after all.

Kate was on the merry-go-round now. That's what they'd always called it anyway. It wasn't a real merry-go-round. It was a round flat platform on a sprocket of some kind, which you turned while other kids rode on top of it.

"Twirl me," she said.

"OK," he said, getting up from the swing. His feet were dragging across the ground as if he were very tired. Kate had always expected him to push her on the swing or twirl her on the merry-go-round. She expected him to be there for her. And he always had been. And probably always would be, he thought, as he grabbed the metal railing and began pushing the platform around. The grinding noise was the same as he remembered.

"Faster," Kate cried out.

"You want fast," he said. "I'll give you fast." The metal was cold in his hands. He held on to it and ran alongside the merry-go-round, pulling it with him.

"Wheeee," Kate said.

George stopped and watched the contraption circle under the steam he'd provided. He gave it another quick push. And another. He thought of the dedication in Kate's book. He thought of their dig at Thompson Street. He made her go faster, pushing harder and harder.

"Enough, George," Kate said. "I'm dizzy. It's your turn."

Did she really think he would sit on that thing and let her spin him around in circles? He kept her going.

"Stop," she said. "George." She called him as if she were calling the dog in for supper.

He gave the merry-go-round another push to keep her going. He had her just where he wanted her.

"I'm getting off," she said.

"No," he said. "Not until I say so." His arms were getting tired. His shoulder was going to start acting up again. He'd better not waste any time. "Say you love me," he said.

"I love you," she said.

"Tell me I'm the center of your life," he said.

"You are. You're the center of my life."

"Apologize," he said. "Say you're sorry." The merry-go-round was slowing down now.

"Oh, George," she said. "You know I'm sorry. You don't have to feed me lines. I love you. I do. I've been such a dope."

"Why didn't you tell me about your book?" he said.

"What book?"

"The dedication," he said. "The dedication in your book. Why didn't you tell me?"

The merry-go-round came to a halt. Kate sat there, holding its center, in no hurry to get off. "What's wrong with the dedication?" she said.

He looked at her. She was an arm's length away. It was too far. She whispered something. He didn't hear her. He sat on the soft earth as if pulled by an anchor. Maybe he

272

would roll under the apron of the merry-go-round and rest for a minute. Kate's legs hung over the side. He saw her feet touch the ground. She slid her body down next to his. She said nothing. He felt her tongue in his mouth counting his teeth.

· TWENTY-FOUR ·

George turned from her and rolled over away from the merry-go-round.

Kate sat up, cracking her head on one of the metal girders. "Damn," she said. The pain echoed through her scalp and settled in her forehead.

George sat quietly in the grass rubbing his knees. The ball field lights were still on.

Kate moved over next to him. The grass was wet. "I hit my head. Do you think it'll knock some sense into me?" She hadn't told George about the dedication. But why was he making such a big deal over it?

"I'm going home," he said and got up.

She rose. The mud on the knees of her jeans had already hardened. She remembered the afternoon she'd typed out the dedication page. It was a long time ago—before Charlie, before her surgery. She hadn't wanted to be sentimental, but a simple *To George* hadn't been enough.

He was walking toward his bike now. She followed. Her feet were soaked.

"George," she called. He didn't turn. "Do you remember that time I went to Girl Scout camp?" He reached down and picked a blade of grass. "It was the same summer we had the chameleon," she said.

He put the grass in his mouth. "I hate it when you get grass stuck between your teeth," he said.

"I wet the bed the first night and was too ashamed to tell anyone," she said. "I never even told you." She wondered what their dead chameleon looked like in its cigar box. She wished now that they'd opened it.

George spit the grass out expertly. She couldn't see where it landed.

"So I slept in a wet bed for a whole week," she said. She knew her face was scarlet. Her forehead still ached where she'd hit it.

"I'm going home," he said. He got on his bike. He reached down and picked a handful of the wet grass and stuffed it into his pocket. Was he going to chew it on the way home? Or leave a trail for her?

She remembered the feel of the cold, wet sheets as she climbed into them. Why was she telling him this now? She had never told anyone. Of course, she had also learned to dive off a high board during that time at summer camp. She had mastered the back flip. She had worked on her swan dive. The lights on the playing field went off now. She looked at George. But George was pedaling across the grass. He was leaving.

She called after him. He didn't stop.

"Damn," she said. She mounted her bike and bumped across the playground. Her calves were stiff and her thighs ached. She could hardly see.

By the time she caught up to him, they were on Washington Street again. The stores were all closed. "George," she shouted. "I slept in a wet bed for a whole week." A high-school kid in football pads and jersey stared at her from the sidewalk. He carried his helmet as if it were an extra head.

George had slowed down enough for her to catch him. But still he said nothing. His back was caked with dirt. For the first time, she noticed that he wore his good trousers. They were ruined. Her own clothes must be just as bad. But it was worth it. The treasure. The swings. The merry-go-round.

"When we get home," she said, "we'll bury our clothes in the backyard. We'll make a map."

He turned right onto Walnut Street past the place where the old Brigham's used to be—where they had made her favorite ice-cream shop into a parking lot.

"We'll have a little ceremony," she called ahead to him. She imagined them naked in the yard. They would bury their clothes. They would not say *Dominus vobiscum.* Her legs pushed up and down. Why wasn't George answering her? She rode up alongside him. Her toes were going to break right through the canvas of her sneakers. She and George were past the section of small stores in Newtonville now and into the residential section. There were no cars on the road. Up. Down. Up. Down. Some of the dirt dropped off her legs in flakes as if she were molting. If George could only get used to a moped. If only he could see that you didn't have to work so hard at everything.

"Shall we dance by the light of the moon?" she said, looking at the sky. There was no moon.

"You never loved me," he said. He pumped harder, switched gears, and bolted ahead of her.

What could he mean? "Of course I love you," she said. But he was already too far away. She stood up on her bike pedals. "Do you believe that?" she said to a man walking a Pekingese. She was moving faster now. George was hunched over the front of his bike. She went through a red light by City Hall. A rock in the road jolted her, and for a moment both wheels were off the ground. She would probably get a flat tire and then she would never catch

277

up with George. Well, if she did, she would force him to consider a moped. Her ankle grazed the bike chain. Up. Down. She was breathing hard. She was actually panting, like that day she'd pulled Charlie out of the ocean. He couldn't think she loved Charlie, could he? Well, maybe she did love Charlie. She sat down. Why couldn't someone invent a comfortable bicycle seat? They sent monkeys to outer space. You'd think a bike seat wouldn't be too difficult. So, maybe she did care for Charlie. But not the way she loved George. She stood up again and pumped harder as she passed the town cemetery. Damn. You could love more than one child at a time, couldn't you? More than one friend? Two parents? Rules. She had spent her whole life breaking the rules. Charlie had nothing to do with George.

She was gaining a little ground. "I've loved you forever, George Cummings," she shouted, as she passed under a streetlight. Was he slowing down? *You never loved me.* He had said that. He couldn't really mean it.

He turned onto their street. Most of the houses were dark. What time could it be? She leaned down. Her head was almost over the handlebars. They made it to their driveway at the same time. The dog came bounding out to greet them.

"You jerk," she said, kicking his rear tire. "How could you not know I love you? It's self-evident. It's true. It's a given." Was she shouting? His spokes were tangled pickup sticks in the darkness. She had never seen how much she had hurt him. He was always so calm, so sensible, so sane.

He looked back at his rear wheel. He just stood there. Clancy was licking his hand.

"Don't just stand there," she said. "Admit it. Admit you know. Tell the truth. Talk to me." Her head was pounding again.

George was walking his bike to the garage. The dog followed. "Where's your pheasant, Clance?" he said.

"What?" said Kate.

"The dog," he said. "I was talking to the dog. She was stalking a pheasant when we left."

Kate wheeled her bike inside the garage and rested it on the kickstand. The bike wobbled and clattered to the cement floor. The bell on the handlebars rang. She sighed. "You know, George," she said, "more than anything, I hate to look stupid." She laughed a half laugh as she considered her muddied appearance. She could still taste the wax of the guardian-angel candle on her lips.

George had put his bike in its usual place. He had found a flashlight. The dog clung to his side.

"No," Kate said. "It's not looking stupid I mind." She picked her bike up off the floor and lined it up next to George's.

He sat down on an old sawhorse, which moaned under his weight but held together. He turned the flashlight on his feet.

"What I can't stand," she said, leaning her spine against a vertical beam, "is being out of control." If she had time, if she only had time right now, she would sit down and prepare a convincing testimony. *You never loved me.* She would make his favorite meal, his favorite dessert. Maybe two desserts. Boysenberry cobbler. Linzer torte. Black Forest cake. She would remind him of her daily love: the coffee by his bed each morning. Maybe that's all she could do: feed him, hold his hand each night.

George shone the light on her face. She squinted. The dog ran back and forth between them.

"Like wetting the bed that time," she said. She was shivering now. There was no question but that the summer was over. The garage was damp and cold. "I'd have died before I'd have told anyone."

George directed the beam of light up at the rafters now and swung it around like a searchlight. The fragile spider webs had been swaying there forever.

She couldn't see him. "Loving you is like that wet bed," she said.

"What?" He put the spotlight on her again.

"Do you remember when we played flashlight tag? When we tried to catch one beam with another?" Her legs were so tired. How long could she stand here?

"Flash tag," he said. "I remember."

"You must know how I feel about you," she said. "Say you do. Say it." Her voice was rising again. She would stay here for as long as it took.

He put the light under his own chin. It distorted his features. "You compare me to a bed full of urine. Oh, yes. I know how you feel," he said. He turned the light off.

She stumbled across in the dark to him. Her legs didn't buckle. She put her palms against his cheeks. The dirt had turned chalky since they'd left Thompson Street. "You're not anything like that bed." She was always searching for the right analogy. Why didn't she just say what she meant? She stood between his legs and felt their support by her calves. How could he sit on that narrow horse for so long? A patrol car drove slowly down the street. The dog ran out to the curb.

"It's like your legs holding me up now," she said.

"Legs," he said. "Beds."

"Well, come on," she said. "You're the psychiatrist. You know what I mean." She was snapping at him. Would she ever learn self-control? She could never match his patience.

"No," he said, standing up, pushing her back against an empty carton, "I don't know what you mean."

A policeman came up the driveway. The dog was barking at his heels.

"I love you, George," Kate said.

"Just stay right where you are," said the uniformed man. His flashlight must have used at least five batteries.

"Oh, God," said George. He walked out toward the garage door.

"Stop." The voice meant business.

"Well, hello, Officer," said Kate. "We've been bike riding." She brushed her hands against her jeans.

"Don't move." The man sauntered toward them. His shoulders were broad. He wore a moustache. The dog was still barking.

"We live here," said Kate.

"Sure you do." The policeman turned the garage light on and flashed his badge. His name was Joe Stone. George and Kate had no identification on them. A neighbor had reported the break-in.

"I'm George Cummings," said George. "I'm a psychiatrist." He looked at Kate. "I live here. This is my wife." Kate wondered if he still had the grass in his pocket.

"It's midnight," said Joe Stone. "What are you doing in here at midnight with a flashlight?" He cracked his knuckles.

"He thinks I don't love him," said Kate. A pile of her textbooks lay on the floor behind the sawhorse.

"You two been rolling in the dirt?" said the policeman.

"See this?" Kate picked up one of her books and waved it in the air. "I wrote it. See this?" She turned to the dedication. "To George, whose love makes everything possible." She said each word distinctly. "He's George." She pointed.

Joe Stone looked from one to the other. He cracked his knuckles again.

"If we go into the house," George said, "I can show you my identification. The back door's unlocked."

"See what I mean?" said Kate. "He won't believe me. My liaison with Charlie had nothing to do with him."

"Who's Charlie?" said the officer. His neck was thick, as if he were a weight lifter. "What's a liaison?"

"Let's go to the house," said George.

The dog lay down on Kate's foot.

"I guess it won't hurt to check out the house," the policeman conceded. The two men turned away from her and began walking. They were the same height.

"George," said Kate to his back. "It makes me so vulnerable, loving you. Like if anyone knew about the bed."

George stopped.

"What bed?" said Joe Stone.

"It scares me." She dropped her book on the floor. It landed with its pages open. What was the matter with her? She had never been afraid of anything.

George turned around. "Scared?" he said. "Vulnerable? You?"

"Are we going in the house or not?" said the policeman.

She approached George. She shook him by the shoulders. Had he never seen her weaknesses? "Do you hear me?" she said. "I couldn't love anyone the way I love you."

"I hear you," he whispered.

The policeman's mouth was open. His hand was on his holster.

· TWENTY-FIVE ·

On the first day of the fall semester, Kate noticed the zipper
on her favorite pair of tan slacks was manageable. She made
herself a cheese and mushroom omelet for breakfast and
looked over the morning paper. George was already in his
office. He had squeezed fresh orange juice for her. *The Globe*
reported what everyone already knew: that so far, despite
the cool nights, September was a record month for heat.
The Red Sox were twenty games out of first place. A man
had drowned in Natick while being baptized in Lake Cochi-
tuate. None of this could alter Kate's good spirits. As she
lifted the stainless-steel kettle from the burner and poured
the water for her tea, the distorted reflection showed the
red of her cheeks and the bright yellow of her blouse. It
was going to be a splendid day.

Once in the lab, she put her white lab coat over her
slacks and blouse. She smoothed the starched coat over
her stomach. The lab was sparkling. The students were filing
in with their new books and scrubbed faces. They looked
you straight in the eye these first few days, as if you were
starting out even. Then, as they found out how much they
had to learn, small traces of doubt and resentment hovered

about their irises. Kate was pleased with the prospect of getting to know still another crop of young people. As they'd become younger than Ellen, she'd enjoyed them even more. Perhaps she and George ought to have had more children.

They were starting with the cat this semester. Her lab assistant paired the students and distributed one specimen to each pair. The formaldehyde was a friendly, familiar reminder that she was back where she belonged, but as she saw the students' reactions, she remembered that not everyone felt the way she did.

She had each student say three things about herself. It was a good way to begin. The cats lay, bellies up, on their trays. There were several foreign students. What a time they were going to have learning the origins and insertions of every muscle in the body. *Sternocleidomastoid* was a big enough mouthful in English. As they spoke, she tried to think what three things she would say about herself if she were a student. Well, it would not be anything about music. That was certain. Each student seemed to have to declare herself in terms of musical preference. "I'm into hard rock," one said. "Punk's my thing," said a girl with a pink streak of hair and four earrings on one lobe. No. Kate wouldn't even mention music. Would she say she had a daughter older than they were? Well, that wasn't really anything about herself, was it? She liked taking things apart and putting them back together. She could say that.

She walked up and down the aisles of the lab. The young women sat stiffly on their high stools, not unlike the refrigerated cats they would soon dissect. "I have fourteen brothers and sisters," one student was saying. Kate thought about the boy she'd seen on a street corner as she was driving to work this morning. As a brown leaf floated down on a stream of air, he had lifted his hand to pluck it, as if it

284

were an apple on a tree. Then meeting Kate's eyes through her car window, he'd blushed, embarrassed to be caught. People were always invading the private moments of others, weren't they?

The students were finishing their introductions. How similar they were. They liked this kind of music. Or that kind. They had three brothers and sisters. Or two. They wanted to be nurses. Most were eighteen or nineteen. They even looked alike. She saw now that there was one older woman in her class. It was just getting to be her turn. She had a smile hiding in the corners of her mouth. She was the only person in the lab with a skirt on.

"I'm Louise Scott," she said. "I'm a mother and a wife. Also, I'm a person. And soon I'm going to be a nurse. At the risk of alienating all of you forever, let me say that my tolerance for loud music is minimal." Her smile spread over her wide face.

Kate introduced her lab assistant and herself. She gave her usual spiel about the course, its lectures and labs, the materials, exams, grading procedures. She had said this preamble to her course so many times she was able to think of other things while she spoke. She wondered where Mr. Hansell, the custodian, was. He'd left a bottle of Moxie on her desk this morning. She'd brought him a tin of oatmeal cookies. And what was she going to do with all those clocks she'd ordered because she thought her students should take apart something they could reassemble? Would she ever learn to curb her impetuosity?

"Today we'll start by skinning the cat," she said. Some of the students grimaced. Beginning the term with a lab before the first lecture was unusual. "We use the cat because its systems parallel those of humans. Same organs. Same blood vessels. Same sets of muscles." She had become an expert in cutting things open. How was she going to feel this time when they slit their animals from stem to stern with their new scalpels? Her stomach was reasonably flat now. But when was she really going to recover? How had Rhoda done it so many times?

The students were unsnapping their lab kits and removing their instruments. Some of them were naming their cats. The older woman, the woman who was still younger than Kate, had paired up with the student who appeared to be most reticent. They'd be good for each other.

"What if I make a mistake?" a puffy-faced girl in front said.

"Nothing is forever, you know," said Kate.

"It won't be fatal," the other, older woman said, patting the belly of her dead cat.

Kate considered telling them the story she'd read in this morning's paper about the blind surgeon. He'd been blinded in an accident and had continued to perform surgery anyway. Imagine if Dr. Parks had removed her uterus without his eyesight.

A student, the shy one, had fainted. There was always one the first day. "Stand back, everyone," said Louise Scott. "I know CPR." Kate was surprised to find a small tattoo of a daisy on her left hand.

At the end of the day, satisfied she'd gotten her students off to a good start, pleased to have seen old students and colleagues, she welcomed the solitude of her small, cinderblock office. She ought to be tired, but was still as keyed up as when she'd begun her day. She walked from one corner of the room to another, considering its space. If she moved the desk along the far wall, it would give her more room. She dragged the bookcase into the empty hall. Her stomach was not going to weep this time. She listened to the building. All quiet. Many teachers had only cursory meetings with their classes the first day and let them leave early. She pushed the metal desk across the multicolored linoleum. She was humming "Pomp and Circumstance." Taking her shoes off, she edged the desk in front of the only window in the room. The magnolia tree just outside it was one of the first campus trees to blossom in spring. She swung the bookcase back into the room and pressed it against the far wall. Yes, there was much more space now. The four-drawer file cabinet would have to stay where it was in the corner; she wouldn't even attempt to move it. As she pushed her old wooden chair toward her desk, its wheels creaked and the pillow on the seat slid to the floor. She reached to pick it up and a bead of sweat rolled off the end of her nose. Her "elegant nose," Charlie had called it.

She sat in the chair, rolling back and forth. Charlie. She wasn't going to think about him. She opened the bottle of warm Moxie and took a swig. In her briefcase she found a No. 3 pencil and a pad of graph paper. UNFINISHED BUSINESS she wrote at the top of the page in capitals. She began her list. CHARLIE. Would she ever see him again? She reached into her lab-coat pocket and crumpled the slips of paper with his phone messages. She erased his name.

CANCER. She couldn't write small enough to stay in the squares. Cancer took up three lines vertically and fifteen horizontally. She moved her hand to her breasts, jabbing herself with the pencil. No lumps. She felt her legs. How had Rhoda known about her legs? She got a small mirror from her purse. Could a face like that have cancer? Never.

Next she wrote the G of George's name and then erased it. "You dope," she said to herself. Making these lists was only a comforting illusion. She tore the top sheet from the tablet, as if it were a Band-Aid stuck to a difficult wound. *Unfinished Business.* It was one of George's psychiatric terms.

She folded the paper in half and then in quarters. Everything was unfinished. You could never know how things would turn out. She drank some more Moxie. She thought about George again. He would be at home now in his office with his last patients of the day. She considered her plan for dinner: veal Marsala. One of his favorites. Was George the best part of her life? Had she really meant the dedication in her book?

There was some noise on the other side of her wall. The office was occupied by a new man in the chemistry department. She'd met him last week at a faculty meeting and had liked the way he talked with his hands. She figured him to be about thirty-five. She picked up her feet and swiveled three hundred and sixty degrees in her chair. Well, she was entitled to her own fantasies. Even Jimmy Carter had admitted to lust.

Her fingers went to the phone. She dialed home, but hung up when George answered. He would think it was one of his patients. Next door, a chair screeched on the linoleum. The sound was nasal, such as a large bird would make, and without thinking, she peered out the window skyward for the geese flying south. But it was too early for that. She looked down at her carefully folded list. She tried to spear it with her pencil. The point broke. She picked up the paper and tore it into small bits. Standing, she threw the confetti over her head. "So much for unfinished business," she said aloud.

A button popped from her lab coat as she took it off. They always ironed the buttons into crumbs. She knelt on the floor to see if the button was worth resurrecting, but couldn't find it until she crawled under her desk. Three quarters of the button remained. It would do. The chemistry man was still rattling around next door.

She sat on the floor, leaning against the desk, and took

the flowered pillow from the seat of her chair. It was some old upholstery fabric her mother had stored away for just such an occasion as an office pillow. Kate ran the heel of her hand across the material. It was still nubby. She put the pillow on the floor and pushed it against the empty space by the wall where the bookcase had been. Lowering her head to the cushion, she felt the blood rush to her cheeks. It was really stupid to get tingly from standing on your head, wasn't it? But as she placed her hands at the correct points to form a perfect triangle with her forehead and felt that special lightness in the tips of her fingers, she knew it was not so stupid. The yellowness of her blouse surprised and pleased her as her chin momentarily touched her sternum. She pushed off with the balls of her feet and rested her knees on her elbows. The blood was surging to the roots of her hair now. She put her legs straight up and let them relax against the wall. On eye level were the tiny bits of graph paper of her list.

A NOTE ABOUT THE AUTHOR

Jean Gould was born in Chicago, Illinois, and raised in Bala-Cynwyd, Pennsylvania. She is married and now lives in Natick, Massachusetts. This is her first novel.